RAVES FOR
JAMES PATTERSON

"Patterson knows where our deepest fears are buried...There's no stopping his imagination." —*New York Times Book Review*

"James Patterson writes his thrillers as if he were building roller coasters." —Associated Press

"No one gets this big without natural storytelling talent— which is what James Patterson has, in spades."
—Lee Child, #1 *New York Times* bestselling author of the Jack Reacher series

"James Patterson knows how to sell thrills and suspense in clear, unwavering prose." —*People*

"Patterson boils a scene down to a single, telling detail, the element that defines a character or moves a plot along. It's what fires off the movie projector in the reader's mind."
—Michael Connelly

"James Patterson is the boss. End of."
—Ian Rankin, *New York Times* bestselling author of the Inspector Rebus series

3
DAYS
TO LIVE

For a complete list of books, visit JamesPatterson.com.

3
DAYS
TO LIVE

JAMES
PATTERSON

GRAND
CENTRAL

NEW YORK   BOSTON

Copyright © 2023 by James Patterson

Hachette Book Group supports the right to free expression and the value of copyright. The purpose of copyright is to encourage writers and artists to produce the creative works that enrich our culture.

The scanning, uploading, and distribution of this book without permission is a theft of the author's intellectual property. If you would like permission to use material from the book (other than for review purposes), please contact permissions@hbgusa.com. Thank you for your support of the author's rights.

Grand Central Publishing
Hachette Book Group
1290 Avenue of the Americas, New York, NY 10104

grandcentralpublishing.com
twitter.com/grandcentralpub

First Edition: February 2023

Grand Central Publishing is a division of Hachette Book Group, Inc. The Grand Central Publishing name and logo are trademarks of Hachette Book Group, Inc.

The publisher is not responsible for websites (or their content) that are not owned by the publisher.

The Hachette Speakers Bureau provides a wide range of authors for speaking events. To find out more, go to hachettespeakersbureau.com or call (866) 376-6591.

ISBN 978-1-5387-5274-6 (trade paperback) / 978-1-5387-41863 (large-print trade paperback) / 978-1-5387-52760 (ebook)

LCCN is available at the Library of Congress.

Printed in the United States of America

LSC-C

Printing 1, 2022

Contents

3 DAYS TO LIVE

James Patterson and
Duane Swierczynski

CHAPTER 1

MY LIFE FELT like a dream. I guess that happens when you elope, hop on a plane, drift off to sleep, and wake up in a foreign country.

Adding to the dreamlike effect: my watch had decided to stop working somewhere over the Atlantic Ocean, and not knowing the exact time was driving me a little crazy. My body was telling me it was the middle of the night, but the midday winter sun blazed bright over the historic center of Berlin.

"Do you see a clock anywhere?"

Kevin Drexel, my loving husband of eighteen hours, smiled and squeezed my hand. "You may have forgotten, but we're on our honeymoon. No schedules, no cell phones, no plans, just us—remember?"

"True. But if I knew it was... say, four o'clock, then we could check into the room. And I could take my shoes off already."

"The Adlon said the suite would be ready in a couple of hours. Let's get the lay of land."

"Interesting choice of words," I replied, raising my eyebrows. I slipped my arms around Kevin from behind and squeezed him tight. He turned to face me. As a woman who has always been on the freakishly tall side, it felt pretty amazing to have found a partner who a) was just as freakishly tall, and b) didn't mind seeing eye-to-eye. Literally.

"You know there's something seriously wrong with you," he said, bringing me in for a kiss.

"Yet, you married me anyway."

"I sure did."

We'd left everything—our bags, jackets, my useless watch—to take a stroll down the Unter den Linden while we waited for our room to be ready. Interesting, the things you learn about your spouse on the first day of your marriage. I knew Kevin was a very chill guy, and I was sure by now he'd picked up on my obsessive need to plan everything down to the microsecond. But had I known Kevin Allan Drexel would be *this* chill...okay, don't get me wrong. I still would have married him. But I would have also packed an extra watch battery.

"Isn't this amazing? I never get tired of this city," Kevin exclaimed. "Where we're walking right now used to be nothing but a field of rubble, just after the war. Now look at it!"

"It's not exactly Paris," I teased.

"That's exactly the point!" Kevin said. "Paris is always the same old Paris. But Berlin is never the same city twice."

I'd never been to Germany, let alone Berlin. But Kevin had spent a lot of time here because his best friend and former business partner, Bill Devander, lived here. The whole flight over, he'd been gushing about how excited he was to show me the city.

"Looks like that church over there has been here quite a while."

I gestured at a huge and elaborate Gothic pile situated next to the city's iconic TV tower.

"That's the Berliner Dom," Kevin said, "and it's kind of a

miracle the old cathedral is still standing. During World War II, a wave of Allied bombs blew out the windows, and another explosion destroyed the roof. We're now in what used to be East Berlin, by the way, so the communist government wasn't all that worried about restoring it. They're still trying to raise funds to restore it to some of its prewar glory."

"You think maybe there's a clock somewhere inside that cathedral? One the Allies didn't destroy?"

"I don't know. But ooh...you have to see the organ!"

"Now *that's* what a bride wants to hear on her wedding night."

Kevin laughed—one of his trademark, unrestrained boyish giggles that made me fall for him. "You're impossibly naughty."

"*Is* it our wedding night?" I continued. "Or is it the day after? See, without my watch or a phone, I have no idea..."

Kevin touched my hand. "You know what this is, Samantha? It's the beginning of the rest of our lives."

If I could go back in time and live in a particular moment, it would be this one. Kevin holding my hand. The sound of his laugh still hanging in the air. The endless possibilities.

CHAPTER 2

THERE WERE NO clocks inside the cathedral, but otherwise the hulking place of worship *was* kind of fascinating. (Not that I'd ever admit it out loud to Kevin.) We gawked at the grand organ, with its intricately carved wood encasing the metal pipes reaching up to the heavens. Which I suppose is the idea with church organs.

"Wilhelm Sauer's masterpiece," Kevin was saying. "He designed over a thousand organs during the so-called Romantic period, but this one was considered his best."

Kevin's business was engineering, so anything well-built and ridiculously complex seized his attention. (I like to think these qualities are what attracted him to me, too.)

"I hope you never grow bored of me," I said.

"Impossible."

"I can be pretty boring."

"I find that hard to believe."

We had given up our lives for each other, in one way or the other. After eight years of my high-pressure job, I was ready to try something...normal (if that was even the right word). Kevin, too, was looking for a change. He'd just dissolved a fifteen-year business partnership developing aerosol technology that had

had him chained to a desk, in favor of a new venture that would allow him to see the world. We'd first met on vacation, both on the same Mexican beach while considering what to do with the next chapter of our lives.

The solution we came up with, after a series of salt-rimmed margaritas? We'd *stay* on vacation. What started as a boozy, flirty joke turned into something real when we planned to meet up again a week later, this time in Key West. And then again two weeks later, on Ibiza, and so on, for the next six months until we finally decided to elope. After which Kevin Drexel whisked away the former Samantha Bell to honeymoon here in Berlin, his favorite city.

"You want to see the crypt?" Kevin asked. "They have caskets down there dating back to the sixteenth century."

"Why, Mr. Drexel, are you trying to get me alone in a dark, confined space?"

"That was sort of the idea, Mrs. Drexel."

"That's *Ms. Bell-Drexel*, if you please. And if we're going to do that, I'd rather not be surrounded by dead Germans."

"In that case, shall we make our way back to the Adlon and see if our room is ready, Ms. Bell-Drexel?"

I threaded my arm through his, and leaned in close. "You know what I like best about you, Mr. Drexel?"

"My rakish good looks? My devil-may-care attitude?"

"No. You're a quick study."

We left the cathedral and made our way west down the Unter den Linden with a little more urgency this time. Kevin made a big deal of pointing out the former communist parade grounds, now a proper garden called—wait for it—the Lustgarten. I told my husband he was making this far, far too easy.

Finally, we checked into the hotel. The Hotel Adlon was

every bit as gorgeous as Kevin had promised. Kevin told me that the Adlon, like the Berliner Dom, had been pretty much destroyed by the Allies during World War II; and since it was on the East German side, a stone's throw from the Berlin Wall and directly across from the Brandenburg Gate, almost nothing had been left of the hotel except a grassy field until after the Wall fell. They eventually rebuilt in the 1990s, with a similar design to the original.

So, in short, we were apparently honeymooning in what used to be Enemy Territory. But Kevin was right; Berlin was in a forever state of birth, death, and rebirth.

"Okay, so we're in Berlin for seven days," I said. "Let's stay in this room the entire time."

Kevin smiled. "Well, at some point I'm going to have to meet up for a quick drink with Bill. He lives nearby in Simon-Dach-Kiez, just a neighborhood or two away."

I pulled him close, whispering in his ear, "You're not going anywhere," then giving him a long, searching kiss.

CHAPTER 3

FIRST ORDER OF business: washing the air travel and Unter den Linden off my body. The tastefully ornate bathroom was bigger than most studio apartments; Kevin and I could practically take up residence here. And as the warm water cascaded over my body from multiple directions, I was beginning to seriously entertain the idea. So I barely heard him when Kevin stuck his head in to say something.

"What was that?"

"I said I'll be right back," Kevin replied. I couldn't quite see him through the steam, but I could imagine him grinning.

"Where are you going?"

"Just a quick errand. Something I forgot."

"Please, Mr. Bell-Drexel. You don't forget *anything*."

"Okay, guilty as charged. I want to pick up some flowers and an outrageously expensive bottle of wine. What's a honeymoon suite without them?"

"Flowers and wine are nothing compared to this shower. You should take off your clothes and join me."

"I will. Just as soon as I return."

"Promise?"

Either he didn't answer, or the water muffled his reply, but the next thing I knew he was gone. I thought about washing my hair a second time, just for the excuse of lingering in this shower another twenty minutes, but I didn't want my groom to return to a shriveled-up prune.

I toweled off and pulled on a robe, then glanced out the window at the street below. We were on the third floor, kinda lousy for city views, but fairly excellent for people-watching. Directly beneath our windows was the red awning of the hotel entrance. From habit, I found myself picking out random passersby and trying to ascertain everything I could about them from physical details: their clothes, how they walked, their body tics. Examples: The middle-aged guy hate-chewing a piece of gum and wearing an ill-advised "trendy" jacket? Recent divorcée trying to kick a nicotine habit because younger women in the dating pool tended to avoid smokers. Oh, and the attractive slender woman wearing the designer dress and zip-up stiletto boots, keeping her face visible to the passing crowd? Most likely a prostitute. Her face is her billboard, and she's hoping to attract the attention of a wealthy tourist staying in the nearby five-star hotel (the boots are sexier than flats and less work than strappy high heels).

After a while, I shook myself out of it—if I was going to settle down to a "normal" life, I was going to have to learn how to unplug this part of my brain.

To distract myself, I unpacked our luggage. We both traveled light; I'm sure we'd both read the same articles on how to live for a month out of a suitcase that fits in the overhead bin. At one point, I'd reached the master level of packing for a week in the Middle East in a single oversized *purse*.

So unpacking took me all of three minutes.

A half hour passed. At least I think it did—my watch was

still DOA. I turned on the flat-screen TV, then flicked it off again. Kevin was surely taking his time with those wine and flowers. Unless...he was surprising me with something else, which would very much be a Kevin Drexel thing to do. Months ago, I'd made myself turn off my internal lie detector around Kevin, so the poor guy could actually surprise me from time to time.

While I waited for Kevin to return, I figured I'd go do something practical. Like find a new battery for my watch or a charger for my phone, so I could finally feel grounded in this city. I quickly dressed, pulled my hair back, slipped on flats, and headed out the door.

Kevin's body was sprawled out in the hallway.

CHAPTER 4

EVERYONE EXPERIENCES SHOCK differently. For some, it's crippling. For others, galvanizing. I like to think of myself as belonging to the latter category.

Right now, I was all about saving my husband's life.

"Kevin! Can you hear me, baby!?"

I dropped to my knees and felt Kevin's neck for a pulse. There was none. Checked his mouth and airway; no visible obstructions. His skin was cold and clammy. I pushed away the fear and told myself this didn't mean anything. *I can still bring him back.*

But as I prepared to give him CPR, a strange array of sensations overcame me. My head spun. It felt like my heart was trying to jackhammer its way out of my chest. My arms and legs tingled as if they'd fallen asleep, yet my fingers felt completely numb. *What was going on?* If I didn't know better, I'd say they were classic symptoms of shock.

"Come on, Kevin, *please* . . ." I begged, then shouted, "Help! Please, call an ambulance!" hoping someone in the adjoining suites would hear me. Then I repeated it again, this time digging deep in my memory for the German words: *"Hilfe! Einen krankenwagen, bitte!"*

But as I glanced down the hall, I realized our next-door neighbors were in no position to phone for help either. Sprawled out just inside the open doorway leading to the next suite were two other people: a gray-bearded man and a young woman, maybe in her twenties. Their limbs were akimbo, like puppets whose strings had been quickly clipped, leaving their bodies to fall to the carpet in awkward heaps.

As I fought a wave of nausea, I tried to make sense of what I was seeing. Was this some sort of outbreak? An electric shock running through the corridor? A gas leak?

Once I knew the source of the problem, I'd know how to save Kevin.

But I couldn't focus. My brain felt fogged over. Even my vision was starting to blur. The numbness in my fingers spread throughout my hands. This wasn't shock. This was something else.

Only then did I realize that whatever happened to the three of them . . . *was now happening to me.*

CHAPTER 5

THIS CAN'T BE it, I remember thinking. *This cannot be how our lives end—just at the very moment they were truly beginning.*

The animal part of my brain screamed at me to crawl backward, away from Kevin, away from all traces of this invisible killer. There was a strange scent in the air, one that cut through all of my other symptoms and stirred up a violent nausea. *Was this what had taken my husband and the strangers next door?*

But I hesitated. I had to take a mental snapshot of the hallway, as awful as it was. If this was the last time I was ever going to see my husband, I wanted every detail burned into my retinas.

Something here just wasn't right—well, aside from the obvious. Something not right about Kevin's body ... what was it? What was I missing?

There was one detail that gave me hope: I was still conscious. Whatever mysterious agent had killed Kevin (and was working on me) hadn't finished the job. But my only chance at survival was getting out of this hotel hallway as quickly as possible.

In the end, the animal inside of me, the part that wanted

very badly to survive, took control of my limbs. I crawled backward, out of the hallway and into our suite.

Going back out into the hallway was not an option. And as much as I'd loved the shower, hiding in there would likely do nothing to protect me. I'd just be dying in a place that was slightly easier to clean.

No, there was only one way out.

I was suddenly grateful that Kevin had chosen a suite on the third floor.

I staggered to my feet, fighting the pounding waves of dizziness and nausea that washed over me like foamy surf. There was nothing in the room I could use to break the window.

Except me.

There was no guarantee I was going to survive this, anyway. If I wasn't able to control my fall onto the hotel awning below, I could break my neck or any assortment of limbs. Or maybe whatever that airborne toxin was I'd ingested would kill me within seconds, no matter how much fresh air I managed to belatedly suck into my lungs.

So I figured I might as well take the odds.

I tightened my fists and pumped my legs. If I didn't build up enough momentum to propel my body through the window, I'd either bounce off the glass or die while being cut to shreds.

I focused on this one task: crashing through this window. I tried not to think about Kevin, even though most of me wanted to stay here and spend my final moments holding his hand.

I remember very little about the next few seconds: the rush of breaking glass, a dozen slashes across my forearms, the sensation of the world tilted on its axis . . .

And then nothing.

CHAPTER 6

THE DARK WAS an impossibly vast ocean, and I was completely lost in it.

Then, suddenly: sounds. Muffled at first, like hearing someone speak underwater. It was a voice in a language other than my own, but that I could sort of understand. German. I knew enough to understand that they were talking about me.

Where was I? It was not entirely clear. My mind felt disconnected from my body, tethered in the most tenuous of ways. One jolt, and I feared that tether could easily slip away, flinging me out into the dark ocean forever, with no hope of rescue.

I couldn't feel my hands, so there was nothing to cling to. Nothing except the German words spoken around me, which my brain automatically translated for me: "I don't know why we're bothering to hurry. She'll likely be dead before we reach the hospital."

"You don't know that."

Hurry. This meant that my body was being transported in an ambulance. How could I not know that? Was my link to my physical self so weak that I couldn't tell if I was badly hurt, or even feel the bumps in the road, or hear the sirens?

"This one is not like the others. She didn't get as much gift. They found her outside, on the hotel's awning!"

Good to know my desperate self-defenestration had gone according to plan. But what was this about a "gift"? Was I mistranslating that word?

"With a gift like this, I don't think she stands much of a chance."

Finally, I remembered that "gift" was German for poison.

"But she's a large woman. Looks strong."

Groß is the German word he used, which could mean large or heavy...or simply tall. I'm too terrified to be properly insulted.

"Doesn't matter. I don't think she can survive. Look what happened to the others at the Adlon. I hear the target was a politician from—"

"Why don't you focus on your job and save the gossip for the media?"

No, no...conjecture away, my pessimistic friend! The more you speculate, the more I can try to understand what's happening to me. And please, please, please say something about my husband! Is Kevin here in this same ambulance with me?

If not, then I was a widow, dying in a foreign country. The people who were conveying my body to medical treatment didn't think I would likely survive.

"Look! She's convulsing!"

I am?

"Quick! Give her some midazolam!"

No! Do not give me a sedative that will slow my brain activity! I have a tenuous connection to my body as it is, and I'm terrified that drugs will sever it completely. Please, stop!

But the medics must have given me the injection, because the ocean around me stirred itself, pushing me even deeper into the darkness. The voices faded to nothing. After another moment or two, so did I.

CHAPTER 7

SEARING PAIN JARRED me into full consciousness, and I quickly realized that I had never felt so horrible before. Imagine your worst body-wracking flu...then dial it up to a thousand.

When I was last conscious, I'd felt like my mind was attached to my dying body by a few spindly threads. Now it felt like someone had taken my brain and brutally stapled it to my skull, with little care or attention to reattaching the neural pathways.

I couldn't tell whether I could move at all, or if it just hurt too much.

What time was it? What day was it? Where was I? I had no idea. I was in some kind of hospital room, and I could hear the tick of a clock somewhere nearby, but a curtain blocked my view.

And what about Kevin? By some miracle, had the EMTs been able to save him as well?

As I lost myself in these frustrating thoughts, an entourage of doctors and nurses entered my room. They were all clad in disposable gowns and surgical masks and gloves. *Why the precautions? Was I infectious?*

I could predict what the next several minutes would entail: the team running down their checklist, asking stupid questions, trying to draw out my mental condition. I considered playing unconscious so that I could simply listen to them discuss my medical condition amongst themselves instead. It would be the fastest way to learn the truth.

"Miss Bell?" one of the doctors asked in English. "Are you awake?"

Instead, I went for the direct approach and opened my eyes.

"It's Ms. Bell-Drexel."

"I'm sorry?"

My voice was dry and weak; no wonder the doctor had a difficult time understanding. I gritted my teeth and swallowed, but it felt like razor blades were sliding down my throat.

"I haven't updated my information yet. Where is my husband?"

The doctor hovering in front of my face hesitated for a moment, and his strained facial expression told me everything I needed to know. When good people have to tell someone bad news, they flinch a little, as if they're about to deliver a punch.

"I am so, so sorry."

The doctor's voice was full of genuine sorrow, expressed like an American. He'd probably been elected to speak with me because he appeared to be fluent in English—possibly schooled at Johns Hopkins or Baylor. I realized that I was fixating on his accent because I didn't want to focus on his words. Meanwhile, his colleagues busied themselves taking my blood pressure and checking my other vitals.

"Where am I?"

"St. Hedwig's. You were brought here earlier this evening."

"Tell me *exactly* what happened to my husband."

"We don't have all of the answers yet," the doctor said. "But you and your husband appear to have fallen victim to a chemical nerve agent that was released in the hallway of your hotel."

"What? Released by who?"

"I do not know. That is not my field of expertise. Perhaps Interpol can tell you more. Our goal is to keep you stable and as comfortable as possible."

"Tell me more about this nerve agent. There was a strange smell in the hallway when I found Kevin."

"As far as I know," the doctor said, "these agents are usually odorless, but again, I don't know the exact type we're dealing with."

"Soman? VX? Novichok?"

The doctor blinked in surprise. "Do you know a lot about nerve agents?"

"I do a lot of reading. So which one is it?"

"Our guess is that this agent is similar to Novichok, in that it attacks the skeletal muscles, leading to respiratory or cardiac arrest. And we've given you galantamine, which has been proven in some studies to counter the effects of soman and Novichok."

"The look on your face tells me it's not working."

"The fact that you are conscious is a very positive sign. We weren't sure we would get you back."

If only I'd been able to bring Kevin back, too.

"Have you compared samples with the database at the Organisation for the Prohibition of Chemical Weapons?" This was the intergovernmental group, based in The Hague, that worked toward the worldwide elimination of chemical weapons.

The doctor raised an eyebrow. "We did. There were no matches. I'd ask how you know about that organization, but I have a feeling you'd tell me about your reading habits again."

It was an attempt at levity, but it fell flat. I needed answers. "If this agent is so powerful, why am I not dead?"

"You didn't receive as large a dose as your husband," he said. "And the dive out of your window probably saved your life."

But not Kevin's. While I was killing time inside the suite, my husband had been fighting for his life in the hallway just outside, and I'd had no idea.

What if I had opened that door just a few minutes sooner?

CHAPTER 8

IT WAS A strange thing, being at the center of an international incident. "An American couple"—that's how they referred to us on cable news networks. Our names had not been released to the public. Some of that probably had to do with my former career. Although the TV broadcasts were in German, I understood enough to glean a few facts:

The intended targets were apparently a wealthy Russian oligarch and his daughter—the strangers next door. Kevin and I, the "American couple," were considered collateral damage, tourists who'd been in the wrong place at the wrong time. *Yeah, you don't say.*

As the hours passed, I began to mark the presence of non-medical personnel amongst the doctors and nurses. Oh, they were wearing the masks and gloves and the white coats, and pretended to check charts and vitals. But they didn't carry themselves quite the same way, and they were trying too hard to observe me without drawing attention to the fact that I was being observed.

Good luck with that. I was in a negative-pressure room, just in case any traces of the mystery nerve agent remained on my skin. The walls were mostly windows, making me feel like an exotic creature in an aquarium. I was keenly aware of being watched at all times, and it was driving me slightly insane.

I took stock of my own condition. I still felt like death slightly warmed up, don't get me wrong, but my limbs were responding to my brain's commands more frequently and reliably. Could the effects of the nerve gas be wearing off?

Right about the time I was mulling the idea of attempting to swing my legs over the side of the bed, someone entered my fishbowl room. It was the same English-speaking German doctor from earlier. Now I could read the ID clipped to his robe.

"Hello, Dr. Hoffman."

There was movement beneath the doctor's face mask. Maybe a grin. Or a grimace. It was hard to tell. He pulled open the curtain surrounding my bed so that I could see more of the room.

"Hello, Ms. Bell-Drexel. Your vision is improving."

"May I call you Jonas?"

"Only if I may call you Samantha. Listen, I have something very important—"

"Jonas, who are all of those people who keep staring at me? I know they're not hospital employees."

"Oh? How do you know that?"

"They don't carry themselves like they're approaching the end of a twelve-hour shift. They might be jet-lagged, but otherwise they look like they spent the night in a decent hotel, not a couch in the break room."

Dr. Hoffman nodded noncommittally. "To be honest, I don't know who they are. None of them have taken the time to introduce themselves to me."

"I suppose my name raised some red flags."

"Why? Are you some kind of international terrorist, Samantha?" he joked.

"No, Jonas. I'm a retired CIA agent."

I could see Dr. Hoffman cycle through the usual reactions to this news: humor (*no, really*), disbelief (*wait, really*) and finally acceptance (*wow, really*).

"The sooner I can get out of this bed," I continued, "the sooner I can figure out who murdered my husband."

"That's what I came to talk to you about, Samantha." Jonas hesitated, summoning some inner strength just like he had before telling me about Kevin.

I had no time for that. "Whatever you're about to say, please don't dance around it."

But even I couldn't have predicted the words that next came out of his mouth.

"Samantha . . . you have three days to live."

CHAPTER 9

I PROCESSED DR. Jonas Hoffman's words through a thick, gauzy wall of shock and disbelief. Part of my brain disconnected again, wanting to escape, flee this room, be anywhere but here. From far away, I heard him continue to speak.

"Although your skeletal muscles are recovering, and you are not contagious, the chemical agent is still very present in your system and showing no response to the galantamine..."

With the curtain open, my eyes finally found the clock on the wall inside my glass prison. It was fifteen minutes before 7 a.m., which meant shift change was coming. Jonas would be leaving. Going home to his life. Possibly a loved one, children. And I would be here, waiting to die, with my husband's body in the morgue.

"The chemical agent is attacking your internal organs, one by one, and based on the rate of progression, our best estimate is that within seventy-two hours..."

Seventy-two hours from when? Right now? Or has the clock been ticking this entire time, since the attack? Although of course it's only an estimate, doctors grappling with a nerve agent they've never encountered before, one that doesn't show up in any database? I might have sixty hours. Forty, perhaps. Or even less than a day...

"And while there is no known antidote or way to halt the progression, we can keep you comfortable..."

I have to get up out of this bed. I don't belong here. This is not my life. This is not my reality. I can't breathe. Why can't I breathe? Has the toxin compromised my lungs already? If I could just catch my breath I could get out of this bed...

Jonas was still explaining but I was done listening. He and his colleagues were wrong. They *had* to be wrong.

I gathered all of my strength and pushed myself up into a sitting position, gasping for air. My muscles needed oxygen to work. And I needed my muscles to work, if they were going to propel me out of this nightmare.

The world spun around me like a carousel. I caught flickering glimpses of Jonas signaling outside the fish bowl, gesturing for help. *No thank you, doctor. I don't have the time to sit around and listen to you and your theories. As soon as this ride steadies, I'm leaving.*

"Samantha, *no*..."

But then the ride abruptly flipped over on its side, and cold linoleum floor rose up to slam into my body.

CHAPTER 10

KEVIN HADN'T BELIEVED me, either, when I first told him I was CIA. It's the kind of thing people joke about, not the kind of thing that turns out to be completely true. *You look a little young to have been with the Company for eight years*, he had said with a sly smirk, at which point I knocked him off balance and put him in an inescapable chokehold, right there on the beach.

But it was the truth. I was one of those "prodigies" whose high test scores at my prep school caught the eye of a recruiter named Quentin Marr, who was somewhat of a living legend in the world of spycraft. When I should have been picking out a gown for my senior prom, I was consulting in counterterrorism think tanks. For the next eight years I helped foil terrorist plots large and small, all by Quentin's side. I tangled with the most sinister minds on the planet—including some within my own department.

And much to my own surprise, I had natural skills when it came to field operations. Genetics played a part, to be sure; both of my parents had been tall and athletic. But Quentin taught me to approach physical combat and gunplay and raids the same way I approached think-tank challenges: all were merely puzzles to be solved.

I'll bet you know a dozen ways to kill me, Kevin once said, caressing the side of my neck with his fingertips, just the way I liked.

Again, I replied, *you underestimate me.*

Come on. How many?

I lovingly detailed those ways, one by one, with gentle touches and caresses that left him not only surprised and shocked, but a little turned on, too. Okay, more than a little turned on.

You've just murdered me twenty different ways and I want you more than ever, he'd said. *What is wrong with me?*

But by the time I met Kevin on that Mexican beach, I was burned out. Solve enough life-and-death puzzles and you begin to realize you've essentially solved them all; the only thing that changed were the variables. So I retired, at the advanced age of twenty-six.

Quentin was surprised, but said he completely understood. He knew better than anyone that a life of counterterrorism is a grind that chews at your soul. *Why do you think I left the field and became a recruiter?* he'd said.

But it wasn't just that. I began to wonder about the road I'd abandoned, the so-called normal world. The world where I would have gone to that prom, to an Ivy League school, and maybe even met a guy like Kevin Drexel.

I'll bet you know a dozen ways to kill me.

Perhaps, my love, but I never would have guessed how you'd actually be killed, less than a day after we exchanged vows.

CHAPTER 11

I SNAPPED AWAKE to find myself back in my hospital bed inside the fishbowl, lying in a puddle of my own sweat. As I twisted my body a little to glance at the clock, my body screamed in agony, as if to say: *Oh, no you don't. You shouldn't be moving. You're dying.*

It was now 11:03. Hours had passed since I'd fallen onto the floor and passed out—more precious time squandered.

What did I have left? A couple of days and change...if even that much? What would it feel like when my organs began to fail, one by one? Which would be the last to go? I'm guessing it wouldn't be my heart, because that had already been ripped out and torn to pieces.

I stared at the clock and pieced together a rough timeline.

Our marriage, from our vows to those last moments at the Hotel Adlon, had lasted all of twenty-one hours. My husband was gone, and I'd be following him into the grave in just two days.

This had been preceded by six months of globe-hopping romance—easily the happiest time in my life. Before that, eight years of service to my country.

Was this my reward? To see the man of my dreams die,

cursed to mourn him even as my own body rebelled against me and closed up shop, one piece at a time? What was the point of any of this? Why couldn't I have been snuffed out during a training exercise when I was eighteen, before I knew any better?

And then I realized: I was caught in a spiral of self-pity.

This was not me.

Whoever this pathetic being was, she was *not* the Samantha Bell I had known for the past twenty-six years.

I checked the clock. I had wallowed for approximately twenty minutes. That was enough; I would not give another single moment to it.

Doors to my negative pressure room opened and closed. Vitals were taken. Pillows adjusted, IV lines checked, sympathetic looks given. And all the while I planned my future, no matter how little of it I had left.

I thought about the crime scene. My husband's body, as well as those of the Russian father and daughter next door. They were the largest pieces of the puzzle, but there were others:

The strange scent in the air, despite all other indications that this mysterious nerve agent was odorless and undetectable.

The nagging suspicion that something about the position of Kevin's body was off; something was missing, something I couldn't yet identify.

The brazen attack on the Russian oligarch, which strongly suggested his enemies needed him dead, regardless of the collateral damage.

I didn't know how these all fit together just yet. But I wasn't going to just lie here and wait to die.

I checked the clock again. It was almost noon.

I vowed to spend whatever time I had left avenging my husband.

CHAPTER 12

THERE WERE A few pressing items on my to-do list:

1. Convince my body that it was in our mutual interest to be mobile, despite the multiple attacks being waged on its major organs.
2. Break out of this hospital.

Item number two could not happen without the first, to be sure. I didn't think literally crawling out of this building would be a good idea. But I had to tackle both if I was going to achieve the third item on the list:

3. Identify and punish those responsible for my husband's murder.

So while I pushed the limits of my body, forcing my limbs to obey my commands—despite numbness in some places and nerve-splitting pain in others—I plotted my escape.

Looking outside the fishbowl, I focused on the nonmedical personnel. Lip-reading was something Quentin taught me early; I was astounded at how much you could learn from a complete stranger, even if you were sitting on the opposite side of a noisy, crowded bar. They were looking at me with increasing frequency, these mysterious agents. Saying things like...

...her to a more secure wing...

...facilities here at St. Hedwig...inadequate...

...trained asset, could be of use to us...

...she doesn't have long...

...one of Quentin Marr's prodigies...

So they knew exactly who I was. I'm guessing I had Dr. Jonas Hoffman to thank for keeping them at bay while I fought for my life. But if, as it appeared, I was about to lose that battle, they wanted to wring every last drop of intelligence from me before tossing my corpse onto the pyre.

Sorry, gentlemen. I have my own mission to complete, and dying inside an interrogation room isn't going to work for me.

Here's another thing Quentin taught me: no matter the situation, you can bend the environment to suit your needs. Here's what I could determine about my environment:

. St. Hedwig's was heavily guarded, not only by its usual security team, but by an unknown number of intelligence agents and their support staff. I needed to sidestep them somehow.

From what little I could see through the windows, I judged myself to be at least three or four stories above the street. I couldn't see myself rappelling down the side of the building— not in my sorry condition.

The vents were way too small for my athletic frame—even if I were physically capable of shimmying through them (I wasn't).

Impersonating hospital staff would be difficult, and there

was no time to counterfeit identification badges or hack into the surveillance systems. I would be caught immediately.

Meanwhile, the minutes continued to tick by. I couldn't waste more time plotting; I needed to start acting now, or I was never going to complete my final mission.

And then, all at once, it came to me.

CHAPTER 13

I WAS *NOT* alone in Berlin.

I'll admit that, when we first arrived, I'd been half-hoping not to get roped into having dinner with him. But now, I realized, the legendary Bill Devander was my only prospect.

Kevin had told me that he and Bill had been best friends since their freshman year at Duke. They'd met at student orientation and soon were inseparable, nursing each other through final exams, failed relationships, and epic hangovers. They became so like-minded that Bill even talked Kevin into changing his major to engineering (from history) so that they could go into business together someday. Which is exactly what happened. Funny how impulsive decisions made in your youth can dictate the course of your life.

But after fifteen years, Kevin needed a break. He'd decided to leave the company just before our whirlwind romance. There had been a few near-misses between us and Bill at various ports of call, but he and I had never managed to meet face-to-face. So up until that moment, Bill was myth and legend.

But now I prayed that the man behind the myth would turn out to be worthy of the praise Kevin had piled upon him. Bill

Devander, according to said legend, was cunning, fierce, and a true business negotiations savant. I hoped this was the case. Because there was something I really needed Bill to sell.

I pressed the call button and asked the nurse in my shaky German if she could send in Dr. Hoffman right away. Her reply: *The doctor is with other patients, is this an emergency?* I wanted to scream at her: *Yes, this is an emergency—I'm dying here!* But that would get me nowhere, except an impromptu psych eval. Instead I asked to see him as soon as he was available.

My exhaustion was strong, and I was worried that I would doze off. The Arctic-level air conditioning wasn't helping much, either—my brain was begging me to hibernate for the winter. But I stayed awake long enough to pounce on Dr. Jonas Hoffman the moment he stepped into my room.

"Doc, will you do me a favor?" I asked.

"That depends on the favor."

"You're seriously going to deny a dying woman her last wish?"

The doc was wary. "Oh, boy."

"Relax, it's nothing dangerous. Can you contact an American businessman named William Devander? His company is headquartered here in Berlin. So it's not even a long-distance call."

"Who is William Devander?"

"Family."

A small lie that wouldn't hold up in court, but I was hoping it would do the trick in this moment. And in a strange way, it was also true: If Kevin and Bill were basically brothers, that made Bill basically my brother-in-law, right?

"I'm sorry...I can't."

"What do you mean, you can't?"

"The hospital staff has been given explicit instructions. No information about patients can be shared outside these walls."

"But this patient, lying right here, is giving you permission."

"You know what I mean."

I did. But if I couldn't reach Bill Devander, my chances of leaving this hospital floor were close to zero.

My other options? I'd hoped that news of my situation had reached Quentin by now. But the radio silence meant he was embroiled in some kind of mission in some remote part of the planet. (Last I heard, he was knee-deep in some North Korean intrigue and very unreachable.) Anyway, I couldn't afford to wait for my mentor to rush in and save the day. He'd taught me better than that.

"I don't want to die alone."

"Look, I can ask the government liaison if—"

"Jonas, *please*. I don't want to have to apply for permission to say goodbye to a member of my family. He doesn't even know anything has happened to us!"

"I'm telling you, *I* can't call anyone."

I was still puzzling out Dr. Hoffman's strange emphasis as he left the room. In fact, I was downright furious—until I realized that Jonas had left his personal cell phone on my bedside table.

CHAPTER 14

"THIS ISN'T QUITE the way I thought we'd meet," Bill Devander said.

"Yeah, this isn't quite how I pictured it, either," I said. "I thought there would be cocktails involved."

Using Jonas's "forgotten" phone, I'd been able to reach Bill quickly—or rather, his curt executive assistant, who took my message with zero promise of a return call. Instead of calling me back, Bill himself appeared in my chilly hospital room less than thirty minutes later.

Bill wasn't as boyishly handsome as Kevin, nor as tall. But he did his best to make up for it with a bespoke suit, professionally tanned skin, and a haircut carefully designed to hide the thinning going on up there.

Bill gave me a wide smile. "There's that sense of humor Kevin was always talking about. Even now..."

His smiled faltered as he spoke Kevin's name, and I could see tears beginning to form in his eyes. No. We couldn't do this now. We could both grieve for Kevin later. Right now, my objective was to make it out of this room, and I needed Bill to be clear-headed enough to help me.

"I'm so sorry, Samantha," he said. "There are no words for what happened..."

"Yes, there is," I replied. "The word is *murder*. And I'm going to find the bastards who did this."

Bill blinked. "I'm sorry...? I think I misheard you."

"I'm going to find them and make them suffer."

A grave look fell over Bill's face. He gingerly lowered himself onto the side of my bed and held my hand just as carefully as if I were made of porcelain. Clearly he'd been told I was not contagious; just hopelessly fragile. There was something familiar about him...His mannerisms were all so...*Kevin*. But it made sense. Spend years in the close orbit of someone and you begin to share traits. It was eerie yet reassuring to see tiny pieces of my love reflected in this total stranger.

I was also embarrassed that he was touching my hand, because I was suddenly sweating uncontrollably. Which is crazy, considering my room felt like a freezer. Was this yet another delightful symptom of the chemical agent?

"Samantha," Bill said, "listen to me. I know you're hurting, worse than anyone has a right to hurt. But there are professionals working hard to find out who did this. Even if you were in any condition to help, you'd only be duplicating their efforts. Maybe even getting in the way."

"I'm a professional, too," I said quietly.

The tell was small; just a slight widening of the eyes. And Bill quickly tried to cover for it by wiping away a tear. But I knew instantly that he knew. Despite the promises he'd made, Kevin had told Bill I was former CIA.

"When did he tell you?" I said.

"Tell me what?"

"That I'm a Company woman."

Bill gave an embarrassed grin. "Not long ago. I practically had to beat it out of him. But you have to understand, Kevin and I had no secrets from each other. And he was so proud of you."

"He told you, even though I swore him to secrecy?"

Not that it really mattered now, but I was disturbed about this. Kevin and I had had a long, serious talk about keeping that part of my life between us, and he'd sworn to never say a word. We joked a lot with each other, but not about this.

I'm sure Bill could read my unease. "Look," he said. "Kev and I may have gone our separate ways in business, but he was, and will always be, my closest friend. And I know he'd want you to focus on getting better. On healing."

"That's funny."

"What did I say that was funny?"

"Didn't they tell you? I'm not going to heal. This is about as healthy as I'll ever be."

The shock on Bill's face was real. No attempts to hide it now, because he had no idea what I was talking about. "What do you mean?"

"The same chemical agent that killed Kevin is slowly doing the same thing to me. I have a couple of days left, at the most. Hell of a way to spend the rest of my honeymoon."

"That is not going to happen, Samantha," Bill tried to rally. "I'm going to find help, and you're going to beat this thing."

I ignored his platitudes. "There *is* something you can do, actually. Which is why I called."

I reached over to my bedside table and picked up the note I'd been working on before he arrived.

CHAPTER 15

"ARE YOU SERIOUS? You want me to say *this*?"

I had written a script using all of the hot-button words guaranteed to cause a panic. I knew they would, because these were some of the words I'd been trained to look for when intercepting communiqués from hostile powers.

"Yes. Word for word. On a prepaid phone. Then break the phone in half, wipe the pieces down, and toss them into separate waste baskets. Burn the script I gave you. Then watch the news, if you want, to see that it worked."

Bill looked as if I'd asked him to go streaking in front of the Brandenburg Gate. But I'd given this much thought. A phoned-in threat was the only thing that would work—if you knew the right buttons to push. Clearly, I couldn't make the call myself. So the task fell to this complete stranger, the closest thing I had to family here.

"And what are you going to do?"

"Break out of this place."

"Are you *sure* there's no other way?"

"Believe me, Bill...if there were, I'd be doing *that* instead."

"I have a feeling Kevin would kick my ass if he knew I was leaving you to fend for yourself. Let me see what I can do about getting you transferred to another hospital. There *has* to be some kind of treatment."

"And what if there's not? Then I waste the little time I have left on this planet just...dying? No. Kevin would kick *my* ass if he knew I was just giving up."

"You're a CIA superspy," Bill said. "Pretty sure you could take Kev."

It was meant as a moment of levity in all of this serious, end-of-the-world talk. But the joke landed wrong for both of us. Yes, of course I would love to take Kevin. Take him away from all of this madness. But that was impossible, because he was far beyond my reach. There was nothing I could do to help him. I could only avenge him.

"Promise me you'll do this, Bill."

Bill squeezed my hand. His touch was warm, just like Kevin's.

"This is absolutely crazy, and I'm probably going to end up in jail for this...but I'll try my best," he said. He lingered for a moment, looking like he was wondering what to say next. Because whether this plan worked or not, this would probably be the last time we'd ever see each other.

"The sooner you call," I said, "the sooner this will be over."

Bill nodded, understanding. Time was of the essence. He left without another word. Without looking back. Pretty sure he didn't want me to see him crying. Which was correct. I couldn't believe I was forcing Kevin's best friend to put himself at risk like this. Bill Devander was a civilian; there were so many factors that could spin out of control, no matter how careful he was.

But now it was time to prepare to play the biggest wild card of all:

My dying body.

I closed my eyes and focused on my breathing as well as my training. In short: the mind-over-matter techniques I'd honed over the previous decade to give myself an edge over my opponents. In theory, your brain should be able to command your body to run and fight and leap and climb despite the injuries it has sustained. Gunshots, stab wounds, broken ribs, whatever. After all, your body was only dumb meat that responded to commands from the brain via the nervous system. The stronger the brain's will, the further the dumb meat could be compelled to go.

That was the theory, anyway.

I tried to relax and fool my dumb meat into trusting that everything was normal, that my brain was in total control. Breathing slow and deep, taking in all of that sweet oxygen, expelling all of that awful carbon dioxide. In through my nose, and out my mouth. Oxygen-rich blood pumping through my veins. *See, all is fine here. All systems go.*

I don't know how long I was in this regenerative state. I don't know if my body was buying any of my mental BS. But I knew a considerable amount of time had to have elapsed, because all at once I heard them, shrill and ear-splitting.

The hospital alarms.

CHAPTER 16

GOOD JOB, BILL Devander. You came through for me.

Okay, dumb meat—you're up next.

I pulled the IV out of my arm, swung my legs over the side of the hospital bed, and sat up. Which was my first mistake, because just like last time, all at once I felt the room defy the laws of physics and rotate in two different directions at once.

Okay, keep it calm—right this ship immediately.

Breathe in, breathe out.

Perception resides in the brain, and the brain is the boss, I reminded myself.

I stood up for the first time since I had crashed through the window of my honeymoon suite. The world threatened to tilt on its axis again, but I breathed in deep, clenched my fists, and all but dared the universe to pile any more misery on top of me right now.

That's right, Universe. You took away the human being I loved most in this world, and then you tried to kill me, too. Are you honestly going to deny me the right to walk out of this hospital room on my own two feet? How much pain can you inflict on a single human being?

I took a step, and then another, and still another. The

universe, as always, acted indifferent, as if it didn't care whether I walked or fell over.

Good, Universe. You stay in your corner, I'll keep to mine.

By the time I reached the doorway I realized everyone had scattered and left me unattended. I also realized I was on the verge of throwing up. The piercing alarms made me feel like the decibels themselves were drilling down deep into my skull. I could feel the rivulets of sweat running down my back from the effort, which under normal circumstances wouldn't be much effort at all. The dumb meat of my body wasn't as easily fooled as I'd thought. *Whoa whoa whoa—you're asking me to do* what, *now?*

I stepped out of my room and turned my head to the left. The hallway seemed like it stretched into infinity. I checked the other direction, and it wasn't much better. How was I supposed to travel such an impossibly long distance?

Breathe in, breathe out.

I flipped a coin in my head and went with the left, taking slow and steady steps as if this was perfectly normal, everything was fine. Nobody had noticed me . . . yet. Which was my only advantage at this point.

If Bill had called in that threat exactly as written, the medical and support staff would be in a frenzy, following a series of protocols to protect the integrity of the hospital in the face of a catastrophic attack. Checking in on little ol' me wouldn't be a high priority at this point. If you're in a sinking ship, you try to patch the hole—not worry about individual passengers. I had maybe three or four minutes to slip through the cracks and leave this place.

As I moved down the hallway, the floor stabilized beneath my feet. This was progress. I was nowhere near free. But I was also not passed out on the floor in a pool of my own puke. You take your victories where you can find them.

I pushed through a door I assumed would take me to an exit. Instead, it was a nurses' break room, with a coffee machine, a worn couch, and lockers. I realized this was even better. It was just what I needed. What had I been thinking, that I'd just stroll down the Alexanderplatz in nothing but a flimsy hospital gown, flashing my derriere all over town? I needed to change into something less conspicuous.

Dressing myself took a lot of coordination. But I managed to find a hospital scrub top adorned with a cartoon character I didn't recognize—was it a German thing?—and slipped it over my head. I even located a pair of scrub pants that were roughly my size. *I was unstoppable.*

Which was of course the exact moment two Interpol agents burst into the break room.

"What are you doing out of your room, Miss Bell?"

CHAPTER 17

THERE ARE ONLY three things you can use in a close-quarters fight with two armed human beings:

Your weapon.

Your body.

Your surroundings.

I had no weapon. Which left the other two on the list. As for my body...well, I wasn't exactly in tip-top shape. All of my muscles were laughably weak. The ground beneath my feet still felt barely firmer than vanilla pudding.

That meant I'd have to lean heavily on my surroundings. But this was the nurses' break room. What could I do? Subdue them with paper coffee cups and a pair of rubber Crocs?

"You shouldn't be wandering around by yourself," said the taller of the two agents. "You could hurt yourself."

"I heard the alarms," I said, blinking my eyes as if I were trying to make sense of reality. "I got scared so I went to look for help..."

"Come with us, Miss Bell," said his partner. "Everything will be okay."

I pretended to swoon as if I were unsteady and about to collapse onto the floor. (This didn't take too much pretending, mind you.) The taller one did the chivalrous thing and tried to catch me.

I was wrong about not having a weapon. I was holding it in my hands: the pair of scrub pants that were just my size.

I looped them around the taller agent's neck and used it to propel his forehead straight into the face of his partner. The crack of hard skull crushing nose cartilage was unmistakable. Both cried out, swearing in German.

I dropped to the ground beneath them, and let me tell you—that felt like dropping three stories to the cold hard sidewalk. Searing pain shot through my entire body and for a moment there I thought I would pass out. This taught me an important lesson: my tolerance to pain, which used to be fairly high, had dropped to near zero. If one of these Interpol agents landed a punch, it'd be all over.

So I had to make sure neither of them got the opportunity.

I spun my body around, sweeping the legs out from under both of them. In two seconds we were a tangle of bodies on the floor of the break room. I still had a slight advantage: they were utterly baffled about what had just happened.

I had four, maybe five more seconds to use said advantage.

Quentin had trained me to take advantage of my size. My arms and legs were long and bony. *In close-quarters combat, your knees and elbows will be more useful than your hands*, he'd said.

I struck at both agents with a flurry of elbow and knee attacks, aimed directly at their heads. I didn't want them in pain or temporarily hobbled; I needed them completely unconscious.

Fingers clawed at my face. I hurled an elbow back, hoping to connect with the owner of those fingers. I heard a crack and felt one of the bodies go limp. *One down.*

But my vision was beginning to fuzz out. I was doing too much, too soon. And the shorter Interpol agent was beginning to untangle himself from me. If he succeeded, this would all be over, and I'd be handcuffed to a hospital bed until the day I died. (Which would be two days from now, more or less.)

"Hey!"

That grabbed his attention. The agent lifted his head, giving me a target: his temple. More precisely, the area behind his eye and alongside the zygomatic bone. I drove the bare heel of my foot into that area as hard as I could.

His eyes fluttered and his body sagged, like someone had just flipped the off switch on a toy robot.

My body threatened to do the same. I dug into the last of my strength to push away from the unconscious agents. Climbed to my feet. Found shoes and a jacket. Stole a clipped pass from the waist of one of the agents. And then, finally, left the hospital.

With every step my body warned me: *Never do that again.*

I told my body I couldn't make any promises.

CHAPTER 18

I WALKED THE dark and chilly streets of Berlin without direction. I had been so preoccupied with the task of escaping the hospital that I'd given very little thought to where I'd go once I got out.

My search for the killers ought to have begun back at the hotel, but that was still very much an active crime scene. I didn't know how I'd manage to get anywhere near the place, let alone upstairs to our honeymoon suite. I was sure Interpol had entire floors sealed off. So where to, then?

A blaring horn snapped me out of my reverie. I heard the screech of tires as headlights washed over me. *Oh, no...*

I propelled myself out of the way and almost tripped into the path of another oncoming vehicle. My limbs flooded with my final reserves of adrenaline and I somehow managed to barely leap out of the way just as the immense bulk of a delivery truck sped past, honking his horn as if to chide me for almost being crushed under his wheels.

I tumbled down onto the sidewalk, scraping the palms of my hands as well as my knees through the thin fabric of the scrubs. Strangers rushed to my side and I heard voices, in German:

"Are you okay?"

"Miss, you need to watch where you're going!"

"I'm going to fetch a doctor..."

I found the source of that last voice and shouted "*Nein!*" That was the last thing I needed—to end up right where I'd started.

Two things were clear. For one, I couldn't continue to count on finding hidden reserves of strength. I had none left. No snappy CIA mind-over-matter trick was going to bypass human biology. My body needed to recharge.

Second: I needed a *place* to recharge. If this were any ordinary operation, I'd have access to fake identities, complete with passports and credit cards, to allow me to check into any hotel in the city undetected. But now I possessed nothing except my stolen clothing.

Where could I pass out in peace and not be discovered by the authorities?

If I didn't make a smart choice soon, the matter would be taken out of my hands. My body would shut down without my permission. And it could happen any second now...

CHAPTER 19

I WOKE UP inside a coffin.

Many of us human beings enjoy a wonderful and temporary bit of amnesia upon waking. A gentle case of forgetting can be truly blissful, especially when the sun is shining and you apparently have no troubles or worries. All you know is that you've risen to face a brand-new day, and the possibilities are endless.

Well, that didn't happen for me.

The moment I woke up, I knew I was in a world of hurt and trouble. I had little more than a day to live. And I was tucked inside a wooden box.

Okay, not exactly a box...more like a chamber. And I'd placed myself here the night before.

I could hear Kevin's voice in my head:

Wilhelm Sauer's masterpiece. He designed over a thousand organs during the so-called Romantic period, but this was considered his best.

The cathedral was the only hiding place that made sense. I had slipped inside the Berliner Dom right before closing time, and crawled around the massive organ (yes, I could practically hear Kevin giggling right now) until I found a cubbyhole large enough to accommodate my aching, exhausted body. I don't even remember trying to fall asleep.

The Berliner Dom had survived the mighty bombing campaigns of the Allied powers. And my body had somehow survived the punishment of the day before. We were two tough dames.

I crawled out of my cubbyhole now and stretched my body. I won't lie to you: I was still feeling miserable. But a night's sleep had restored some of my strength, and sharpened my mind a bit.

I unfolded the stolen coat I'd used as a pillow the night before and pulled it onto my body. Then I made my way to the first row of pews and sat down. I'm not the praying type—though I was tempted to make an exception.

No, I needed a moment to strategize. If I were going to quickly solve a case that had so far stymied Interpol, the German government, and who knows how many other intelligence organizations, I needed a plan of attack. As well as information.

Also: some nutrients and water, sufficient to keep my doomed body going long enough to avenge my husband.

I stared up at Sauer's organ and thought again about Kevin. Was it really only the day before yesterday that we'd been strolling around this cathedral, flirting like teenagers and gawking at something constructed in another century? Had the Berliner Dom herself looked down upon us with pity, knowing the ultimate truth?

Love may be powerful, but nothing lasts.

CHAPTER 20

AS I MADE my way toward the Hotel Berlin Alexanderplatz, I swiped a few copies of today's international newspapers to read the latest on the attack. (Had the story of my own escape from the hospital made the news?) *Der Spiegel,* the *Guardian,* the *Washington Post, Le Monde,* the *Sydney Morning Herald.* I spread my thievery over a series of news agents. To the untrained observer, I was just a harried nurse on her way to the hospital looking for a little reading material for her commute. Okay, a *lot* of reading material.

By the time I wrapped up my little crime spree, I was crossing the lobby of the hotel and looking for the breakfast buffet. Almost every hotel has them. Very few make you present proof that you're a guest of said hotel.

As I loaded my plate with enough protein and fruit to sustain me for the next twenty-four hours, the macabre thought struck me that this was probably my last meal. Not the one I would have gone with by choice; I'd have preferred grilled swordfish, sautéed mushrooms, and an ice-cold Hendrick's martini with Kevin by my side. Instead I sat alone, eating runny scrambled eggs, overcooked sausages, and melon slices.

I absorbed every story about the attack. But nothing in the

news made sense. The murdered Russian from the suite next door to ours had apparently been loyal to his government, with no known enemies. He'd been visiting Berlin to take his twenty-five-year-old daughter on a birthday shopping spree.

It was entirely possible that the real story was being kept out of the press. Perhaps that young woman was a mistress rather than a daughter. Or the oligarch was an American asset, and our side was trying to keep that fact quiet. But there was no hint of anything rumbling in the background—none of those quotes from anonymous sources, "officials close to the investigation," etc.—that usually indicated something else was going on.

Too many questions were left unanswered. Who would do this? And why? And who funded it?

I forced down more eggs and pushed the stack of newspapers away from me. They were useless.

So I flipped it around. Say *I'm* the individual carrying out this attack. I have a highly experimental chemical agent. I'm headed to the Adlon to kill a Russian oligarch and possibly other people…because that's how chemical agents work. There is almost always collateral damage, though it can be minimized, which is why I unleash the weapon in a hallway where there will not be many people.

Wait. Why not play it completely safe and unleash it in the oligarch's own suite? A person of my experience and skill should be able to break into the room easily. Otherwise, I wouldn't be trusted with a chemical agent. I'm no lackey. I'm a professional killer.

Yet for some reason, I choose the hallway. Why? What advantage does that offer? This puzzle piece refused to fall into place.

Then it struck me: *What if I was the actual target, and not the oligarch?*

Had some terrorist scumbag decided to take revenge on me during the happiest day of my life? Had I been traced through my new husband? Did the scumbag wait until Kevin was about to open the door, knowing that if he tried to break into the room when I was inside, I'd take him apart a dozen different ways?

All at once I was overwhelmed with the feeling that I was going to lose the breakfast I'd just eaten. It couldn't be true... but sadly the pieces fit.

I did this.

CHAPTER 21

"YOU KNOW I'M in Berlin hunting you, right?"

"I expected they'd send you."

"And now you've practically turned yourself in to me."

"It would appear that way."

"Why?"

I was sitting across the café table from the closest thing I had to a rival at the Company. Her name was Zoya Gage, and she'd spent the past ten years trying to undermine me at every turn.

Which I appreciated, frankly. It kept me on my toes. Zoya was the prodigy Quentin had discovered just before me, so when I was brought into the fold, I became an instant threat. This taught me a lesson: there will always be someone smarter, younger, and tougher than you. People who seem to be rewarded more than you. It's important to accept that and focus on your own unique strengths. Otherwise, it will unravel you.

"Tell me everything you know about the attack," I said.

"You know more than I do. After all, you were there."

"I want to know what kind of chatter you're hearing. Possible suspects, motives, anything. Is anyone looking into my case files?"

Zoya leaned back in her chair. Behind her was the iconic television tower of the Berliner Fernsehturm, and from my angle, it looked as if Zoya had a giant spike sticking out of the top of her skull.

"Ahh," Zoya said. "You think this is all about you, don't you?"

"The thought had crossed my mind."

"Look at the ego on you. Even in your condition."

"Are you saying the Company believes the oligarch was the target? If so, what's the motive? Who wanted him dead?"

"I don't know anything about that. I'm just here to bring you in."

I must have shuddered, because all at once Zoya had the strangest expression on her face. It was genuine concern.

"So it is true," she said softly. "You really are dying."

"That's what they tell me."

"I should be happy, finally seeing you like this. Weak. Alone. *Desperate.* I always thought Quentin put too much faith in you. Must be why you flamed out six months ago."

"Thanks."

Truth is, I was barely paying attention to Zoya. Instead I was clocking the gunmen slowly converging around our café. Three...no, four now. It hadn't taken them very long.

"But I'm in charge of bringing you in safely, and that's what I'm going to do. Otherwise I'm going to have to answer to Quentin. Maybe I can get us on a jet to the CDC and some big brain there will be able to figure out your condition..."

"Uh-huh."

Five now. Arranged around us like the points on a pentagram. Zoya was so busy relishing her superiority over me that she failed to clock the enemy agents gathering around us.

Then she cursed.

"I take it you just noticed them," I said. "I'm counting five..."

"I see them. Who are we dealing with here, Bell?"

I wasn't entirely sure, to be honest. All I knew was that whoever they were, they'd definitely be able to give me some answers about the chemical agent. This had been my goal all along. I'd carefully orchestrated this moment. Reached out to Zoya on an open line. Chosen an outdoor location that could easily be surveilled. Made a small show of using code words, but nothing any foreign op worth a damn couldn't easily figure out. Hell, I had to make it easy enough for *Zoya* to understand.

(Okay, that was a little catty. But she deserved it.)

"Where's your backup?" I asked.

"You told me to come alone."

"I didn't think you'd actually listen to me."

(Ugh, she was such a stickler for the rules.)

"What do we do now?"

"Let's see what they want," I said.

Zoya, however, didn't like being in a situation that was rapidly spiraling out of control. I saw her reaching for her weapon at the same time she was pushing back away from the table. Before I had the chance to tell her to stop being foolish and stand down, Zoya was muttering more expletives, flipping over the table, and opening fire.

CHAPTER 22

IN REALITY, THE firefight probably last all of twenty seconds, tops. But it felt like forever.

Pedestrians were screaming and running for cover. They needn't have worried; the gunmen were interested in pinning us down and forcing our surrender, not plugging a bystander. We were all trained killers, but we were also professionals.

"I think we're dealing with the SVR," Zoya said, before lifting her gun over the edge of the overturned table to return fire. I heard an anguished scream as she hit her target.

SVR—Russia's foreign intelligence service.

"Makes sense," I said.

"*Nothing* about this makes sense," she replied, and reached around the table to fire three more shots. I heard two more screams. Three down, two remaining. Zoya was nothing if not efficient.

Which was another reason I chose her. For all of my grousing about her capabilities, Zoya was an amazing marksman. And as a professional, she wasn't shooting to kill—just a little harmless maiming, enough to force the agents' retreat.

You see, there's an unspoken code between opposing field agents—a kind of a dance we do. Zoya had slightly breached that code by shooting first when they made their presence known. So the agents sent a message in return, based on the trajectory of their bullets: *Relax, we just want to talk.* Zoya's response, written in the bullets that sliced through biceps, shoulders, and thighs: *Well, we don't wish to speak to you right now. Back off.*

Even with three of their own down, however, the remaining two pressed the issue. Bullets zinged closer to our heads. If they wanted to, they could have taken headshots a minute ago and ended this all at once. The fact that they hadn't done so meant they wanted us—or at least me—alive. Which was the first hopeful sign I'd had in two days.

"If only Quentin could see us now," Zoya said, almost giddy. "Me, saving your tail!"

"Yeah, well, too bad Quentin's in North Korea."

Zoya furrowed her brow. "North Korea? Who told you that?" she said as she took down the penultimate agent, knee-capping him. The poor bugger howled. This was a more serious message, along the lines of: *No means no, pal.*

When she spun the table around us to line up her final shot, I took *my* shot—an elbow right to her temple, knocking Zoya unconscious.

Now the real fun could begin.

CHAPTER 23

AFTER ZOYA COLLAPSED to the ground, I reached for her gun. The final SVR agent had had enough by now—he'd just watched four of his comrades win trips to the hospital within the past thirty seconds, and he wasn't about to take any chances on me. I had to act fast.

"Don't dare!" he yelled at me in broken English.

I tried to put him at ease by responding: "Take it easy! I'm surrendering!"

"Oh, *now* you surrender? Couldn't you have done that *before* your incredibly sadistic friend hurt my friends?" (He responded in Russian, so I'm not completely sure what he actually said, but that's my best translation based on his tone.) In English, he added, "How about I place bullet in *your* leg? See how *you* like it?"

"Buddy," I said, "that would be far from the worst thing that's happened to me over the past two days."

While he puzzled that one out, I slowly climbed to my feet, showed him my palms, and surveyed the scene. Civilians were still sheltering in place, behind overturned tables and behind huge planters. I saw smartphones taking photos and recording videos. Not good. I had to wrap this up quick.

"I'm coming to you."

I took a step forward and wobbled a little, trying hard to maintain my balance.

"What is wrong with you?" he said in English. I must have been an awfully pathetic sight. He'd just pivoted from wanting to put hot lead in my thigh to inquiring about my well-being.

"I'm kind of working with an expiration date here, and it's fast approaching."

"I'm sorry? I don't understand."

"If you have a vehicle nearby, I strongly suggest you put me in it and take me to your superiors. Because I'm not going to be alive much longer."

CHAPTER 24

A HOOD OVER my head, a push into the back of a white van—it was nice to have the opportunity to finally get a little more rest, at the very least. The back of the van smelled like bleach. As if a body had been disposed of recently.

The length of the drive indicated I was being taken somewhere deep behind the former Iron Curtain—back when the Soviets controlled this half of the country. The Wall fell and all of that, but I knew the Russians kept a secret black site interrogation room or two around, just for old times' sake.

I was glad they hadn't bothered to take Zoya, too. She couldn't tell them anything useful, and she'd probably just have annoyed them until they killed her. I didn't want to spend the afterlife with her giving me nasty looks.

Several sets of hands rudely pulled me from the back of the van and dragged me down a long corridor. Guess they didn't care that I was a gravely ill woman and not being difficult for the fun of it.

Soon, I was stripped down to my undergarments and secured to a chair with thick bungee-style cords. I wanted to tell them this was overkill; frankly, at the moment I'd have a hard time breaking through dental floss, let alone industrial-grade rubber. On the plus side, I'd already suffered the indignities of the hospital, so the petty torture of being exposed to strangers in my underwear didn't bother me too much.

I kept repeating one of the only phrases I knew in Russian: "I will only speak to your section chief."

They went in a little harder with the torture—bending my fingers in directions that nature didn't intend them to go, using rubber batons on pressure points, and so on. What they didn't understand was that thanks to the effects of the chemical agent, I was feeling increasingly numb as the time passed.

"I will only speak to your section chief."

There was a psychological component to my numbness. When you feel like the fates have already dealt you the worst hand possible, you don't fear the turn of the next card. Pain didn't mean much. Pain was a mere annoyance next to the true horror of losing Kevin. Especially if I was somehow to blame for that.

Which was the whole reason for this ruse—meeting Zoya, allowing myself to be captured, stripped, and tortured. I wanted all of this, because I needed to find out the truth, if nothing else, before I died.

Any minute now.

"I will only speak to your section chief."

The agents eventually left the room, which turned out to be the worst torture of all. I didn't know how much time was passing, because there was no clock in the interrogation room. Was it hours? Mere minutes that felt like hours?

When you have precious little life left, you don't want to squander it in a former Stasi interrogation room. I almost wanted the torturers to return, just to give me something to help pass the time.

CHAPTER 25

"WHO WAS HE?" the section chief asked, in English.

After enough time passed that I was certain I would indeed be dying in this musty room in the old East Germany, the SVR chief entered the room and ordered my binds loosened. I was even given a set of clothes—workout gear that fit surprisingly well. I knew it was a tactic meant to instill a sense of gratitude toward my captors. But you know what? It worked.

"I don't understand the question."

"The man in the hotel, posing as your husband. Clearly you were using him as some sort of cover. So Samantha Bell, 'former' agent of the CIA, I'd like to know why you chose him."

"I chose him," I said, "because I loved him."

The section chief had at least twenty years on me, with lean, hard features and a severe military crew cut with salt-and-pepper temples. But there was also a tenderness in his blue eyes, and slight skin discoloration around the fourth finger of his right hand. Which told me he either removed his wedding ring before torturing people or was recently single.

"You say you loved him, yet you murdered him to stage an attack on one of our own citizens?"

"And kill myself in the process? Think about it…what is your name?"

"Oleg."

Now we were on a first-name basis. The personal touch. That was an interesting play.

"Oleg, a suicide mission would be easy. I would have delivered the chemical agent directly, not caring if I perished in the attack."

"But your government created the chemical agent, Samantha. Clearly, you would have an antidote on hand. Which brings us back to why you chose to kill this innocent businessman, Kevin Drexel."

Was this an attempt to coerce a "confession" out of me? If the SVR *did* murder the oligarch and were trying to pin it on me, then of course they'd want to build a narrative around the possibility that I'd somehow snared a wealthy businessman in a honeypot-style operation, then killed him to cover my tracks. Except I'd been caught in the crossfire, and had accidentally succumbed to my own chemical weapon.

I asked Oleg: "How long have you been married?"

He covered it well, but there was a moment of surprise on his face before glancing down at his right hand.

"I was married," he said, "for twenty-two years."

Emphasis on the word *was*.

"How long has it been?"

"Not long at all," he said quietly.

I realized his line of questioning was not about building a frame-up narrative around me. No, he was getting personal with me because this was personal for him. Oleg and his wife hadn't divorced; death had taken her away from him.

I sensed that Oleg wanted to look me in the eye and figure out how I could so blithely murder a spouse, when all he wanted in the world was to bring his own back to life.

Which told me something even more important: the SVR and the Russian government actually believed the Americans were responsible for the attack in the hotel.

I was beginning to believe it, too.

CHAPTER 26

"YOU THINK *I* did this?"

"You, or your government," Oleg said.

"My government doesn't make chemical weapons."

"So you claim. We have evidence that says otherwise."

"What kind of evidence?"

"A clandestine lab running experiments, funded by shell companies. We've known about it for a while. Maybe you could shed some light on why you decided to act now with this public demonstration. Do you have buyers gathered here in Berlin?"

"This was not a demonstration," I said, angrily. "This was a murder. And I had nothing to do with it."

"I know you're not trying to insult my intelligence, Samantha, but look at it from my point of view. You're right at the center of this incident."

"Listen, I'm going to be dead in less than a day, Oleg. If I did this, then I really wasn't thinking ahead."

"So, you're saying your government set you up? You can prove it?"

"I can't prove anything at this point," I said. "But let me tell you something. I left the employment of the CIA around the same time I met my husband. I'm starting to believe that my superiors didn't like the idea of me leaving."

Oleg shook his head. "That doesn't make much sense. A sloppy attack on foreign soil, with the potential for collateral damage? No. There are many ways your superiors could have punished you. This strikes me as a foolish option."

He was right, of course. Quentin used to relish detailing the numerous ways he could kill me, some of them downright surprising and gruesome. It was his way of teaching me to keep my eyes open for any possible threat. Plus, I think he got a big kick out of it. (He was always a little weird that way.) But of all of the methods he'd name, this would never be one of them. Because it *was* sloppy. Because there was way too much room for error.

But if I *was* the target, and the Russians *weren't* to blame . . . then what piece was I missing?

"Help me find the truth."

"You want my help?" Oleg said with a smile. "What could I possibly do for you?"

"If what you've already told me is true, I can eliminate the entire Russian government as suspects. I'd like you to let me walk out of here so I can find the people actually responsible."

"Just let you walk out? You engaged my agents in a firefight so we could have this chat. Good men are in the hospital."

"I didn't know my trigger-happy ex-colleague would open fire. I was hoping my surrender to your men would be a little more . . . civilized. Did she take anyone out of the game for good?"

"No. Your ex-colleague—if that's indeed what she is—happens to be an excellent shot."

"I'm glad to hear it. I don't want any more death on my conscience."

Oleg studied me for a while. Maybe he could sense that I was telling the truth. Maybe he sympathized with me. Maybe he was running scenarios in his head. There was virtually no downside to what I was suggesting, and it might mean justice for the murder of two Russian citizens.

"Go, then," he finally said.

"Thank you, Oleg. I do have one last favor to ask."

"What else may we do for you, Samantha Bell?" The very suggestion seemed to amuse him. What other favor could I be asking him? For weapons? Surveillance gear? Possibly a vehicle? A war plane? All of the above?

"Could I get some clean underwear? I've been wearing the same ones for a while."

Oleg laughed.

CHAPTER 27

THE GOOD NEWS: I was free on the bustling streets of Berlin once again. The bad news: I had no idea where the hell I was. The even worse news: I had less than a day to live. It could even be down to a few hours.

I'll admit that a small part of me clung to the desperate belief this was all just a nightmare. Any second now, I would jolt awake in Kevin's arms, and over breakfast I'd tell him about this deliriously horrible dream I had—how my years as a spy finally caught up with me.

Please, let me wake up now. I've had enough.

Instead, I was stuck in this strange purgatory. Walking down unfamiliar streets, with no watch, wallet, or phone, no identification or cash, wearing shiny athletic gear donated by Russian intelligence agents.

I ducked into the first hotel I came across. A humble two-star place—a glorified hostel, really. But the lobby had a kiosk full of tourist brochures, including local maps to help me orient myself. Apparently, I was now in Weitlingkiez, which wasn't too **far away** from the Berliner Dom. My "kidnappers" must have taken an overly circuitous route to confuse me.

I needed to figure out my next move. I gamed out a few scenarios, but in my heart I knew there was only one choice.

I was going to have to reach out to Quentin.

Years ago, he'd developed a last-resort system of personal communication that didn't require any fancy technology or spy gear—he didn't trust satellites, cell phone towers, or the Internet to be working properly in a crisis. He also needed a system outside the purview of the Company, in case it was ever compromised by a foreign agent.

Quentin's system was simple. There was a person in a room, sitting by a landline. When you called that number, you gave a coded message that would be passed along to Quentin.

(I once asked Quentin about that person in the room—or rather, the several people in that room, who worked rotating shifts. What were their lives like? How much did he pay them? And was a service only used twice a decade worth the expense? Quentin just smiled and said: "They're the best-read people you'll ever meet.")

I picked up the hotel courtesy phone and dialed the number. I spoke into the receiver and gave the message I'd memorized long ago: *"Vergessen sie nicht, Kirschen zu kaufen."*

Translation: "Do not forget to buy cherries."

This sentence included two pieces of information: that I was in Germany, and that my situation was critical (cherries, red).

A female voice responded in a flat Midwestern accent: "I'll make sure he knows that, dear," and then disconnected the call before I had the chance to ask her what novel she was currently reading.

The protocol was to stay near the same landline for five

minutes. If Quentin could be reached, he'd call back. If not, it meant he was deep into some other op and I was on my own.

It felt like I spent forever in that overheated, seedy lobby. A half-dozen college-age kids with backpacks entered at one point, tipsy and rowdy. They sized me up as potential prey, but quickly looked away. Maybe I looked homeless. Or perhaps they could see the death in my eyes.

I thought about what Quentin might say after these past six months. My retirement had been a little awkward; he thought I was making a rash decision. I'd extended multiple invites to meet Kevin, but Quentin had demurred. *"If you're not in this life, I can't be in yours."*

The phone rang. I pushed through the crowd of backpackers to answer it. This took more energy than I'd expected; I was practically out of breath by the time I held the receiver to my head.

"This is Samantha."

"Bell, get out of that hotel immediately," Quentin said. It was the first time I'd heard his voice in months, and despite the words he was speaking, I felt some degree of relief. Quentin had always been something of a father figure or an older brother to me. And right now he was the only family I had left.

"Listen to me. Interpol is closing in on your location."

"Good. Tell them that I can be trusted. I'd love a ride to a safe house."

"You don't understand. I don't trust *Interpol*. There's a lot happening behind the scenes here—"

"What do you mean 'here'? You're in Berlin?"

"I arrived just after you escaped from the hospital. Look, I'll explain everything later when I find you . . . but right now I need you to put down the phone and *run*."

CHAPTER 28

EASIER SAID THAN done, breaking into a sprint when you're at death's door. In my condition the best I could hope for was evasion.

Using the map of the area I'd memorized from those tourist brochures, I zig-zagged my way through the dim streets of Weitlingkiez. I checked every reflective surface for signs that someone (or some vehicle) was following me. I saw nothing. Either I'd slipped away from the hotel before Interpol could pick up my trail, or I was being followed by some truly exceptional agents.

But maybe I was giving myself too much credit. The symptoms I'd felt in the hospital were coming back strong. Maybe it was a combination of rest and sheer willpower that had kept them at bay. But now I felt like I had the night before, when I was almost flattened by a bus. My body was reminding me: *Don't forget, we're preparing to close up shop. Conduct your final transactions before we pull down the metal gates one last time.*

I couldn't stay out here for much longer. Either Interpol would find me, or I'd collapse in the street. I needed a safe place to wait until Quentin could meet me. This was my mission now: tell him everything I knew so that he could avenge me and Kevin after I was gone.

But what would I tell him, definitively? That I had a strong *hunch* the Russians weren't behind the attack? That I had a *feeling* I was the real target? Quentin dealt in proof, not conjecture.

So I thought about the things I'd observed, starting with the moment I opened the door to find Kevin's body.

The position of his body.

The strange scent in the air.

The "something else" missing from the scene.

The problem was that my shock and grief were getting in the way of my rational mind. It was far too raw, too painful, to dwell in that moment. I couldn't force myself to bulldoze past those Kübler-Ross stages of grief. My heart had *exploded* in that hallway two days ago. And every time I tried to access my memories of that awful moment, some kind of self-defense mechanism slammed a door in my face. I had to find the strength to push past all of that if I was going to put the pieces together.

I was also exhausted. Berliner Dom was too far away, and I didn't relish the idea of sleeping in a musical instrument again.

This is when I heard Kevin's voice in my head:

Well, at some point I'm going to have to meet up for a quick drink with Bill. He lives nearby in Simon-Dach-Kiez, just a neighborhood or two away.

CHAPTER 29

KEVIN HAD ALWAYS told me that Bill Devander was a serious foodie who preferred living in places with a wide array of dining options. (*And women who liked to drink*, he'd added.) I could see what he meant the moment I stepped onto the bustle of Simon-Dach-Straße. The narrow street was lined with so many tables and chairs spilling out of nearby restaurants, it felt like one big, bustling dining hall.

At the moment, those tables were full of carefree young couples and students out for a night on the town. I found myself hating them all. How could they be here, sipping good wine and eating good food, pretending everything was right in the world? When I was standing here, dying?

Stop it, I told myself. Self-pity won't help you find Kevin's killers.

I knew that Bill's home address wouldn't be public information; he was a wealthy businessman, after all. But a little social engineering might do the trick. Kevin doubted his best friend would ever settle down; he was too much of a playboy. "Weddings give him hives." I picked a cocktail lounge at random and approached the most attractive female bartender—a lithe woman with purple fingernails who wore her hair in a severe bob.

Now, I was fully aware that I must look like hot garbage. I hadn't bathed since my shower more than two days ago, and I'd since gone from the hospital to a secret interrogation room. Plus my clothes were far from stylish, unless "Soviet Brutalist" had swept the runways during the most recent fashion week. But I tried to use all of this to my benefit now, using my pain to project the image of a spurned date.

"But Bill was *supposed* to meet me here," I said in English, almost in a pout.

"I'm sorry," the bartender replied. "Who?"

"Bill Devander. I am *sure* you know him. He runs a big company here in Berlin."

Of course she knew Bill; I could read the recognition on her face. But she told me she was sorry, she didn't know who I was talking about, did I want a cognac while I waited? I told her I did not.

This same trick yielded zero results at the second lounge. In fact, I'm pretty sure they thought I was going to pull a dine-and-dash scam, because they asked me if I wouldn't mind waiting outside for this Mr. Devander.

But at the third, I found a curly-haired sommelier who was quick to admit she'd had a fling with Bill. In fact, she poured me a very fine glass of 2012 Donnhoff Riesling as she launched into the gory details. At first, it was one for the storybooks: Bill had taken her on shopping sprees. Bill took her out to a new place for dinner every night she wasn't working. Bill promised trips to wine country, just as soon as "some annoying things at the office were ironed out."

"And then he ghosted me," the sommelier said. "He didn't even tell me to my face that he'd grown bored of me and gone off in search of someone better."

"I'm sure that wasn't the case," I said, feeling sorry I'd started this conversation in the first place.

"Was it you?" The sommelier regarded me with both pity and confusion. *He dumped me for this tall, skinny woman in bad workout gear?*

"To be fair, I think our situations are very different."

"So why do you want to see him?"

"He promised me a favor, and I need to hold him to it."

That seemed to satisfy her. "You might try..." at which point she rattled off an address I won't repeat here. "If you see him, tell him Karla with a K says hello."

"Karla with a K," I repeated to myself, and went off into the night.

CHAPTER 30

"SAMANTHA! I'VE BEEN worried sick about you!" Bill Devander exclaimed.

"Not as sick as I am," I replied. "I promise you."

As Bill wrestled with the appropriate response, I tried to put him out of his misery. "Do you mind if I come in? I don't want to die in your doorway."

I won't lie: the feeling of a well-made sofa beneath my aching body felt like a dream. My limbs trembled. Bill offered me a variety of refreshments, from a warm latte to a cold martini—*anything,* he said. His home bar was well stocked. But I told him I just wanted some water and a moment to breathe.

After Bill handed me the glass, he sat down across from me. "I've been in touch with a number of private clinics," he said. "I know you were told that your condition is irreversible, but I really think you need second, third, fourth, and fifth opinions."

"I appreciate that, Bill. But my body is telling me otherwise."

"Then let me, at the very least, take you to a place that will keep you comfortable."

"And what—gently ease me into my own grave?"

"That's not what I meant."

That's exactly what Bill meant. Keep me comfortable until my body gave up the fight. Which could literally prove to be any minute now. But I refused to take the easy way out.

"By the way, Karla with a K says hello."

Bill put it together quickly. "Karla...*That's* how you found me? You could have just called my office!"

"And have Interpol return the call? Karla seemed nice, but a little intense. I can see why you pulled away."

"What else about me have you learned?" Bill asked, annoyance creeping into his voice. I'd touched a nerve.

"I wasn't doing a background check, Bill. I just scammed a lady in a bar to get your address."

"Isn't that what you used to do for a living? Pry into people's lives and expose all of their dirty secrets?"

I would have apologized for prying into his personal life, were I not suddenly overwhelmed with nausea. Bill saw the stricken look on my face and bolted out of his seat, as if anticipating the worst. *Was this near-stranger about to die on my couch?*

Instead I whispered "Bathroom" and Bill pointed me in the right direction. Only my exhaustion prevented me from breaking into a sprint.

CHAPTER 31

DO NOT THROW up, I commanded myself, splashing cold water on my face. *If you're about to die, do it with some dignity.*

Something was wrong. I mean, aside from the fact that my body was shutting down. My blood felt like it had been run through a hot water heater. I was utterly exhausted yet extremely agitated, like my brain was bumping up against something. I knew I couldn't rest until I figured out the precise nature of that *something*.

Have you ever had the kind of dream where you're working frenetically to solve a problem, but no matter how rationally you approach it, you're unable to solve it? Because—well, because you're in a dream, and nothing is rational in that mental landscape.

That's how I felt, standing in Bill Devander's luxurious bathroom. I was missing something *huge*. If only I could pause for long enough to figure it out . . .

I am sorry to report, Dear Reader, that I did indeed vomit. Not my finest moment, and it didn't make me feel that much better, either. I hoped my retching wasn't worrying poor Bill out in the other room. The last thing I wanted was for him to force his way in here, out of concern.

I rinsed my mouth out with tap water, cleaned up the sink, and opened the cabinet under the sink to look for some mouthwash. Nothing under there but high-end cleaning products. I eventually found a small bottle of rosewater mouthwash in the medicine cabinet.

As I swished the fluid around my mouth, I saw that Bill had an array of expensive toiletries: Creed aftershave balm, Erno Laszlo deep cleansing bar. Bill's taste was far more refined than Kevin's—whose own attitude of *why shouldn't I use the same bar of soap to wash my hair* and *my body?* was frugal, but also drove me a little crazy.

After I spit, I saw a bottle of Frederic Malle's The Night. *How fancy, Mr. Devander.* I uncapped it, breathed some of it in. I'll admit, I was curious what two-thousand-dollar cologne smelled like. I also wanted to clear the awful smell of vomit out of my nostrils.

Yet instead of relieving my misery, the expensive scent made me light-headed, and I broke out into a sweat. I quickly recapped the cologne, closed the medicine cabinet door, and gripped the sides of the porcelain sink.

No. Do not pass out. Do not let Bill find your unconscious body in here, because he'll call the paramedics, and then it'll be all over.

I couldn't get the nightmare images out of my head, playing in a messy cinematic loop. The creak of our suite door, opening. The feel of the smooth wood beneath my fingertips. Pan down. Kevin's body, facedown, sprawled on the hallway floor. Sweep right. Further down the hall: the dead father, the dead daughter, limbs akimbo.

Repeat loop. The creak of the door as it opens. The feel of the smooth wood. Pan down, again. Kevin's body, again, as if there could be any other outcome. *But something is missing. Someone left a key prop out of this sequence. What was it?*

I couldn't stop the images, no matter how much I squeezed my fists and clenched my teeth until I thought I would explode. Maybe if I screamed? I realized I was losing my mind, at long last. I had to get out of here. I pushed away from the sink and staggered over to the bathroom door.

I opened the door to find Bill pointing a gun at my chest.

CHAPTER 32

THE IMAGE WAS so absurd that I thought it was a joke—a punch line to the horror movie loop spinning in my head. My dead husband's best friend, pointing a gun at me? I may have even given Bill a quizzical smile.

"If you want to kill me," I said, "you won't need that. Just wait a couple of hours."

"I can't believe you're making me do this," Bill replied. "This is *not* how it was supposed to happen."

"Put the gun down, Bill. Let's talk through whatever you think is going on."

"You first, Samantha."

"I'm not the one holding a firearm."

"No. I know how you people work. You were in there looking for a weapon. You thought you were being clever, pretending to throw up. Kev told me how resourceful you are."

"I promise you, I have no intention of hurting you. Even if I wanted to, I can barely stand. I just want some answers."

"That's another thing. You seem to be getting around fairly well for a woman on her deathbed."

Yeah, I make it look real easy, I thought. If he only knew what I'd endured these past three days. But enough of Bill accusing me of wrongdoing. It was his turn. The way he'd reacted to me grilling Karla with a K meant that he was hiding more than his address. I'd gotten a glimpse into Bill Devander's life. Dining out and breaking hearts all over Simon-Dach-Straße. The fancy townhouse, the expensive toiletries. None of it conclusive proof, but I was playing a hunch. A hunch built on a dozen details that were snapping into focus.

I took a stab at it. "Fine, we'll try it your way. Tell me—how long have you been stealing from the company?"

I can always tell when an accusation hits home, because the subject will work really hard to appear casual, maybe even puzzled. Or they'll seem relieved, because they've been waiting to get caught. With Bill, it was the latter.

"Kev told you."

Of course he hadn't. But he *had* made a point of coming to Berlin for our honeymoon. Yes, he'd said he wanted to show off a city he loved. But it was still something of an odd choice after our island-hopping romance. Kevin had needed an excuse to see Bill in person. Something that he couldn't discuss over the phone, or via email. Something sensitive and serious. Corporate espionage, a violation of regulatory laws, perhaps.

Embezzlement.

"I was working out a deal to pay him back," Bill said now. "To make things right again. Most important, I wanted to get my best friend back."

"I'm sure that's what he wanted, too. Which is why he met with you in person when we first arrived."

"I haven't seen Kev in months!"

"Wrong. You saw him right before he died."

The look on Bill's face told me I was correct. "How could you possibly know that?"

I realized that I'd known it all along. That was the missing detail that my brain couldn't quite process, because it was the unthinkable.

"When I found his body," I said, "he didn't have wine or flowers with him. That's because instead of going to a store, he actually went to meet you. Or rather, you came to meet him. I know that, because I could smell your cologne in the hallway. You were the last person to see him alive. Which means you killed him."

CHAPTER 33

"NO. YOU'RE WRONG. I'm no killer!"

"Says the man pointing a loaded gun at a grieving widow."

At least, I assumed the gun was loaded. Impossible to know for sure, but I did note that Bill had the safety disengaged. Which meant he was prepared to use the weapon, if he felt threatened.

"It was Kevin's idea to meet with me here in Berlin," Bill said. "I think he wanted all of this awful business sorted out and off his chest so you could enjoy your time together."

"Yeah. Let me tell you, I really enjoyed the last thirty seconds of our marriage. Kevin dying in a hallway. Me leaping through a window. That was a nice wedding gift."

"I didn't kill him!"

"But you *did*, Bill. I *know* you did, as sure as I know I'm about to die in a matter of hours. Want to know *how* I know?" I needed to keep him curious for a few moments longer. I was still piecing it together—but I was very close now.

"Tell me," he said.

"The chemical agent that killed Kevin and the Russians—and is killing me—was odorless. All of the experts agree on that. Yet, I smelled something distinct in the hallway when I found Kevin's body. I couldn't place it then. But I've encountered the same scent twice since. Once in the hospital, where it made me sweat bullets. And once just now, in your bathroom."

"What are you talking about?"

"Your very expensive cologne. A sniff of it unlocked the memories I was suppressing. The memory of you in the hallway, running away from the scene of the crime."

I'll admit, this last part was a bluff. I wanted to see what Bill would do. Confess immediately, or try to kill me? Instead, he tried a different approach.

"That's not what happened," he said coldly. "You're suppressing the wrong memory, Sam."

"I don't think so. What did you tell him, Bill? That you finally agreed to meet me, so he brought you back to the hotel for a quick hello, maybe a friendly drink? And instead, you murdered him right outside our door."

"You have it wrong, believe me. If you don't stop asking questions, you're going to get us both killed."

"Only, you didn't realize that two other people would have the horrible misfortune to step outside of their room at the same moment, so you killed them, too. Because it's bad form to leave witnesses."

I had Bill Devander exactly where I wanted him: on the razor's edge. I could see it in his expression, the way he held his body. The way he held his gun. It was time to bring the mystery to a close.

"There's just one thing I don't know, and maybe you can help me sort this one out."

"Sam, don't do this…"

"How did an American executive in Berlin even manage to get his hands on an experimental chemical agent?"

The question tipped Bill over the edge. The life drained out of his face. He lifted the gun, pointed it at my face, and pulled the trigger.

CHAPTER 34

BY THE TIME Bill fired, I'd already let my body go completely limp and had collapsed to the ground. I heard the bullet shatter the tile wall behind me. Chunks of porcelain drizzled down to the floor.

I imagined Bill was probably wondering how he'd missed. I pressed my left foot against the door frame, then pumped my leg with all of my might, propelling myself deeper into the bathroom. As I slid, I used my right foot to slam the bathroom door shut.

Two bullets punched through the door in quick succession. Then a third, a bit lower than the first two shots.

But I had already rolled to my right, curling my body toward the sink. The three bullets tore up the floor behind me. Bill was firing blind.

I opened the sink cabinet and grabbed a container of some fancy bathroom cleanser. I dumped a small pile of powdered detergent into my right hand. Bill wrenched open the door and approached, gun in hand.

"I'll never forgive you for making me do this," he said, kneeling down to finish me off at close range, which was exactly what I was hoping he'd do. As he got closer, I blew the detergent directly into his eyes.

Now, I don't know if you've ever had the pleasure of calcium carbonate, sodium carbonate peroxide, hydrated silica, and assorted other ingredients blown directly on your naked eyes...but it's a bad chemical burn. Bill's hands flew to his face, and he howled inconsolably.

But the damned gun stayed in his hand. So I did a half sit-up and slapped my palms as hard as I could against both of his ears, which had the effect of a firecracker snapping off right in the middle of his brain.

Still, he didn't drop the gun; I had to give him that. He clung to the weapon like a toddler with his favorite toy. I used the sink to pull myself up to a semi-sitting position as Bill scuttled like a crab out into the living room, moaning all the way. This was not good.

I needed to find another weapon. Any weapon. Something that would incapacitate Bill until I could question him properly. Once I knew where he had gotten the toxin, I could close this case. Report what I found to Quentin. Die in something like peace.

But then I heard a noise that changed everything.

The muffled crack of a gunshot.

CHAPTER 35

I CRAWLED INTO the living room and confirmed the worst: Bill had placed the gun in his mouth and pulled the trigger.

Instinctively, I pressed my fingers to his carotid artery. There was a mild blur of a pulse, about to fade away to nothing. Had it been stronger, I would have called an ambulance. I've seen human beings survive a shocking amount of head trauma over the years. But Bill Devander would be taking his secrets to a German coroner's slab.

Maybe I should have felt relief. After all, Bill had been trying to kill me. Yet what I felt was overwhelming shame that I'd let Kevin's best friend down somehow. Was I so hell-bent on forcing the truth from Bill that I had backed him into a corner? He was just a civilian, after all, not a war criminal. He deserved a trial and prison, not a panicked suicide.

"I'm sorry, my love," I said, as if Kevin were in the room, too. "For everything."

If Kevin was indeed with me, he didn't respond. I couldn't blame him.

I knew I couldn't stay here. This was a tightly packed residential district of townhouses. Somebody must have called in the multiple gunshots by now. My own death was fast approaching, and I *really* didn't want to die in an interrogation room.

Somehow I propelled myself out of Bill's front door and staggered halfway down the block before hearing the singsong of Berlin police sirens. I kept moving, even as the strength drained out of me like blood from a hundred cuts.

Was Kevin's spirit walking with me? I hoped so. Maybe this was how our honeymoon was always supposed to end. The two of us lost souls, refugees from the real world, wandering the streets of Berlin together in the middle of the night.

About five blocks away from Bill Devander's apartment, I collapsed and died.

CHAPTER 36

COME ON, BELL, God said. *Open your eyes. That's an order.*

My body had disappeared. I had the sensation of floating through slightly turbulent air. I opened my eyes. But I quickly realized it wasn't God speaking to me.

"Quentin?"

I was in his arms and he was hurrying us both down the street.

"Good, you're still with us. I'm going to bring you to a nearby safe house. You hang on just a little while longer. You got me?"

I wanted to tell him I appreciated his concern, but that I was a lost cause... only, I passed out again before I could form the words. My mind slid away from my body and disappeared into an impossibly black lake. The water wasn't cold; it felt more like warm, viscous oil. At some point I realized there were creatures down here with me. One of them squeezed my hand in the dark. Jaws clamped down on my wrist...

I jolted back awake in Bill Devander's living room, handcuffed to a radiator.

My first thought was that the last fifteen minutes had been a dream, that I hadn't really escaped from the townhouse after all, and the Berlin police had just arrested me for Bill's murder.

But then I saw Quentin across the room, leaning against a wall, studying the room like a forensic analyst taking in a crime scene. It was a bit surreal, seeing him here, now, after all of these months. He was tall (six foot five) and lean as ever—possibly leaner now. *I'm the one boss you can look up to*, he used to joke.

"Quentin," I said. "We can't be here."

"Don't worry. When the address popped up on the scanner, I had the Berlin police diverted." Quentin gestured down at Bill's corpse, which lay in the same exact position as when I'd left it. "Devander do himself in, or did you make it look that way?"

"All his idea," I said. "Quentin?"

"Yeah, Bell?"

"Why am I handcuffed to this radiator?"

"I have to explain a few things to you, and I want you to stay calm as I explain them. Promise me you'll stay calm?"

"That's impossible," I said. "How can I promise not to react to something when I don't know what it is?"

"Fair enough."

"Start talking. I don't have much time left."

"Yeah, speaking of that...Listen, Bell. I didn't want it to happen like this, but this idiot screwed it up. You weren't supposed to be anywhere near when he dosed Kevin Drexel."

CHAPTER 37

ALL OF THE blood in my veins turned to ice.

"*You* had my husband killed?"

"He wasn't your husband, Bell. Not the way you think he was."

"If there's one thing I know for sure, it's that four days ago I married Kevin Drexel, whom I loved with all of my heart. And now you're trying to tell me what—it was all a figment of my imagination?"

"What I'm trying to tell you is that the only reason you married Kevin Drexel, or even met him in the first place, is because *I* sent him to you."

"That's truly amazing, Quentin. I always knew you were a narcissist, but I had no idea it was this bad. How do you pass the Agency's psych evals every year?"

"Let me explain, because it's important you understand what's happened over the last six months. I think once the fog of so-called true love has faded away, you'll see that I was acting in your best interest."

As Quentin talked, I tried to figure out a way to escape my handcuffs. One cuff was around my left wrist; the other was snapped around the thickest pipe of the radiator unit. If I couldn't pick the lock, it would take superhuman strength to rip the radiator out of the floor with my bare hands and beat him to death with it.

"Both Kevin Drexel and Bill Devander—this suicidal idiot on the floor here—worked for me. Cutout company based in Berlin. I'd cultivated Devander years ago as an asset. He was a useful idiot. In other words, my favorite kind of asset. Only later did I bring Drexel into it."

Cutout company: in other words, a front for Quentin's various operations.

"Right," I said. "So one day you decided to say, 'Hey, random business guy who runs my cutout, why don't you go off and marry one of my field agents?' "

"I knew you were eyeing the door, Bell. Look, it happens all the time. An adolescence cut short, followed by eight years in a high-intensity job? Of course you'd be looking to leave. It's practically textbook. You wanted to know what the road less traveled felt like. I knew it before *you* knew it. And you're so stubborn, I knew I wouldn't be able to talk you out of it. You had to see for yourself."

"So you hired Kevin to what? Break my heart?"

"I wouldn't put it that way, but essentially . . . yeah. He was supposed to show you a good time, then do what *all* men do eventually—dump you for a younger model. See, this is a lesson you never learned, because you came to work for me so young. But I didn't want your heart broken by some random civilian. You deserved much better than that."

What I *deserved* was something I could use to pick open this handcuff. But Quentin was too careful to leave anything within reach. I was cuffed to this particular spot because he had determined that escape would be impossible. He was right.

"But Kevin fell in love with me for real," I said, "so of course you had to kill him. To what, teach me a lesson? Punish me?"

"No. I was happy for you. If Drexel turned out to be the exception to the rule, and the man of your dreams, who was I to stand in the way?"

"So what happened?"

"While you and Drexel were globe-trotting, the idiot on the floor here started embezzling."

CHAPTER 38

"THIS IS ABOUT money? You have to be kidding, Quentin. You have unlimited access to funds. Each year, the government hands you the biggest blank check in the free world!"

"You're right. It wasn't about the money."

"You were afraid Kevin would tell the police?"

"No. I was afraid Kevin would convince the corpse here to dissolve the company. And I couldn't let that happen, because that would...well, let's just say a very delicate operation would start to unravel."

"If this story goes on much longer," I said, "you're going to be talking to another corpse. Tell me what all of this misery was worth."

"You'll be fine, Bell. I have an antidote."

That revelation almost stopped my heart right then. Not because it was a new lease on life. But because of what it implied. Namely, that everything I knew was wrong. For the moment, though, I let Quentin play things out his way.

"There's been an antidote this whole time? So I'm not going to die. Not tonight, anyway."

"Yeah, and I would have given it to you in the hospital if

you hadn't decided to escape. You really don't know what I've been through these past couple of days."

"Poor baby. Why did your cutout help me escape the hospital?"

"Because it was the best way to get you away from Interpol. I knew you wouldn't just lie there and wait for the end."

"And *why* did you murder my husband?"

"See, you're still looking at it the wrong way. Drexel was going to bring everything down! And as you know, he was a very smart guy. If he saw me coming, he'd know something was up. Devander had to do it. Only, he was supposed to do it discreetly. And boy did he screw that up."

And at that point Quentin looked down at Bill's body. "It's not mace, you idiot. You were supposed to release a tiny amount in his drink, not dose him like you were spraying for weeds!"

"Why would you give a civilian an experimental chemical agent?"

"Devander insisted on it. He wanted something quick and painless for his best friend."

"How would he even *know* about it?"

Quentin stared at me. "What did you think the cutout company was secretly funding? We weren't wasting our time developing aerosol technology, I'll tell you that. The money paid for the development of this weapon. We can't let the Russians have *all* of the fun."

Which confirmed my suspicion: Quentin happened to have the antidote on hand because he'd *created the damned thing.* Oleg and the Russians had had almost everything right—the experimental labs, the cutout company, the funding. They just had the wrong motive. It wasn't a demonstration. It was a cover-up.

"Did Kevin know?"

"Not until very late in the game."

"Now your story finally makes sense. I know why you killed him."

"I *told* you why Drexel had to die," Quentin shot back. "He would have compromised the entire operation."

"That's not why. You killed my husband because you were afraid he was going to tell *me*."

CHAPTER 39

"LISTEN—YOU WERE RIGHT earlier, when you said there isn't much time. Which brings us to the point of our conversation. Come back to work for me, and I'll give you the antidote."

"And if I don't?"

"You'll retire for good, quite suddenly. In about two hours, I suspect. But listen...I *know* you, Bell. You're a survivor. Look how far you've come in the past three days, pushing yourself to extremes, calling on reserves of strength you didn't even know you had. When Devander told me you wanted his help escaping the hospital, I was impressed."

I stayed silent. I closed my eyes.

"Look...I have the antidote right here. I'll be honest, I wish it hadn't come to this. Nobody was meant to encounter this stuff and survive. You're going to need monthly booster shots of the antidote for the rest of your life."

Thereby guaranteeing my indentured servitude to the Agency. And to Quentin. Literally until the day I died.

"Shall we? You've suffered enough, I think."

I didn't answer him, because I was too busy convulsing and foaming at the mouth.

CHAPTER 40

"NO!"

Quentin ran across the room. He pulled a syringe from his jacket pocket, then uncapped it and flicked the side to make sure there were no air bubbles.

"You're not going to die on me, Bell. Not today! I've put too much love and care into you. No no no..."

Quentin had to kneel on my hand and grab my upper arm to make it stable enough to inject me.

"You're the girl who can survive anything. I knew it the moment I met you. And I knew we were meant to be together. Forever."

With those words, I finally understood why my husband had been targeted for death. Maybe Quentin really had been afraid Kevin and I would expose his highly illegal and revolting weapons program. That was motive enough. But the real reason? Quentin couldn't stand to see me with anyone else. For the past eight years, his interest in me had not been about fatherly affection. It had been *obsession*.

"You wake up now and let me take you home."

His dream was about to come true. I would be his forever.

CHAPTER 41

WHEN I OPENED my eyes, Quentin jolted. *Surely*, he must have thought, *the antidote couldn't work that fast!* He'd be right. The convulsions and frothing at the mouth had been just a ruse to bring him closer.

I used the elbow of my free arm to jackhammer his head into the metal radiator. *Elbows and knees, Quentin, just like you taught me.* The resulting collision seemed to reverberate throughout the entire plumbing system of the townhouse.

Even so, it was just meant to stun him and muddy his judgment enough for me to grab the back of his head and pull him close, almost as if I were about to deep kiss him.

Instead, I jammed the palm of my left hand—the cuffed one—against his chin. Quentin's eyes widened in surprise. He knew better than anybody what was about to happen next. After all, he was the one who taught me the most effective way to break a man's neck.

His final words were spat out machine-gun style: "Samantha-wait-you-don't-understand-I'm-in-lo—"

I twisted as hard as I could. The last thing he saw was the ceiling. His limp body fell against mine.

After I pushed him away, I searched his suit for the hand-cuff keys. *Right trouser pocket*, I guessed correctly. I'd spent the past decade observing his patterns of behavior. That's what he trained us to do. Look at the small details, he'd said. They add up to *everything*.

But the tiny details hadn't told me that I'd been in the employ of a monster all these years.

I climbed to my feet and shuffled through the living room. I tried two doors before I found what I was looking for: a bed-room. I couldn't take many more steps without some rest. Maybe the antidote was working. Maybe not—maybe Quen-tin had lied and I was still a walking corpse. Either way, I wanted to lie down on something soft. Would I wake up tomorrow morning? No way to know for sure. Now that the two men responsible for my husband's murder were dead, it didn't really matter if I went on living.

But before I could lie down, there was one more surprise waiting for me.

You see, Quentin had prepared the bedroom. A dozen nutrient-rich pressed juices in a cooler. An air purifier. An IV pole and gear. Flowers. On the bedside table rested a selection of herbal teas and a cast-iron teapot. On top of the pot was a tiny cream-colored card with a handwritten note:

Love, Q

He'd managed to say it after all. This was to be the bed in which he'd nurse me back to health. In which he'd work on my mind, and convince me that he'd had my best inter-ests at heart this whole time. That Kevin and Bill were the real enemies here. And then, when he was finished taking my mind apart and putting it back together just the way he wanted, we'd consummate our relationship.

I swept everything off the table with my arm, kicked over the IV pole, and collapsed into bed.

CHAPTER 42

THE NEXT MORNING, I strolled down the Unter den Linden as the sun crawled up out of its grave. I heard Kevin whispering excitedly into my ear:

Where we're walking right now used to be nothing but a field of rubble, just after the war. Now look at it!

I walked past a Gothic pile situated next to the city's iconic TV tower.

That's the Berliner Dom, and it's kind of a miracle the old cathedral is still standing.

Just like me. The world had tried to kill me, and failed. I lived to stroll another day. What would I do now?

I'd given that a lot of thought since waking up this morning. Even though my former mentor was dead, his secret chemical weapons operation was presumably up and running. There were almost certainly illegal tests being conducted in this city or somewhere else in Europe. Perhaps he had even gone as far as soliciting clients. Some of the chemical agent may even be out there in the world, waiting to be deployed in a bustling hotel or crowded stadium. Lives were on the line, and I was the only person who knew the truth.

If Quentin was right, and I had to be injected with the antidote on a regular basis, I had about thirty days to live.

Plenty of time.

WOMEN AND CHILDREN FIRST

*James Patterson and
Bill Schweigart*

PROLOGUE

CHASE WELDON STOOD outside his lovely townhouse, holding a 9-millimeter pistol pressed to his leg.

The lightening sky reflected off the dark, blunt edges of the building in the Dupont Circle area of Washington, DC, where years ago he and his wife, Shay, had settled when Madison was young and Luke was just a baby. At this moment, in the predawn beginning to glow the barest color of rose, Chase wanted to be anywhere but home.

A wave of nausea rolled through him. When it passed, he straightened and fit his key into the lock, then stepped inside.

Though it was dark in the foyer, he knew the location of every hazard. Where Madison dropped her knapsack. Where Luke kicked off his cleats after soccer practice. The pause he took to let his eyes adjust was a farewell.

To his world before it shattered.

But it was either his world, or the whole world.

And in control of that world was a commanding voice on the phone. The voice had been painfully clear about the requirements—and explicit about the consequences if instructions weren't followed.

Chase had no reason to doubt the capabilities behind the voice. He'd seen ample proof already.

Girding himself, he climbed the stairs.

Chase entered the master bedroom first. He was startled to find his wife fully dressed in her work slacks and blouse and leaning back against a mountain of pillows, working on her laptop with papers stationed around her in ordered stacks.

He had been hoping, praying even, she'd be asleep.

She was staring down at the screen. The family joked that when Shay was working, she was on a seven-second delay. But now, as Chase stared at his beautiful wife of twenty years—her face clear of makeup, a pencil poking through the twist of dark hair on top of her head—Shay looked up.

She pled and shouted. Begged him to think of the children. Nevertheless, he raised his gun.

"I'll always love you, Shay."

He fired twice. The noise was startling, like thunder erupting in their bedroom. Shay fell limp, one arm knocking her laptop to the side, a flailing leg kicking a stack of papers into the air.

In the silence following the gunshots, he heard stirring from the children's bedrooms. Feet hitting the floor, concerned voices calling.

Tears streaming, Chase Weldon turned to finish the job.

Several Days Earlier

CHAPTER 1

THE WELL-DRESSED MAN watched the spectacle unfold on the field at the Nationals' brand-new baseball stadium: Avalon Park in Southeast Washington, along the Capitol Riverfront. The bases were loaded when a slugger launched a ball into the upper decks, and as the runners now trotted down the third base line to home plate, the local fans were on their feet, railing first at the visiting team and then their own beleaguered pitcher.

The man sighed, resigned to the prospect of another losing game for the Nationals. Even the new stadium couldn't help. He pulled out his phone and opened Twitter. He typed:

This umpire . . . think it's time to bum-rush the field and beat on the brat with a baseball bat. #Wildcats #AvalonPark

He thought about it for a second more, then added a third hashtag to his tweet—#RamonesForever—and released it into the wilds of cyberspace. *I may be provoking assault and battery,* he thought, *but I'm no plagiarist.*

He noted the time, then slipped the phone back into his blazer and sat back to enjoy the late-April afternoon, if not the game. Against the crisp blue skies over the stadium, the manicured outfield shone neon green and the sandy clay infield glowed a rich brick-red. Colorful ads flashed from the LED displays that lined the stadium's bowl, a welcome distraction from the action on the field.

He felt a strong hand grasp his shoulder.

"Sir, would you mind coming with us?"

The well-dressed man looked up into the stern face of a giant in a yellow ball cap and a matching yellow windbreaker. The large security guard loomed over him, blocking out the sun. A second guard, a younger, lanky man, stood beside him.

"Is there some sort of problem?" asked the man. "I'm minding my own business."

"Just come along, sir."

The well-dressed man felt the hot sensation of eyes on him. To the Nationals fans in his section he smiled and shrugged— *no big deal*—with the intent of turning their attention back to the losing game.

The two guards positioned him between them. The first guard led the way, the second followed behind. In a taut line, they descended the stairs to the concourse level, past several concession booths, to a security door.

The first guard punched in a passcode, and suddenly they were *inside* the stadium. A warren of corridors led to a holding room. The second guard opened the door, revealing a lone table and chair, then peeled off to another location. The first guard gestured for the well-dressed man to sit.

"What's this all about?" asked the man.

"It'll just be a moment, sir." The massive guard faced him while blocking the door, his hands clasped to the front. *The fig leaf pose*, thought the man.

"Something funny?" asked the guard.

"Am I being detained?"

"Again, just a moment."

"Marty, I'd like to speak with your supervisor."

The guard made a quick, snorting sound, but said nothing. Then he stiffened. The skin around his eyes tightened as he scrutinized the well-dressed man seated at the table. "What did you just say?"

The well-dressed man watched the guard glance down to double-check whether he was wearing a nametag. He wasn't.

"I didn't tell you my name."

The man smiled. "You didn't need to. I already know that your name is Martin Reyes. That you drive a green 2010 Toyota Camry. That you live at 822 South Veitch Street in Arlington. That on your way home later, you plan to stop at the Lost Dog Tavern for trivia night and a couple of pitchers with the guys. And you *definitely* didn't tell me that on your Tinder profile you claim you actually prefer daiquiris."

The well-dressed man regarded the bulky guard. "You know, Marty, I didn't picture you as a frozen-drink guy, but after all these years it's refreshing to be surprised every now and then."

Marty didn't seem to agree. He advanced toward the table with his fists clenched.

This was fun, but time to move along, the well-dressed man thought. He held up a finger. "*Marty.* Your supervisor? Tell him Chase Weldon from the FIRST Group is here."

CHAPTER 2

AVALON PARK'S CHIEF security officer burst into the room, nearly pushing the door off its hinges. He didn't deign to introduce himself, but Chase knew his name was Barry Daniels.

"I just have one question," said Daniels, dropping into the chair opposite Chase while Marty loomed behind him, his arms crossed across his wide chest, his face a hard mask.

"Shoot," said Chase.

"Don't tempt me." Daniels leaned forward, getting into Chase's space. *"Who the fuck are you supposed to be?"*

"I'm Chase Weldon, president and CEO of the FIRST Group."

"Never heard of you. And you have two seconds before I walk out and lock you in here with him," said Daniels, jerking his thumb at the big guard.

Chase shrugged. "Marty and I are bros."

"No, we're not," said Marty, unamused.

"Fair enough," said Chase, removing a business card from his jacket and sliding it across the table. "The FIRST Group—short for Fully Integrated Risk Strategy Team—conducts comprehensive risk assessments for high-end clients. During Phase One, we scrutinize your operation from every conceivable angle—your security practices, engineering, cyber hygiene—before you even know we're looking. If you want to be the best in risk mitigation, you have to be FIRST."

"You're really in love with that acronym."

"Passion is only part of what earns me executive pay."

"So illegally surveilling my staff is Phase One?"

Chase looked wounded. "Is it illegal to follow someone to a crowded restaurant, sit close enough to eavesdrop, then see where they live?"

"Yes," hissed Marty. Daniels looked up at the guard, who was now red in the face.

"*Actually,*" Chase pointed out, "it's all open roads and public spaces, so it's technically within the law, but I'm going to give you a pass on that one because you're very large and I can tell you're still kind of miffed at me."

"If that's Phase One, what the fuck is Phase Two?" asked Daniels. "Kidnapping?"

"We make our approach," said Chase, spreading his hands. "Voilà. Then we work together to identify your vulnerabilities to any and all physical or cyber threats, or any convergence of the two. For example, I sent out a particularly mean tweet—a cyber threat. Actually jumping onto the field to beat up the umpire would be a manifestation of that cyber threat in the physical world—aka convergence.

"Continuing with that very simple example, I tweeted and Marty dutifully arrived. But it took two at-bats. Four minutes and thirty-seven seconds, to be precise. That's almost five full minutes before your social media team picked up on the tweet and contacted your operations center, who then dispatched Marty, who did a hell of a job by the way. But Marty's heroics aside, if I was a lunatic—"

"You *are* a lunatic," said Daniels.

"If I really was a lunatic or a truly bad actor," continued Chase undeterred, "that would have been *all the time in the world*. You need a faster, more nimble response. That starts with better social media monitoring software. I can recommend some systems."

"I'll jot that down." Daniels remained seated with his hands folded in front of him. "So, let me get this straight, this was what, an audition?" He chuckled, and Marty, for the first time, cracked a smile. "Did you really think I was going to fucking hire you after this little stunt?"

Chase let them have a laugh at his expense, then said, "I'm already hired."

"Not by me," said Daniels, and the two men laughed even harder.

"By Miles Gillen."

The laughter stopped.

"Miles Gillen? The owner of the Washington Nationals and Avalon Park, Miles Gillen?" asked Daniels.

"And CEO of Avalon Communications," added Chase. He leaned forward and stared intently at Daniels. "Miles Gillen is deadly serious about the safety of Avalon's venues, as well as the resilience of Avalon's products and services, which now touch nearly every American household. And believe it or not, I am even more serious. My goal is to make Avalon Park the most secure ballpark in the country. I don't mean gates, guards, and guns.

"Do you know that *secure* comes from two small Latin words—*se,* meaning 'without,' and *cura,* meaning 'care'? I want every patron who passes through your gates to be without care, knowing that they are safe. I want you and your staff to go to sleep at night without care, knowing you have the best procedures, training, and equipment possible. And I want Miles Gillen to be without care, knowing he got his money's worth and the Avalon Communications brand remains above reproach."

Daniels stared at him for a few moments, looking like he had indigestion. "All right, Mr. Weldon, I'll play along. Let's say you're actually working for Mr. Gillen—and I'll be vetting you while you cool your heels in here with Marty—what's next? Inspections?"

Chase shook his head. "FIRST does not *inspect*—we *assess* and *educate*. This is not punitive. We're not looking to embarrass you."

Daniels sighed. "Doesn't sound like I have much of a choice. What Miles Gillen wants—"

The chief security officer was cut short by a dull roar from overhead. The three men each cocked their heads toward the ceiling. Chase heard fast footsteps echoing through the corridor outside, heading in their direction.

The door burst open, revealing the lanky guard from earlier. "Sir, come quick! It's chaos topside!"

"What the hell's going on?" asked Daniels.

"Shooter!"

CHAPTER 3

DANIELS KNOCKED OVER his chair and shoved past Marty, ordering his security team into a full run. The men did a double take—Marty, a triple—when Chase appeared beside them, breathing easily.

Chase had been an 18E in the Green Berets—a communications sergeant—in a highly secretive special-operations intelligence unit. Though no longer an active participant in the Global War on Terror, once a Green Beret, always a Green Beret. He kept in top physical shape, partially out of habit, partially out of vanity. Plus Shay, his wife, would kick his ass if he developed a spare tire.

"What the hell are you doing?" growled Daniels, already winded.

"I was hired by Gillen to conduct a comprehensive risk assessment," said Chase. "Seems to me like you're at risk."

The knot of men bounded up sets of stairs until they arrived on the 200 level. Up here, the cries of the crowd were sharper, louder, filled with fear. The guard who had alerted them sprinted ahead on long legs to a sealed door, waved a badge in front of a reader, and held the door open.

"Just stay out of the damn way," said Daniels as they all filed inside.

The first thing Chase noticed when he entered the operations center was the space. He'd been in all manner of OPCENs, from high-tech communications suites in the back of roving vans to command centers that were obviously afterthoughts—basements and conference rooms and large closets never intended for their makeshift use—but the Avalon OPCEN was state-of-the-art, as befit a tech company. Miles Gillen had built out a luxury suite for the command post. Safety and security were typically red items in a company's ledger, and it wasn't every CEO who would cede such prime, profitable real estate to such an operation. But Gillen had.

Chase fought his way through the rows of workstations to east-facing windows overlooking the stadium.

He took in the ominous view. Chaos.

The massive HD LED video displays were wiped clean of advertisements and crowd-friendly messages to cheer for the home team and stretch during the seventh inning. They'd been reset to a single, dire warning:

ACTIVE SHOOTER: SECTION 111.

Chase scanned the entirety of the stadium bowl. His heart was in his throat as he scanned the area where he had been sitting earlier. Chase pulled his phone from his pocket and checked the screen. The top text read:

Safe exfil. RV at Angelo's.

He breathed a sigh of relief. His family had evacuated. Behind him, Daniels was shouting. The flat screens rimming the walls each depicted a different camera feed showing terrified Nationals fans in flight. All being broadcast into homes around the country.

Daniels turned to a woman in khakis and a Nationals polo who appeared to be his deputy. "Give me a SITREP, Connie!"

"No sign of the shooter yet," said Connie. "Or any victims."

"How is that possible?"

"I don't know, Chief. I didn't sanction this."

He stared at her for a beat, confused, then called to the room. "Put every fucking camera on 111 right now. Keep panning until you pick up the trail."

Chase turned from the windows to the screens. The figures of the yellow-jacketed security personnel appeared life-size on the displays, surging against the fleeing crowds like brightly colored fish swimming upstream. They converged on 111 from different directions, arriving and scanning the section, weapons drawn, then looking at each other in confusion.

"Where's the shooter?" raged Daniels. "Who called it in? What the hell is going on down there?"

"That's the thing, Chief," said Daniels's deputy. "We're not sure..."

Daniels spun on a panicked young man hunched over a console. "Who authorized you to put that message up?"

"Sir, I didn't." His eyes were huge behind his glasses.

The chief security officer grabbed the young operator by the shoulder and jerked him aside. The operator's wheeled chair spun backward as Daniels muscled in.

Before he could take a closer look at the display system's controls, a fresh round of screams sounded outside. The security feed showed the crowd looking at the LED screens lining the walls. Chase turned back to the windows. Outside, the main LED screen had changed.

ACTIVE SHOOTER: SECTION 302.

The remaining fans surged in the other direction, like schools of fish turning in unison.

"I didn't touch anything!" the operator began, but Daniels was already yelling into his radio.

"Can anyone confirm shots fired? Does anyone have a visual on a suspect?"

Across the bowl, in the tier above them, Chase watched the yellow jackets converge on Section 302. The reports were coming back in. *No sign of a shooter. No sounds of shots fired. None injured except from the panicked exodus.*

From behind him, Chase heard Daniels. "*You,*" the bullish chief security officer growled.

Chase turned as Daniels slammed him against the windows. The back of Chase's head bounced off the thick glass. It smarted.

"This is you, isn't it?" Daniels demanded through clenched teeth.

Chase calmly reached across Daniels's fists with his right hand and seized the wrist at his left side. With his left hand, he reached across and grabbed Daniels's forearm, then drew his arms down, pulling Daniels to him, exerting steady, crushing pressure. Daniels tried to break free, but realized Chase had his arms trapped. Chase spoke low enough that only the chief security officer, whose eyes were now wide, could hear him.

"This was not me. We are in this together. And right now Avalon's ass is in the wind, on national television. Nod if you understand."

Daniels nodded quickly.

Chase released him. "Kill the network feed," he said. He

pointed at the control console operator. "And you, pull the plug."

"It's not that simple . . ." said the operator.

"Emergency shutdown," ordered Chase. "Right now."

The operator shot Daniels a wary look for confirmation.

The bullish man was rubbing his wrists, his jaw clenched, but he nodded.

"Do what he says."

CHAPTER 4

CHASE WALKED INTO Angelo's, a pizza restaurant on the Southwest waterfront. In full military sweep mode, he scanned the dining room, his mood sour as he struggled to pinpoint the source of the uneasy feeling at the back of his mind.

He felt *behind*.

He didn't like it.

It had been a beautiful day for a baseball game and an even better day to cultivate new business, until he'd been jolted from his favored position left of *boom*—where he could stay ahead of nefarious activities *before* they occurred. He had waltzed into Avalon Park smack in the middle of a nasty *boom*.

Determining whether today's incident was a glitch or something more sinister would require a deep probe into the system. In the control center, the entire security team was poring over every console, checking every display, but even the main operator was only a highly skilled technician, not a software engineer.

There was nothing left for Chase to do but let Daniels try to clean up the mess, and to get out of his way while he did it. He was frustrated. When he was deployed and found himself squarely in *boom* territory, he could always take out his frustration by finding the enemy. That wasn't an option here.

A waving hand reached above the heads of the other diners, and at the back of the restaurant he found what he was looking for.

His family.

Chase relaxed into his civilian self and smiled his relief at seeing them safe. His nineteen-year-old daughter, Madison, and his twelve-year-old son, Luke, were sitting with their backs turned.

Madison was tall and lithe with a shock of pink hair. At least, it was pink today. Tomorrow it could be blue or purple or some outlandish combination of colors. He was used to it now, but when Madison first began experimenting with her hair, Shay had had to remind Chase that he was no longer in the army, Madison was never in the army, and their daughter's flavor of self-expression wasn't hurting anyone.

Shay had a point. She usually did.

Madison had been way ahead of them both. Constantly changing up her look—and keeping her parents, and the world at large, on their toes—forced everyone to reckon with her intelligence, her wit, and, most of all, her character. A brilliant strategy, really.

Beside Madison sat Luke. His hair was a floppy shag, but so far still a natural brown. Luke was the most introverted member of their family, quiet and serious. He could be even more intense and inscrutable than his mother. He was equally content, and adept, with a soccer ball or a video game controller.

And then there was Shay, seated with her back to the wall. As he made his way toward the table, he kept his eyes on his striking wife, her long, dark hair pulled back, her green eyes and full lips, and a sensuality that even a crisp business suit couldn't conceal.

She smiled when Chase caught her eye. Even after twenty years of marriage, that smile never failed to make his pulse quicken. She was a formidable woman, currently using her razor-sharp mind as an attorney in the service of Avalon Communications. While he would have liked to believe that FIRST had landed its contract with Avalon Park on their own scrappy merits, Chase suspected it had more to do with the CEO's esteem for Shay.

By the time he joined his family, Shay's expression had settled into a smirk, one eyebrow tantalizingly lifted.

"What. Did. You. Do."

It wasn't an invitation. It was an interrogation.

Chase held his hands up in a gesture of humility and innocence. "I didn't do anything."

"You've always had a flair for the dramatic," said Shay, but her arched eyebrow began to settle.

"You honestly think I would cause a stampede? There are safer ways to get someone's attention."

She gave him a final suspicious glance, but her smirk was now dangerously close to breaking into a wide smile. As he slid into the booth beside her, he noticed Luke passing a five-dollar bill across the tabletop to Madison.

"What's this?" asked Chase, pointing between them. "Why is money changing hands?"

"Luke lost a bet," said Madison.

Chase looked at Luke. "Did you honestly think I could screw up that badly?"

Luke shrugged and Shay burst out laughing.

"He gets that from you, you know," Chase said to Shay, who

offered Luke a consolatory fist bump from across the table. "At least my favorite daughter had my back."

"The bet wasn't that you didn't screw up, Dad. Only that you didn't screw up in that particular way."

"Appreciation rescinded."

Two large pies, each missing several slices, stood on pizza stands. The family had started without him. He didn't mind. Madison had dusted her pizza with enough parmesan cheese to conceal the tomato sauce. Luke folded his slice in half lengthwise and took a massive bite.

Shay squeezed Chase's hand under the table. He returned the squeeze, then leaned over to kiss his wife. She kissed him back.

"How did the approach go?" she asked.

"It was going just fine until all hell broke loose."

"You didn't alienate Daniels?"

"Have a little faith, babe. I'm actually quite good at my job."

"Just ask him," quipped Madison.

"Don't bother," added Luke, "he'll tell you anyway."

Chase reached across the table and pinched them both.

"Seriously though, it wasn't contentious?" asked Shay.

"He knows we're on the same team." Chase leaned forward. "You could say he even embraced me."

Madison looked suspiciously at her father, then reluctantly slid the five-dollar bill back over to a delighted Luke.

They spent a long, leisurely time at Angelo's. Shay ordered some wine for the two of them and gelato for the kids. Chase stepped to the front of the restaurant to pay the bill, then, as he waited for his family at the exit, pulled out his phone.

Though by now the afternoon's embarrassing mishap had bloomed into a very public black eye for Avalon, he ignored the news and social media to scroll through his missed messages.

Starting at the top, Chase read the All Clear notice from AlertDC, the District of Columbia's communications system, as well as fire, police, and EMS, all of which he subscribed to. He went backward in time, noting how and when the various agencies sent the emergency warnings of a potential active shooter at Avalon Park. He reread Shay's text from earlier, letting him know that she and the kids had safely evacuated the park and would rendezvous with Chase at the pizzeria. An earlier text caught his eye, one he had missed during the melee. It was from a blocked number and displayed just two words.

BANG BANG.

Chase stared at the message. It seemed to have been sent simultaneously with the first warnings displayed inside the park.

Just then, Shay sidled up to him and wrapped her arms around one of his. "You okay?"

Chase gave her his most winning smile, then leaned in for another kiss.

"Couldn't be better," he lied.

CHAPTER 5

"TEAM, I HAVE some good news and some bad news..."

Chase stood at the head of the main conference room table in FIRST Group's headquarters, in an eleven-story high-rise in CityCenterDC, the District's $950 million mixed-use development. The neighborhood, encompassing ten acres in the heart of downtown, was one of the most ambitious real estate projects of the new century.

Shay had chastised him for leveraging so much of their personal capital to secure such premium office space—complete with terraces and a landscaped roof—until she saw the boutiques lining the street. Hermès, Dior, Gucci, Kate Spade, even a Tesla dealership. It wasn't long before her disapproval thawed and she began visiting the offices more frequently for lunches with Chase, followed by a retail digestif.

In for a penny, in for a pound, Chase had thought. If FIRST was to be the first name in tailored risk assessments to *Fortune* 100 companies, he needed to look the part, and that included a prime address.

He looked around the state-of-the-art conference room, equipped with an expensive bank of 4K display screens opposite the floor-to-ceiling windows, and tried not to dwell on his family's future financial well-being. He didn't even want to *consider* the ceiling, embedded with invisible speakers and microphones, or the wall behind him that acted as a capacitive touch surface—a high-tech whiteboard.

"Why do you keep saying 'team'?" asked Madison, FIRST's only other employee. "It's just the two of us."

In addition to Madison's colorful hair and her collection of superhero T-shirts—today's was Captain Marvel—his daughter possessed a breathtaking fluency with computers that put Chase's own proficiency to shame. When he compared his own hard-earned information operations skills from his army days to Madison's natural cybersecurity gifts, it put him in mind of the opening scene of *2001*, when the film transitioned from cavemen to astronauts.

Brilliant as she was, Madison was in a mood today. She was coming down with a spring cold and her normal high wattage was dimmed. Chase overcompensated with cheer.

"And the two of us are a team. Positive visualization, Mads." He gestured at the empty seats around the too-large table. "These seats will be filled soon enough, mark my words."

"Start with the bad news," she said and sighed.

"I received an early morning call from Avalon's CEO and he's decidedly apoplectic."

"Do I look like a thesaurus?"

"Gillen's super-pissed." Chase grimaced, and continued, "Apparently, when thirty thousand fans flee in terror from your brand-new ballpark, it tends to make you cranky. I reminded him—between his epithets—that we were only contracted a month ago to assess Avalon Park, and were still in the information collection phase. I explained that I had only made the introduction yesterday."

"Yikes. What's a billionaire in a rage like?"

"Considering Gillen makes about $1.5 million per hour, let's just say it was the most expensive ass-chewing I've ever had. In a weird way, I'll savor those seven minutes."

"Didn't you say there was *good* news?"

"We're not fired yet," said Chase, raising his arms in mock triumph, as Madison groaned.

"Jesus, Dad," she said, "you really need to work on your sales pitch."

Chase sat down at the head of the table. "Gillen wants us to fast-track the assessment and assist with Avalon's internal investigation. Figure out who did what—then stop it from ever happening again."

"So where do we start?"

"What can you tell me about the jumbotron?"

"First of all, it's not a *jumbotron*," she said, as if the word was a personal affront. "That's like calling a Corvette a Chevy. We're talking about an Avalon/Techtronics Echelon 4."

"Fine, what can you tell me about the fancy jumbotron?"

Madison rolled her eyes as she tapped on her keyboard, then spun her laptop around to show the screen to Chase. "Bleeding edge, integrated LED system, with scoreboard and displays in-bowl, around the concourses, and outside the stadium."

"Can it be hacked?"

"Anything can be hacked," she said and shrugged, "but an Echelon would be tricky. It's a closed system, operated by a trained controller. If I could get a peek at it—"

"Today's your lucky day. A Techtronics field rep is arriving this morning to go over the Echelon with a fine-tooth comb— I want you breathing down his neck. Gillen says you can take the damn thing apart and put it back together again to your heart's content."

Madison rubbed her hands together. "Merry Christmas to me. What are you going to do?"

"Talk to anyone and everyone who had access to the Echelon, starting with yesterday's controller. Daniels grilled him pretty hard, and the poor guy seemed legitimately shaken, but I want to take another crack at him. And anyone else who has access to the Echelon."

As Madison headed for the door, Chase stopped her.

"Can you run a quick diagnostic on this before you go?" he asked, handing her his smartphone. He gave her the passcode as she scrutinized the device.

"Any particular problem?"

"I received a strange text from a blocked number."

"That's not really a performance issue, Dad."

"No, but it could be an OPSEC issue."

"I'll take a look under the hood." Madison stopped short. "Wait…" she said, turning in the doorway, her brow knitted. "You mean strange like this?"

She held up the phone, and Chase saw a new text that had just appeared on his screen:

BOOM.

CHAPTER 6

CHASE SENT MADISON to her office—basically a computer lab—to run diagnostics on the phone. As soon as she was gone, he activated the screens in the conference room and pulled his laptop toward him. He began scrolling through Twitter. It wasn't long before he saw the first notices from AlertDC hit his screen.

Explosion reported near Fort Dupont Park. Avoid area.

Chase brought up a map of DC on the 4K display screen. He typed in "Fort Dupont" and zoomed in on the Southeast neighborhood. At its center was a swath of green that denoted Fort Dupont Park, the grounds of a Civil War fort, now an urban greenspace with miles of hiking trails. To the west, the Anacostia River. To the north, Capitol Street. Finally, to the east, Chase found what he was looking for among the churches, community centers, and apartment buildings that populated his map.

The DC manufacturing plant for Avalon Communications.

He would bet a year's worth of his exorbitant CityCenterDC lease that Avalon's DC hub was where the explosion had occurred. The unease Chase had felt since the false alarm at Avalon Park congealed in the pit of his stomach. These texts—BANG yesterday and BOOM today—felt obviously connected to the phony shooter event and the apparently real explosion.

But why? And what did it mean?

"Hey," said Madison, poking her head into the conference room. She tossed the phone at him. He caught it one-handed.

"Squared away?" he asked.

"L7," she said, pausing to sneeze violently. "Ready to go?"

"You know, if you're feeling under the weather, you can check out the fancy jumbotron later. Go home and get some sleep."

"You think I'm going to cancel a date with an Echelon over the sniffles?" she said. "I'd like to think I'm a little tougher than that. I'll see you at home later."

"Now who's acting the billionaire in a rage?" Chase asked.

Madison was the most capable young adult he knew, but she was still his daughter and he didn't want to frighten her. He had his suspicions about the source of the texts, but decided to keep them to himself. For now.

Once Madison left for the stadium, Chase tuned each of the 4K screens to a different local station. *I didn't buy this equipment to watch daytime talk shows and soap operas*, he thought ruefully.

It wasn't long before WJLA cut in to a telecaster standing in Southeast in front of a yellow police tape cordon, a plume of dark smoke rising above a line of fire trucks in the distance.

The breaking-news chyron read: FIRE RAGES AT FORT DUPONT AVALON PLANT.

Chase watched as one by one, each network had a reporter on the scene to inform viewers that this was the second Avalon incident in as many days, and *"Could they be connected?"*

Chase mentally criticized the reporters for resorting to pure speculation to fill airtime, then conceded that they were probably right.

When every 4K screen along the conference room's wall was flashing those red lights and that dark, towering plume, he reached for his phone. He found the last text and typed a reply.

You have my attention.

Within seconds, his phone rang.

CHAPTER 7

"THIS IS CHASE Weldon from FIRST," Chase answered.

"I think we both know I'm not a potential client, Mr. Weldon," the caller said. It was a digitized voice.

"You know my name and I don't know yours," Chase said. "That's hardly fair."

"Very clever," said the Voice. "As advertised."

"I'm too busy for a personality assessment," Chase replied. "One of my high-profile clients is facing unexpected security concerns stemming from some unfortunate accidents."

"I think we both know those weren't accidents."

The digitized voice laughed. The sound of it was like metal scraping metal. It gave Chase the creeps.

"In the coming hours," the Voice continued, "news will break that a blast furnace in the Avalon plant did not shut down properly. That is true. It will be reported as an unfortunate accident. This is not true. We breached the plant's network and seized their industrial control systems."

"Who's *we?*"

"Don't waste time on stupid questions, Mr. Weldon."

"What do you want?"

"We want Miles Gillen to bleed. If not actual blood, *money.*

A hemorrhage. See to it that $100 million is deposited in the link we're sending, or the evening commute will be a real gas."

"You're extortionists. I'll be hanging up now so I can call the FBI."

"Well then, I hope your daughter feels better."

Chase sat bolt upright, every muscle in his body tensed. The threat was an electric jolt. He fought to control his breathing, so as not to reveal his mounting fear to the caller.

"Do I still have your attention?" asked the Voice. That grinding laugh again, like pocket change falling into gears. "The deadline is 6 p.m. tomorrow. No cops, no tricks. Or the next bodies ripped apart will be your family's."

"Do not threaten my family," Chase growled.

"Then keep them safe. Get to work."

"Why me?"

"You have access to Gillen."

"Lots of people have access to Gillen. I'm a consultant. Not part of his inner circle."

"Because you're the one who wanted to be *first*, Mr. Weldon."

The line went dead.

CHAPTER 8

CHASE SPENT THE rest of the day and most of the night trying and failing to connect with Miles Gillen and Avalon Communications' chief security officer, Alex Teague.

"It's crucial that I speak to Mr. Gillen," Chase told Gillen's executive assistant. "Regarding the plant and the stadium. He needs to hear what I have to say."

"He's unavailable, Mr. Weldon," said the EA. Her voice was singsong, as if she were talking to a kindergartner. Or a conspiracy theorist. "He's flying in from the West Coast to assess the damage from the accident."

On the Avalon corporate jet, no doubt, he thought. *Completely reachable. If Gillen won't talk, time to bring out the big guns.*

He called Shay.

As one of Avalon's corporate attorneys, she guarded Gillen's private number like the crown jewels. Even over the phone, he could practically hear her eyebrow raising, but to her credit, she didn't question the seriousness of his ask, just gave him the number with a simple warning. "Be good."

"Always, babe."

Chase's first call went to voicemail. He kept his tone calm and measured, but laden with authority, summoning his army command voice. Green Beret Chase, not "Sales" Chase from keynote speeches at security summits.

"Mr. Gillen, Chase Weldon. I have information regarding your Southeast plant and Avalon Park. They are related incidents, and neither were accidents. I believe a third situation to be imminent. It is imperative you call me back immediately, sir."

When no return call came, Chase rose slowly from his seat and moved to the windows, scanning the park below, then looking across to the windows of the surrounding office buildings. He didn't know what he expected to see, and no external threat was apparent.

But he couldn't yet rule out the chance that he was vulnerable from the inside. He turned and examined his conference room, assessing every familiar object for potential danger.

Chase began walking through the office, turning off every electronic device—phones, laptops, monitors. Next he walked down the hall to a small, locked supply closet. He keyed in a series of numbers and the door swung open. Instead of cleaning supplies or spare printer cartridges, the space held a small armory. He scanned the shelves until he found what he was looking for—a small black box.

He walked to the far end of his office suite and powered up the device: a radio frequency detector. The device was top-of-the-line and would detect most commercial bugs, hidden cameras, GPS trackers, or any object that was transmitting a signal.

Unlikely as it was that anyone could have penetrated FIRST's spaces undetected by him or Madison, he had to accept the possibility. Certainty meant hubris of the kind that had caused shame and humiliation to many a base commander during his JSIVA days.

Chase would know better than most. His unit's mission was to conduct clandestine assessments—of American military bases.

JSIVA (Joint Staff Integrated Vulnerability Assessment) had recruited Chase based on his proficiency in direct action, counterterrorism, and special reconnaissance. Meaning Chase was a good guy who'd spent his days thinking like a bad guy—surveilling, probing, and gathering intel just as a terrorist cell would—in order to spot the potential risks before the real bad guys did.

His time at JSIVA had planted the seed for FIRST. It also taught him that complacency kills.

Chase swept his offices twice but found no sign of surveillance. He returned to FIRST's armory, to retrieve a 9-millimeter pistol, a waistband holster, and two magazines, before securing the door once more.

His mind was racing as he planned his next sweeps: his house and his family.

CHAPTER 9

CHASE DIDN'T SEE the figure rushing at him until it was too late.

As he opened the front door to his home, he registered the blur of movement down the long hallway. Chase closed the door behind him and kept his weapon holstered as he dropped into a defensive posture. Knees bent. Balls of his feet. Hands floating.

Luke came at him fast, dribbling a neon soccer ball from foot to foot, almost too fast to see.

Keep your eye on the ball, Chase...

Luke juked left. Chase feinted right.

Somehow, in the space of a second, Luke zigged, zagged, then zigged again. Chase was defenseless as Luke shot the ball right between his father's legs—a nutmeg. The ball bounced off the front door with a loud smack.

It was a frequent father-son ritual, Luke trying to "meg" him in a one-on-one contest. Occasionally Chase's defenses held.

Today was not that day.

"Knock it off!" called Shay from the kitchen. "I've told you two not to play soccer inside."

Caught, father and son both went silent. Then Luke bolted up the stairs before Shay emerged from the kitchen to issue her next command.

"You," said Shay to Luke, pointing without bothering to turn toward him, "wash up. Dinner in five."

From the landing, Luke caught his father's eye and smiled. Behind his mother's back, he pumped his arms in victory before disappearing.

"Ava," called Shay, "play something relaxing so I don't murder my husband."

Ava, Avalon's proprietary answer to Google Home or Amazon Echo, cooed, *"I'm sorry, I don't recognize 'something relaxing so I don't murder my husband.'"*

"Just play some Norah Jones," Shay said, and sighed.

"Playing Norah Jones . . ."

"And you . . ." said Shay, advancing on Chase as the opening bars to "Don't Know Why" sounded.

"Hey," protested Chase, "one of these days that kid is going to break my ankles."

"Poor baby," said Shay, making a face. She wrapped her arms around his neck and kissed him deeply. Just as Chase was getting into it, Shay pulled away. "Now go get your daughter for dinner."

"No fair."

"No ball in the house."

Chase climbed the stairs to his daughter's bedroom and knocked. When he didn't hear a response, he knocked again and opened the door. She was at her desk hunched over her laptop, large headphones covering her ears. When she saw him, she pulled them free and he caught a storm of guitars.

"You know Mom doesn't like shop talk at the table, so give me the headlines," he said.

"Nothing."

"*Nothing?*"

"Nothing. There was zero evidence of an outside cyber intrusion. I even took the Echelon apart and sifted through every chip like I was panning for gold. No physical tampering either. And the operator didn't do it, I can tell you that. Poor guy had a panic attack just talking to me."

Chase thought back to his time in the OPCEN. When he arrived, the system had already been compromised. The only two people he saw touch it then were the operator and Daniels. Daniels may be a prick, but he didn't seem the type to self-immolate his career.

"Could someone else from the OPCEN have inserted something into the Echelon and then removed it? A flash drive loaded with malware? Something?"

"I mean...it's possible?" Madison made a face. "But someone slipping a drive into a terminal in the middle of a busy operations center? That'd be some serious sleight of hand. And again, no evidence of malware after the fact."

Damn, thought Chase, but he forced a smile.

"Well, that's not nothing. It's something. A deeply unsatisfying something, but something. Things we can check off the list. Let's keep doing backgrounds on everyone in the OPCEN. In the meantime, I have a new assignment for you. The Avalon plant in DC."

"I saw the news. Bad couple of days for Avalon."

"I want you to put eyes on it."

"Did Gillen expand our remit?"

"You leave that to me."

Shay called from the kitchen, "Dinner!"

Madison was out the door before Chase, but she spun on

her heel. She wore a wide grin and had a mad gleam in her eye. "Can I bring the drone?"

"First, it's not a drone. It's a two-thousand-dollar unmanned aerial system. Second, it's not a toy."

"You're the one who named it *Air FIRST One*."

"I'm trying to establish a brand. Need I remind you what happened when you borrowed my car last year?"

"Ah, but the drone has obstacle avoidance software . . ."

"Nice try. No, I want you inside the plant and all over its industrial control system like you were on the Echelon."

"Fine, but your official brand is No Fun. What are you going to do?"

Self-immolate my career, he thought.

CHAPTER 10

CHASE WAS WIDE awake, trying to figure a failsafe against fulfilling his own dire prophecy.

The Voice echoed in his head.

The unspoken threat.

I hope your daughter feels better.

The broad warning.

The evening commute will be a real gas.

As the family slept, he'd quietly shut down every device in the house, just as he had in the FIRST offices. He started with Shay's laptop, Madison's multiple computers and tablets, then Ava, Luke's video game console, even the damn complicated smart refrigerator that seemed like more trouble than it was worth.

No bugs.

Unless it was a bug sophisticated enough to beat his high-end RF finder, a potentially catastrophic setback Chase wasn't yet ready to consider.

There was nothing left to do but continue what he'd started at FIRST's offices: conduct a risk assessment of DC's sprawling transportation system.

No big deal.

By the Voice's own admission, it had masterminded two cyber operations with physical manifestations. Cyber/physical convergence. Chase's research showed that terrorist attacks on transportation systems were primarily physical. Still, he couldn't discount "old school" methods.

If past was precedent, Chase should expect another breach. But where? Metro, traffic lights, bridges, airports? Mechanical and digital machines were increasingly, inextricably linked.

London, 2005. Four terrorists conducted suicide attacks with IEDs carried in backpacks—on three Tube trains and one double-decker bus, killing fifty-two and injuring over seven hundred.

Madrid, 2004. Ten IEDs exploded almost simultaneously in the commuter train system at morning rush hour, three days before Spain's general elections. Nearly two hundred people were killed and two thousand injured.

Tokyo, 1995. The Aum Shinrikyo cult released sarin gas into the subway, killing over a dozen and injuring thousands.

These didn't even account for the rash of vehicle-ramming attacks around the world in recent years...

As dawn broke, Chase settled on a course of action. A risky one.

Madison was still sleeping when he left a note in her bedroom: "Contact Will Shannon at Metro. He's an old friend. Tell him to QUIETLY conduct full security sweeps on the Metrorail, Metrobus, and MetroAccess systems. Remind him he owes me a favor. Will explain later."

Will was another JSIVA friend, a former navy pilot and championship rifleman, who, upon retiring, went to work for the Metro Transit Police Department as an emergency management consultant. The Washington Metropolitan Area Transit

Authority (WMATA, or Metro to the locals) was a massive transportation system serving the District of Columbia, the State of Maryland, and the Commonwealth of Virginia. WMATA would listen to Will's security recommendations. Convincing him to sound the alert was another matter, but Madison's reminder would hopefully jog Will's memory of the debt he owed.

The Voice had said no cops and no tricks, but waiting for another call or, worse, another attack would put Chase at distinct disadvantage. Preemptive action was simple fair play.

Now he took a sip from the monstrously large coffee sitting in the cup holder of his Acura as he crossed the Key Bridge against DC morning rush hour traffic, heading toward the Rosslyn neighborhood of Arlington.

He was on his way to pay Miles Gillen a personal visit.

CHAPTER 11

AVALON HEADQUARTERS SHIMMERED iridescent in the morning sun. Superstar CEO Miles Gillen and Avalon had a familiar origin story—he'd created the telecommunications juggernaut in his garage decades ago—but now they were housed in an all-glass modern structure, a beautiful blend of art and commerce.

Chase had only met the man once before, when he'd attended Avalon's annual holiday ball as Shay's plus-one. That night, the building was shining with LED lights, but no glow was bright enough to camouflage a bird as odd as Gillen.

The CEO had stood out among the crowd—tech geniuses and a few of Shay's lawyer colleagues—as even more uncomfortable than Chase. When in full-on sales mode, Chase excelled at working a room, but this kind of holiday party wasn't his scene.

Gillen was the CEO. What was his excuse?

Shay made the introductions, then immediately drifted away in the swirling currents of revelers, temporarily stranding Chase. He suddenly felt like a grade-schooler set up on a play date.

"Some party," said Chase.

"I hate parties," said Gillen.

"It's *your* party."

"It's *their* party," he said, gesturing to the black-tie crowd. "I'm normally in bed by now."

Chase laughed. It was barely 9 p.m. The man was maybe a few years older than Chase, but hardly ready for the early bird special. "Seriously?"

Gillen glared at him, narrowing his famously ice-blue eyes.

"I wake up every day on the dot at 4:30 a.m. I journal, I meditate, I exercise. I own the morning so that I can own the day." Gillen said it by rote, as if it were an interview question he'd answered a hundred times before.

Chase got the feeling that people had stopped talking to Gillen like a human being a long time ago. He tried a different tack.

"You have me beat by thirty minutes." He hoisted his beer at the CEO. "And a few billion. Maybe I should set my alarm earlier. Sounds like that half hour makes a big difference."

Gillen took another look at Chase, chuckling as he sized him up, suddenly curious, engaged. "Why do *you* wake up so early?" he asked.

It was a genuine question, so Chase gave a genuine answer. "To prep the battlefield."

Intrigued now, Gillen turned to face Chase.

"For what exactly?"

"I don't know, but an early wake-up is a small price to pay for vigilance." He nodded at Gillen. "Or innovation."

The CEO grew animated. "After breakfast, I have a session of deep work—an uninterrupted period of focused concentration. I get into a flow state. That's where I solve the world's problems," he said with a grin. "I take a break, have lunch, go for a run, and then another afternoon session of deep work."

Chase sighed. "That sounds pretty great. With my schedule, I couldn't—"

Gillen cut him off. "I run my schedule. My schedule doesn't run me."

Chase sipped his drink and nodded. "Says the man isolating himself at his own party."

Gillen faced the room again. "Which he hates."

It came as a surprise to Chase when Shay came home months later with an offer from Gillen himself that FIRST assess Avalon Park.

Chase did his due diligence, reading company and magazine profiles of the daring entrepreneur as well as watching interviews, all routinely portraying Gillen as a maverick who enjoyed bucking the system for the sake of the greater good. Those icy eyes gazed at him from the covers of *Forbes*, *Fast Company*, and the *Economist*, but Gillen was notoriously private, and the information was infuriatingly thin.

I run my schedule. My schedule doesn't run me, he had said.

Chase asked Shay for her thoughts on the CEO, but she couldn't give a solid answer. The man was either true to the vision he professed or exceptionally good at delivering the talking points his PR firm provided. "Either way," she said, "he pays handsomely."

Alex Teague, Avalon Communications' chief security officer, made it obvious that he didn't appreciate the idea of an outsider scrutinizing Avalon assets. The CSO did his best to turn a perfunctory phone interview into an interrogation, but Shay had prepped Chase well, and his hire was a foregone conclusion. Teague was smart enough to realize that when the CEO of a global technology giant makes a suggestion, it's not really a suggestion.

As he approached Avalon Headquarters now, Chase realized he hadn't actually seen Miles Gillen in person since the ball.

This time, Chase was throwing the party.

In his crisp suit, worn with an open-collared shirt and an air of belonging, Chase bluffed his way past lobby security. None of the tech idealists who populated Avalon's ranks challenged him at all. Chase rode the elevator to its highest access point, but the top floor where Gillen and his executive assistant worked was secured. He ducked into the stairwell and climbed upward.

Time for a little covert entry.

Avalon Headquarters may be bright and shiny on the outside, but the spine of the building was the same as any other, and it was subject to building codes. The egress side couldn't be equipped with a latch or lock that required the use of a tool or key. On the ingress side, he gambled that even Avalon hadn't upgraded the stairwells; few in the high-rise likely ever used them except during mandatory fire drills.

He was right. No keypads or badge readers—just a simple lock to pick. Building codes and other people's complacency had kept Chase in business for years.

He would have to point out this vulnerability to Gillen. Right after he told him about the mysterious caller demanding a $100 million ransom. Which would probably be right before the CEO fired him.

He slipped into a hallway on the top floor. He passed a restroom and rounded the corner into the elevator bay, which seemed to stretch the entirety of the floor. But it was an illusion. Most of the partitions were actually glass. He knew Gillen believed in corporate transparency, but this was taking things a bit too literally. Now that Chase had rounded the corner, he'd be spotted by the receptionist.

He straightened, smoothed the front of his suit, smiled his most winning smile, and marched straight toward her.

The receptionist was stationed at a desk in front of a pair of frosted-glass doors. She didn't look much older than Madison.

Great, thought Chase, *young people love me*.

That notion evaporated the second she lifted her eyes. He could practically feel her glare boring twin holes through him.

"Good morning," boomed Chase.

"How did you get on this floor?"

He pointed at the frosted-glass doors. "I have an appointment with Mr. Gillen."

"No, you don't."

"Don't you need to consult your computer? A datebook?"

"*No.*"

He didn't want to lay it on thick, but she wasn't budging, and time was of the essence. He glanced at the nameplate on her desk, then said, "Ashley, I wish everyone in this organization was as efficient as you. My name is Chase Weldon with the FIRST Group. Mr. Gillen has hired us to manage risk."

It was a bit of an overstatement—he had only been hired to assess Avalon Park. Not a lie *per se*, just rounding up. "I have important information regarding the Echelon incident at Avalon Park as well as the explosion yesterday. Mr. Gillen needs to hear it. Immediately."

It was a little like pulling rank in the army. Using position power over personal power. If you had to rely on it, you'd failed as a leader.

Ashley sat back in her chair, eyes wide. "That's...a big deal."

"It is."

"Then you really should have made an appointment."

He rearranged his facial expression from friendly to hardened, suspicious glare.

"Maybe you didn't hear what I said. People are dead. More people might die."

"Sir, Avalon Headquarters is Mr. Gillen's castle. As his executive assistant, I'm his royal guard. I don't know how you made it this far, but you're going to have to leave."

Chase was impressed. The young receptionist was the best security feature he'd encountered so far here—a dedicated employee who was paying attention. He'd tried both personal power and position power. Neither had worked. Only one thing left.

The meg.

"Fine," he said. He feinted for the elevators, then sprinted for the frosted-glass doors. As tough as she was, the receptionist was moving from a seated, stationary position. He slipped through the doors, Ashley fast on his heels and yelling. Once inside her boss's office, the receptionist stopped screaming, and Chase stopped short.

Miles Gillen was sprawled on the floor, unconscious.

CHAPTER 12

"CALL 911," CHASE instructed Ashley, bounding for Miles Gillen's body.

The CEO lay in the center of his vast office, in the expanse between his large desk and the frosted-glass doors. It was a spare, clean space, as streamlined and functional as Avalon's smartphones. Chase's eyes swept the office suite's floor-to-ceiling windows, looking for bullet holes. In the second it took him to cross the distance to Gillen's body, he saw neither blood nor evidence of an attacker.

Possible cardiac event or stroke, thought Chase, his brain shifting into medic mode. The CEO had a wiry muscularity with minimal body fat. Still, heart attacks happened to fit people, too.

Gillen opened one eye. "Savasana," he said.

Does he recognize me? Chase thought. *Is he remembering our conversation from the holiday ball or slurring his words?*

"Savasana," repeated Gillen. "Corpse pose. I take it you're too busy *prepping the battlefield* to practice much yoga."

So he does remember. Chase had to keep sharp.

Gillen raised an open hand. Chase clasped it and pulled the CEO to his feet.

"I'm visiting the DC plant this afternoon and I was taking a moment to get centered. It's going to be a long, sad day and I owe it to my people to be calm. No one wants to see a stressed CEO." Gillen walked to his desk to retrieve a hand towel and patted his brow. "If you don't mind my saying, you seem pretty stressed yourself, Mr. Weldon."

"Do you know this man, Mr. Gillen?" asked the receptionist, who Chase just realized was gripping his elbow. Hard.

"It's okay, Ashley. He did just try to save my life. He's earned five minutes."

"Very well, sir..." It was clear she didn't like the answer. Reluctantly, she left the room. For now.

Chase turned back to Gillen. The CEO was seated behind his desk and gestured for Chase to take one of the empty chairs. He poured a glass of water from a pitcher.

"Rather than be upset that no one on my staff detected an intruder, I'm choosing to be delighted our new risk consultant was able to pass undetected."

Chase jerked his thumb toward the doors. "If you had more Ashleys, I'd have never made it past the lobby. You should give her a raise."

"Noted. Now, what can I do for you?"

"I left you some pretty urgent voicemails last night."

"Digital sunset."

"Excuse me?"

"I turn off my phone and all devices at 7 p.m. No calls, no texts, no emails. Voicemails get auto-forwarded to Ashley. She fans them out to the correct department."

Chase was incredulous. So his message was routed to Alex Teague, who apparently didn't appreciate Chase sticking his nose in. Which further explained why the voicemails Chase left for the CSO had gone unreturned as well. Turf battles he could understand, but he struggled to wrap his brain around the idea that a tech billionaire who designed phones would turn off his own at 7 p.m. People were dying and this guy was talking about yoga and digital sunsets.

"How do people get in touch with you?"

"They don't. That's the point. I make my deepest, greatest natural contribution to society with my tech. I can't be distracted with minutiae."

Minutiae. If this was Gillen's headquarters, and Ashley was his keep, then his assets out in the world like Avalon Park and the manufacturing facility comprised his kingdom. Right now, his kingdom was under siege. And with the latest attack, the explosion at the plant, his subjects were now getting killed. And more were under threat.

"What about emergencies?" asked Chase.

"For those instances where I absolutely must be consulted," continued Gillen, "I schedule short blocks of what I call OPS time throughout every day."

"Operations?"

"'Other People's Shit,'" said Gillen smiling.

"Well, I'm afraid I'm here with a heaping helping of it, Mr. Gillen. Avalon is being targeted. The incident at Avalon Park was no simple glitch and yesterday's explosion at the plant was no accident."

"You're saying someone was able to breach an Echelon *and* the firewall of an Avalon manufacturing facility?" Gillen smiled, a skeptical eyebrow raised. "Unlikely."

The CEO was friendly, but in his expression, Chase read

the boundless confidence and certainty of his skills and in his tech. The competitive streak, too. Avalon Communications was the fastest-growing tech and communications company in the world and considered by many to be the best. It was as if Chase had issued a challenge. Or an insult.

"Teague told me it was an industrial accident," Gillen said. "A terrible one, to be sure, but an accident nonetheless."

"Teague needs to look deeper. No matter how advanced or impenetrable your tech is, it's still used by humans. My best guess is someone went phishing and one of your people took the bait. They sent an official-looking email, an unwitting employee opened a link, and just like that bad actors are in your network. I have an associate who can help confirm that today, but however they got inside the fence line, they were able to mess with the industrial control systems and wreak havoc. Was it the blast furnace?"

The expression on Gillen's face told Chase he was warm. "Teague tell you that?"

Chase shook his head. "The adversary called me."

"What?"

"It gets worse. They want $100 million." Chase pulled his phone from his breast pocket, found the Voice's text message with the link, and placed it on the desk before Gillen. "And they want it sent to this link by this evening. Or else more people will die. That's why I'm talking to you, not Teague. We don't have time for chain of command here."

Gillen leaned over the phone, staring.

"You must be joking..."

"The news is reporting that three people died in that explosion. A hell of a lot more were terrified by the ballpark evacuation. I love a good joke, but nothing about this is funny."

"I'd agree. What are they planning to do?"

"Didn't say. They called from an untraceable number, using a modulated, unidentified, digital voice. With what you've confirmed, I have no reason to doubt their capabilities. Or their determination."

"So I just, what, transfer $100 million to a link? On your say-so? I'm afraid I'm very much in the 'We don't negotiate with terrorists' camp. We're calling the FBI right now, Chase." Gillen grabbed his own phone.

Chase leaned forward in his chair, held up his hand.

"I threatened the same. The caller said no cops and no tricks."

Gillen placed his phone on the desk and scrutinized Chase for a few moments. "How convenient."

"Pardon me?"

Gillen stood and began to pace in the lane behind his desk and the floor-to-ceiling windows. "Chase, do you know what I'm trying to do here? What Avalon is on the cusp of?"

"Roll out more devices, I imagine."

Gillen shook his head. "No. I'm not in the device business, or even the tech business. I'm in the *freedom* business. Everyone knows that there's exponentially more computing power in any car on the road these days than in the Apollo 11 module." He swiped his phone off of his desk and brandished it. "With this, people have all the tools they need to start a business, film a movie, or broadcast their voice around the world and start a revolution. We're preparing the next generation of Ava, with enough features to blow your hair back. It will save people so much time. For the elderly and mobility impaired, it will allow them to be more self-sufficient and to stay in their homes longer. Hell, for some it will be a member of the family. I'm trying to drastically improve people's lives."

"Great speech," said Chase.

"Thanks. A little overblown rhetoric buys valuable time."

Just then, the doors behind Chase flew open. Two beefy security guards marched toward him. They did not look pleased.

CHAPTER 13

CHASE EXHALED, SUDDENLY exhausted. "Panic button?" he asked.

The guards took station on either side of his chair, just behind him. At his four and eight o'clock. They were large enough to cast a shadow over his chair. He glanced back at them for a moment and noticed Ashley holding the doors open, her intense expression now softened with the hint of a smile. He looked back at the CEO.

Gillen shrugged. "Teague said you mentioned a few key safety features in your interview."

The Zen CEO's genial smile was gone. Gillen was serious now. Angry. A man did not build an empire on creativity alone. There was steel in there. "Of all the more established and better-resourced risk firms out there, do you know why I gave FIRST a chance? Because of the incredible respect I have for your wife."

Ouch. Chase had not kidded himself otherwise, but he hadn't expected Gillen to go there. What was the tech motto?

Move fast and break things.

Feelings didn't enter into the equation.

"Of all people, I never figured Shay Summers would have

married a buffoon, but I suppose we all have blind spots. Does she even know you're here?"

"No."

"I'm going to spare her the embarrassment—no, the mortification—and let you tell her."

"Mr. Gillen, I don't think you're taking this seriously—"

"Oh, I'm deadly serious. Good people—*Avalon people*—died in an industrial accident. It's you I'm not taking seriously. You break in with a tale of a 'mysterious caller' who demands I deposit a hundred million dollars into an anonymous account immediately or even more people will die. And when I suggest we contact the authorities, you tell me that's forbidden. All this, the day after an active shooter hoax occurs at Avalon Park. You're not the first person to try to make a quick buck off of me, and this little shakedown is definitely not the most sophisticated. But it is the most sickening. What did you think was going to happen here, Chase?"

Gillen signaled imperceptibly to the guards, who seized Chase beneath each of his arms and hauled him to his feet. Chase allowed it to happen; any other behavior would only escalate the situation and make him seem crazy, proving Gillen's point for him.

"Damn it, listen: More people are going to die," said Chase as the guards dragged him toward the doors.

"No, you need to listen, Chase: You need help."

The men locked eyes before the doors swung shut.

"You're going to regret this, Mr. Gillen."

Suddenly, the doors were closed and Ashley stood before him.

"Have a nice day, Mr. Weldon," she said, dripping sarcasm as the guards shoved him into an elevator.

They held onto him for the long ride down, and when the elevator reached the ground floor, they marched him toward the building's entrance. Chase didn't resist. It would have only made a spectacle, and being flanked by two muscle-bound guards in the airy, brightly lit lobby was humiliating enough as it was.

The pair shoved him out of Avalon Headquarters and onto the Arlington sidewalk, with $100 million even further out of reach and the clock still ticking.

CHAPTER 14

CHASE HEADED WEST on Route 66, trying to make sense of the last forty-eight hours.

Three days ago, his biggest concern was how Luke would do in next weekend's travel soccer tournament. Two days ago, a dangerous hoax at Avalon Park sent 30,000 patrons screaming for the exits. Yesterday, an explosion ripped through a manufacturing plant, killing three and injuring more.

And the cherry on top? Whoever was behind it all saw Miles Gillen as their personal $100 million piggy bank...and Chase as the hammer.

Though not for long. Chase was certain his little stunt had just cost him FIRST's biggest client and his professional reputation. He imagined Gillen picking up a golden phone and convening an emergency meeting of the Billionaire CEO Club, where the only item on the agenda would be blackballing Chase out of future business.

Thinking about his own problems in the midst of a campaign of terror felt selfish, but also oddly comforting, like touching a sore tooth. But Chase had more probing to do.

The evening commute will be a real gas.

Plan A hadn't worked, so now it was time for Plan B.

He took the Dulles Toll Road, then Route 7, speeding toward rural Virginia. The dense environs of the DC metro area gradually yielded to farmland. In Loudon County, he stopped for supplies at a Sheetz convenience store, then continued west toward Bluemont. Near the base of the Blue Ridge Mountains, he pulled onto an unmarked dirt road. After a few dusty miles he stopped before a low, secured gate. He exited his Acura to inspect the sheet-metal sign that read NO TRESPASSING in orange, reflective lettering.

Neighborly, thought Chase, then vaulted over the gate.

He walked several hundred yards before the trees on either side of the dirt road receded, revealing a ranch in the distance. Chase continued toward it. As he drew near to the main house, the dirt road became gravel. Suddenly, a large dog bounded from behind the house, alerted by the rustling sounds of Chase's footsteps. The dog rocketed toward him, teeth bared. Chase braced, narrowing his profile, and reached into his jacket pocket as a high-pitched whistle sliced the air.

The dog halted. An older man, tall and rigid, his face deeply lined, stepped forward from the shadows of the house's porch. He held a shotgun. It was pointed at the ground, but it was there.

"I never had much of an opinion of you, Weldon," said Captain Townsend Wade, "but at the very least I thought you could read."

"You know," said Chase, jerking his head toward the road, "you'd get a lot more visitors without that sign."

"You hear me complaining?"

Chase nodded toward the dog, now sitting a few feet in front of him and emitting a low, steady growl. "What is he?"

"Cane corso. Italian guard dog."

"Can I pet him?"

"Depends. How attached are you to your fingers?"

"That's not very sporting. I can tell you've already poisoned him against me."

"Maybe he's just a good judge of character."

"Well then, let's see," said Chase. He reached slowly into his jacket pocket and produced a six-inch braided bully stick. "An old man, living alone in the woods…of course there'd be a dog. Probably a very mean dog. *Or is he?* Maybe he's just misunderstood. Maybe he just doesn't have any friends beside the grumpy old man. I bet he's not getting enough affection. Regardless, I'd be foolish to come empty-handed. How am I doing so far, pooch?"

The dog's ears were up, and he was no longer growling. A long stream of drool touched the ground.

"That's what I thought. You're a good boy, aren't you?" Chase pitched the bully stick at the dog, who snatched it from the air.

"Titus," said the captain. His tone brooked no dissent, just as Chase remembered. The dog slowly lowered the bully stick to the ground and looked back at his master.

"That's cold," said Chase.

"Titus follows orders. Unlike some."

"There's more to life than always following orders, Captain."

"You always have an answer for everything, don't you? Even if it is garbage. You may've fooled Summers, but you never fooled me. Still don't."

That didn't take long. Chase looked at his shoes and rubbed his cheek, partly to hide his expression, partly to relax his clenched jaw. He'd heard the phrase "swallow your pride," but had never truly appreciated it until now.

"You'll be happy to know," tried Chase, "I don't have all the answers. And I'm in a hell of a jam—"

"One even the slick Chase Weldon can't talk his way out of?"

"It would seem not."

"Thing is, you're not my responsibility anymore. And I'm not buying whatever it is you're selling," said Wade, jutting his chin toward the road, "so why don't you just go back the way you came."

Chase was out of patience.

"You stubborn bastard. If there was anyone else on the face of the earth I could go to, any other option than standing here, hat in hand, with *you,* don't you think I would take it? But the plain truth is I need that big, strategic brain of yours. There's none better. I wouldn't be here if lives weren't at stake, Captain."

Wade stared at him hard for a moment, then looked off toward the tree line.

"I can't help you, Weldon."

"Come on, Captain . . ."

"No. Not anymore. Now shove off."

Chase stood his ground, fists balled, trying to settle on one of the ten profanity-laced insults that bubbled in his throat. Instead, he produced an envelope from his pocket and held it up for Wade to see, then threw it on the ground.

"My number's inside. In case you change your mind, *coward.* And pet your damn dog once in a while."

CHAPTER 15

CHASE STOMPED ON the gas pedal—such was his fury at his old JSIVA commanding officer. No one could get under his skin more than Captain Townsend Wade. And he knew the feeling was mutual. His car fired twin geysers of dirt as it sped away from the ranch.

His phone rang, yanking him from his thoughts. It was Madison.

"I tried, Dad. Honest..."

Oh, no, thought Chase. *What had he put his daughter through?* "I'm so sorry, Mads..."

"I presented myself to perimeter security at the plant. I flash the Avalon ID badge you gave me and explain why I'm there. They usher me in to meet the plant's chief security officer, who seems grateful for the help. And that's when Avalon's Big Security Cheese shows up."

"Teague?"

"Yeah. He examines my badge, then asks me to follow him. He leads me past the wreckage..."

"Are you hurt?"

"I'm fine, Dad. Everything in there, though? Ripped to shreds and scorched. There were some... dark stains, but for the most part the debris was cleaned up. But there were little cones and flags everywhere. To mark the, you know..."

"I know," said Chase. *The body parts.*

"Then he walks me through a door and I'm outside again. 'The grown-ups are handling it,' he says, and slams the door shut. That's when I realize I've just been escorted off the premises. And he never gave back my badge. I'm sorry, Dad."

Damn. Gillen didn't waste any time. Apparently, the first call from his golden phone had been to Teague.

Alex Teague and I are going to have a talk about his gruesome little tour when all this is done, thought Chase.

"I didn't mean for you to see any of that. I feel terrible."

"I don't need a fainting couch, Dad. But what the hell happened? It feels like our remit just shrank."

"You know how territorial these pricks can get. I'll sort it out."

Madison didn't seem convinced, but Chase ended the call before she asked any more questions. He wasn't ready to come clean.

He barely registered the ride back to the District. When traffic backed up suddenly before the Key Bridge, Chase hammered his fist into the steering column. The first blow felt good, so he brought it down again twice more in quick succession. He caught a look at himself in the rearview mirror. Breathing hard. Dark circles around wide eyes. An expression somewhere between rage and terror.

Christ, was this how I looked to Captain Wade? To Miles Gillen?

He closed his eyes and took several deep breaths. When he opened his eyes again, he noticed the driver next to him, a middle-aged woman, staring. She had been angling to get ahead of him as their lanes merged, but the look of horror on her face told him she now thought twice about cutting him off. When the space opened up, he nodded sheepishly and pulled ahead.

Come on, Weldon, he thought. *Get it together.*

So Plan A hadn't worked. Neither had Plan B. That still left plenty of letters in the alphabet.

The phone rang.

He tensed, but it was only Madison again.

"I have good news and bad news," she said.

"Let's start with the good news."

"Your friend Will just called. WMATA found a package with a suspicious substance inside the Foggy Bottom Metro station. They think it's *anthrax,* Dad."

"Jesus. Was anyone hurt?"

"The sweep team is getting checked out, but they were masked and gloved up. Too soon to tell for sure, but they should be fine."

Chase blew out a long breath. "If that's the good news, I really don't want to hear the bad news."

"I'm worried, Dad."

"I know. Me too, baby girl."

"*No,*" she said, the word an angry dart. "I saw the text yesterday. The BOOM. Then today, I'm suddenly persona non grata at the plant. You're hiding something."

"I'm not," he lied.

"I thought we were a team."

"We are. It's going to be all right, Mads, I promise. You just have to trust me."

"Please come home..."

"On my way."

The last mile home felt good. He hadn't gotten the money,

Wade had been a prick, and he knew he wasn't out of the woods yet, but FIRST's actions had disrupted the Voice's plot. At least for now. Buoyed by Madison's call, he swore he'd figure out a way to outsmart the bastard on the phone for good.

For once, the rush-hour bustle of the District held some appeal. The traffic was bumper to bumper, the brake lights of the cars casting a warm, red glow in the shadows as the sun dipped below the tops of the buildings to the west. Along the sidewalks, men and women happy for the end of another work day entered restaurants and coffee shops and boutiques.

He thought nothing of the first police car, sirens blaring, speeding in the opposite direction. The second, moments later, got his attention, and by the third, he began to get a bad feeling.

He arrived home in minutes, took one look at his family gathered in front of the TV in the den, and knew it was bad. Madison was crying. Shay held their son, who for once didn't shrug off the affection. Over the top of Luke's head, her lips were pressed into a thin line.

"Metro," she said. "Collision."

Damn it. He had thought of shooters, IEDs, gas, even another cyber hack with a physical manifestation, but he hadn't imagined an attack this spectacular. Or maybe he simply hadn't wanted to.

BREAKING NEWS. The chyron blared beneath a somber newscaster. MULTIPLE CASUALTIES IN METRO COLLISION.

He barely had time to register the words when his phone rang. The number was blocked. Madison shot him a look, but he left the room.

He took a deep breath, then answered.

"You broke the rules, Mr. Weldon," said the modulated voice.

"The hell I did," Chase hissed, looking over his shoulder to the den.

"No cops, no tricks. We consider tipping WMATA a trick."

How did they know?

Chase locked himself in his study. "Listen, I—"

"The price is now $200 million. Or this collision will be a footnote. A taste. By this time tomorrow, we'll crash ten more. Industrial accidents, power outages, hospital equipment failures, airlines…a digital apocalypse that will grind DC to a halt and bring Avalon to its knees. Then we'll move from city to city."

"If you have that kind of juice, you don't need me. So I think I'll take my chances, thank you very much…"

"That's the price we're asking from Avalon. The price of *your* insubordination is your family's lives."

"I told you, do not threaten my family."

"Too late, Mr. Weldon. They're already marked for death. The only variable is how badly they suffer along the way."

The Voice went into sadistic detail, describing the horrors he and his unseen team would visit upon Chase's wife and children. How there was no escape, how the outcome was inevitable, and how he'd brought it upon himself.

Chase's mind raced ahead, plotting contingencies on the fly, but every plan he conjured was anticipated and mocked by the Voice before Chase could even protest, as if the Voice were reading his mind. It was like getting tangled in vines or falling in quicksand. The more furiously he fought, the harder he was seized, the quicker he was pulled under.

It was uncanny. Worse, it was undeniable.

Chase's heart pounded and his vision swam. For the first time in his life, thinking three steps ahead wasn't enough.

"Wait! Let's talk about this," he said, fighting to keep his voice steady. "We can work something out..."

"Women and children first, Mr. Weldon," the Voice taunted. "Your family dies by sunrise. By your hand or ours. And ours will not be merciful."

Chase tried again, but it was no use. He was talking to a dial tone.

CHAPTER 16

CHASE WALKED ALL night. It wasn't the first time. During FIRST's earliest days, worried that he'd overleveraged himself, long walks were the only way to clear his head.

When in doubt, walk it out.

He headed west until he hit Rock Creek, then turned north and walked along the trail, barely hearing the water burbling over the rocks in the stream below.

Chase had spent his whole adult life calculating risk, mitigating it, mastering it. It was his specialty, his livelihood, his calling. He ran scenario after scenario, trying to figure out an alternative, running the numbers. It was a byproduct of his JSIVA days—the endless search for contingencies, loopholes for the contingencies, trapdoors for the loopholes—and that line of thinking was the very linchpin of the FIRST Group's operations. Making cold calculations before having time to process normal human emotions was the name of the game.

Only tonight, when he most needed the numbers to add up, they had failed him.

He turned back, staggering under the weight of the adversary's promised attacks. On the first day, it had sent a crowd into a full-blown panic just to get his attention. On the second, it had penetrated a network and blown apart a manufacturing floor, ripping three innocent people to shreds. And the death toll from the Metro collision was twenty and climbing. Bodies, crushed and battered, were still being pried from the twisted wreckage or scraped off the tracks. It was an exponential curve rocketing upward and the Voice was threatening thousands now.

But even that paled in comparison to the gruesome descriptions of what the Voice threatened to have in store for his family.

Chase would not allow Shay and the kids to suffer, and with that cold calculation made, there was nothing left to do but get it over with. Sometime before dawn, he rounded his block. He stopped a few houses away from his own, leaned over a low wrought-iron gate, and vomited into an azalea bush. He wiped his mouth and waited for his head to stop spinning. Then he continued to his own front door.

He fit the key into the lock with trembling hands and pushed inside. Standing in the foyer, he paused, listening for activity. Silence. He stood a few moments longer, savoring the familiar smells of his family and their home. He moved quietly to the bottom of the staircase and paused again. His feet felt as heavy as cinder blocks when he set them on the first stair, the pistol as dense as a dumbbell in his hand.

His brain screamed as he used the banister to haul himself up the stairs, frantically recalculating one last time. But the Voice had been clear—his family would be horrifically tortured and then gruesomely killed. He forced his feet onward.

Then, he was standing just inside their master bedroom.

Shay was awake, propped on the bed, still in her business clothes, at work on her laptop.

God, she's beautiful. His resolve wavered. For twenty years, he had been the luckiest man in the world. But sooner or later, luck always runs out.

Then he realized she was staring at him. At the gun in his hand. He was committed.

Shay's eyes went cold. Chase had seen that look before. She was running the numbers too, but never before had he been the threat she was calculating. The pieces of his already broken heart crumbled.

When she spoke, her voice was soft. "You don't have to do this, Chase."

She gripped the laptop—to put it to the side? Or fling it at him? He raised the pistol. She released the laptop and let her hands fall to the bed.

"It's just...I've run the numbers, Shay. There's no other choice. I'm sorry."

"Think of the kids."

"Don't." Chase swallowed and looked away.

"You son of a bitch," she hissed. "Look at me, you coward!"

He looked her in the eye, saw her fury.

"I have to. It's the only way."

"Please," she pleaded. "Don't do this."

"I'll always love you, Shay."

He fired, twice. The noise was shattering. Despite having fired many weapons in his lifetime, no other shots had startled him like this. He backed away as Shay fell onto her mound of pillows.

He heard commotion from the bedrooms, the sound of feet hitting the floor.

The children, he thought.

Chase was sobbing as he headed for them. The job was only half finished.

CHAPTER 17

CHASE FLED. NOT into the street, but deeper into his home.

Climbing the steps, his feet had felt leaden, but now he felt light and feverish. He caught himself on the banister as he slipped and stumbled on the stairs like he no longer had control over his own limbs. When he reached the first floor, he wheeled through the hallway into their large kitchen and found the light switch to the basement with a shaking hand. He descended, closing the door behind him, as if he could somehow shut out what he had just done.

Boxes and clear plastic tubs were stacked against the far wall, loaded with holiday decorations, old electronic equipment, paint cans. He shoved them aside to reveal a steel door that resembled a ship's hatch. Chase swung the heavy door wide, its hinges groaning like the roar of a giant awakening. A cool breeze blew through the basement, and Chase stared into a black hole.

He walked headlong into the darkness, breathing deeply to slow his heartbeat. He switched on the flashlight function of his phone and pointed it farther down the dark passageway.

DC's robust Metro system had over fifty miles of tunnels beneath the District and surrounding suburbs, but its abandoned streetcar tunnels were more esoteric. Chase had been unaware of them until he and Shay originally moved to the District. He'd been delighted to find the weird hatch-like door in the basement, connecting to a network of dark underground tunnels, when they first looked at the townhouse.

In 1949, the District had built a trolley system below Dupont Circle, with tunnels and platforms, running from N Street to the south and R Street to the north. But after little more than a decade in use, the entire streetcar system was shut down, made obsolete by the rise of automobiles. The massive subterranean space had been more or less abandoned since the '60s, despite various attempts to revive the space: as a fallout shelter depot in the 1970s, an underground food court in the 1990s, most recently as a contemporary art installation space.

As a man who had spent most of his adult life assessing risks and looking for contingencies, Chase counted any escape hatch as a positive sign. "Boys and their secret tunnels," Shay had muttered. Still, it was a beautiful home in a great neighborhood, so she'd agreed...with the caveat that she would murder without hesitation any derelict who ascended from their basement, making Chase her next victim.

He felt an overwhelming pang at the memory of her dark joke. Neither of them could have predicted that the greatest threat to their family would come from Chase himself.

His legs felt weak and his head swam. He wanted to lie down.

Instead, he pushed off the hatch and followed his light deeper into one of many spurs connecting to the vast underground complex. He charged ahead, causing unseen animals to skitter before him in the darkness.

He still had unfinished business.

CHAPTER 18

THE SUN WAS low in the sky now, an hour until full darkness. Chase planned to make the approach to the main house.

The advancing private security guards were unlikely to let him.

Crouching behind a copse of trees, Chase watched the two-man, black-clad security detail move. They were not the yellow-jacketed guards of Avalon Park—beefy men with a few hours of crowd management training and a professional certification. These two moved like professionals with real experience. Likely some of the same experience Chase had seen during his special-operations days. They were lithe and light on their feet. Heads on a swivel. They were younger, and there were two of them.

Not good, thought Chase.

The high fence topped with razor wire Chase had scaled to breach Gillen's estate was behind him. There was no escape.

Chase had no intention of retreating. There was no one and nowhere to retreat to. There was only forward now. He hadn't come this far, done all he had done, to walk away now. He had a new mission now.

Make Miles Gillen pay.

After emerging from the tunnels onto N Street and destroying his phone, Chase ran to FIRST's offices to collect the necessary supplies. He gambled Metro PD would still be trying to make sense of the crime scene, but he knew his time in limbo wouldn't last. After a quick spree, he exited the offices, pulled a ball cap low, and headed west on foot. Two cruisers blew past him, blue lights flashing and sirens blaring. They screeched to a halt in front of his CityCenterDC building.

Limbo was officially over. He was a wanted man.

He avoided the Metro with its crush of commuters and taxis with their curious hacks. He kept to the sidewalks, moving relentlessly toward his target.

Gillen's estate.

Set back from Foxhall Road behind wrought-iron gates and bordered on the rear side by a high fence, Gillen's Georgian-style mansion on fifteen acres was its own city on a hill. A private oasis in the middle of the nation's capital.

Chase disappeared into the woods bordering the property. He walked the fence line, assessing the best spot to scale it undetected. He chose a vantage choked with vegetation, then dropped into a crouch on the Gillen side of the fence. The plan was to wait for sundown.

Now, Chase watched the two-man detail split up as they approached, each heading for a far end of the property to do a sweep of the fence line. Eventually, they would converge, then retrace the steps of the other guard and meet back at the house.

Except one of them would discover him first. And the other would come running.

You really didn't think you were going to waltz right into Miles Gillen's private estate, did you, Chase?

With the tall fence behind him, a rolling green space ahead of him with no cover, and the two guards flanking him, they had him in a pretty effective pincer maneuver.

Fortunately, they didn't seem to realize it yet.

With the sun low over the trees behind him, the shadows were long and jagged. With two backward steps, he melted into the darkness. Chase quickly unzipped his pack, found what he was searching for, then straightened up slowly, careful not to move too quickly and draw their eyes.

He looked slowly from one guard to the other. The one to his right was closer, so he sidestepped as silently as he could to his left. If this was going to work, he needed to be at the exact spot where both men converged. He couldn't afford to tangle with one, giving the other ample time to unholster his weapon. Or worse, call for reinforcements. Chase arrived at the spot he thought they would meet, then proned out with his dark hood up. Willing himself to become one with the darkness.

In his head, he was already there. He was going to hurt these men. He searched himself for any part that felt guilt or remorse about it, but he found none.

He heard the footsteps ahead and behind him. He readied himself.

When the footsteps were practically on top of him, Chase slowly reached out his hand, containing a stun gun, from the shadows, and pressed its electrodes to the nearest guard's ankle. He pulled the trigger and sent 50,000 volts through his body.

The guard's back went rigid. He made a sound like every muscle in his body seized at once. Which it did. Then he went down. The second guard didn't realize what was happening as his partner grunted and collapsed. The guard rushed for him, catching him before he hit the ground. It would be nice if the electricity coursed from the first guard to the second, but stun guns didn't work like that.

Instead, Chase exploded from the shadows and rushed the second guard like a defensive lineman trying to sack a quarterback. The guard was faster than Chase thought, dropping his comrade and going for his holstered weapon. Chase had no choice but to drop the stun gun to hold the man's drawing hand in place, stuck by his side. They slammed into the fence. Chase didn't have time to be cute. He drove his forehead into the man's nose and heard a crack, felt the spatter of blood. He felt the hand on the holster lose strength. He released his right hand and flung his elbow upward, striking the man's temple with his forearm.

The man's knees buckled.

Nighty night.

He looked at the two men on the ground. In a fair fight, they probably would have wiped the floor with him. But as Shay had been fond of saying, "Fare is what you pay to get on a bus."

Recalling Shay made his jaw clench. Chase shook thoughts of his wife from his head.

He needed to act fast. He patted the fallen guards down, stripping them of anything useful. Glocks, paramilitary blades, small LED flashlights, portable access tools, even their Avalon watches, which were voice activated. He tossed them all into the woods. Finally, he removed one of their black jackets and put it on.

Chase found his stun gun by the fence and returned it to his pack. He swapped it out for more supplies. He propped the men up and zip-tied them to the chain link fence. Then he duct-taped the mouth of his stun gun victim. He seriously considered taping the mouth of the second guard he grappled with, but the man's broken nose would be useless as a breathing apparatus for a while. He figured he would have a few minutes before they were even capable of calling the cavalry.

More than enough time, he thought.

He marched toward Gillen's brightly lit fortress, the 9-millimeter in his hand.

CHAPTER 19

MILES GILLEN'S FIFTH-GRADE teacher once told the class that Albert Einstein could not remember his own phone number. His fifth-grade classmates cracked up.

Miles understood. There simply was no room in his mind for the inessential.

What was essential to Miles was the future.

As a result, he was never fully present.

Miles was stuck between how things were and how wonderful they *could* be. It was only when Miles felt he was closing the gap between the two that he felt alive, consumed with purpose, radiant.

When he felt the gap widening, he became incredibly irritable.

Yoga helped. As did all the systems he had put in place. The meditation, the journaling, the digital sunsets, but most of all, ignoring the inessential. But when new information—even of the unpleasant variety—disrupted his carefully cultivated routines, Miles prided himself on assimilating and adjusting faster than just about anyone on the planet.

So when he turned from his refrigerator to find Chase Weldon pointing a gun in his face, Miles immediately deemed the development essential and reconfigured the rest of his evening accordingly.

Miles sized him up. Cataloging the man's appearance, sorting bits of evidence into a narrative. Weldon was clearly distressed. More than that, he was disheveled. He wore dark clothes and a dark ball cap—a sort of modified covert uniform—streaked with mud. Miles pictured Weldon lying in wait in the woods behind his estate, away from prying eyes. Weldon's cargo pants were torn at the knee and Miles glimpsed bloody skin. He pictured the loops of razor wire topping the high fence that separated his property from a ravine that emptied into the Potomac.

And, of course, there was the gun.

Teague had already briefed Miles that Chase Weldon had murdered his entire family and was at large. As a precaution, the Avalon CSO had deployed the roving guard force.

The idea of armed security skulking around in the darkness had seemed both unnecessary and unnerving. And apparently ineffectual.

"Chase," said Miles, loading empathy into his voice, "are you hurt?"

Weldon said nothing. Miles decided to press his luck.

"Chase, I heard some very disturbing news earlier. Please tell me it's not true."

Weldon gritted his teeth. "He made me. He said... unspeakable torture if I didn't..." Weldon gripped his pistol tightly. Gillen saw the knuckles going white. "They came out on gurneys. Under sheets. I was a few blocks away, behind a tree. I watched them get loaded into ambulances. Then I came here."

Gillen could scarcely square the self-assured man from his office yesterday with the unbalanced man before him now.

"I see," said Miles. "How did you get here?"

"I walked. After."

After. The word hung heavy in the air between them.

One of the many systems Miles had put in place was rigorous exercise. His latest passion was Brazilian jujitsu. He was quite skilled at it, but rolling around on a mat with an opponent was nowhere near trying out a move with a gun pointed inches from your skull. And Miles knew Weldon had prior military experience. He also knew that if he was a fraction of a second too slow, his significant intellectual property would rapidly exit the back of his head to paint his stainless-steel refrigerator.

He reached deep for empathy.

"Chase, please. You need help. And I can help you."

"You're right. You're the only one who can help me," said Weldon, moving out of striking range, but keeping his pistol level. "The price is now $200 million."

"All this is about money?"

"No!" barked Weldon. He spoke slowly, enunciating every word, as if trying to make Miles *understand.* "It's about saving what lives we still can. The Voice promised a digital apocalypse. Tomorrow."

"Would you show me your phone, Chase? Maybe we can figure this out together."

Chase laughed ruefully. "Smashed it. No more electronic leash."

Gillen sighed. "Look around, Chase. There's no apocalypse, digital or otherwise. I'm going to ask you a question. I need you to really think about it. Are you sure the Voice is real?"

Suddenly, Weldon strode toward Gillen, pistol raised.

Miles shrank back until he was pressed against the

refrigerator, the muzzle an inch from his face. His hands floated up involuntarily.

He let out a breath. He wasn't looking forward to this next part.

"I can't." Gillen sighed.

"Can't? From one of the richest men in the world..."

Weldon cocked the hammer for emphasis.

"It's a skill problem, not a will problem, I assure you." Miles spoke quickly. "I can't transfer that sum of money from here. As soon as I initiate the transaction, it will send an authentication code to a terminal in one of my Avalon towers. To prevent a scenario, well, like this. Remember your interview with Teague? He said you rattled off a few ideas to prove you knew what you were talking about. We listened. I'm still listening."

"Then listen to this," said Weldon. "If you try anything, I'll put you in a permanent corpse pose. Let's go."

CHAPTER 20

LEAVING GILLEN'S ESTATE was easy. They slipped into his garage, selected a car—the CEO's electric Aston Martin Rapide E—then roared through the gate.

They rode across the Key Bridge in silence, Avalon's iridescent tower glowing in the distance.

My castle, thought Miles.

He felt the first stirrings of hope, but then the dragon beside him ground the barrel of the gun into his ribs. Miles wanted to wipe the beads of perspiration forming on his forehead, but he dared not move his hands from ten and two on the steering wheel.

They rolled into Avalon Headquarters unchallenged. It was after hours, and they parked in Miles's underground spot, then rode his private elevator to the top floor, bypassing lobby security.

Everything was automated. After tonight, he would spend some of his deep work time rethinking basic protocols.

If he lived.

They emerged to an empty suite. Miles was on his own, but found himself actually enjoying the urgency. The present had never been so tantalizing.

Miles knew Weldon was deadly with a gun, but the CEO,

in his own way, could be just as deadly with an electronic device. He just had to bide his time.

He led the way to his office suite, and Weldon motioned to the couch off to the side. "Shut up and sit down."

The couch was isolated, save for the coffee table in front of it. Weldon settled himself behind Miles's laptop, the seat of his power, his throne.

The CEO tried not to wince.

Miles was too far from any of his own devices. Weldon had already relieved him of his smart watch and phone, which he now removed from a pocket and set down on the desk next to his pistol.

"Password," said Weldon, fingers hovering over the laptop.

"3xc@1!bur."

Weldon consulted a slip of paper from another pocket. There appeared to be a string of characters scrawled on it, probably the link the Voice had given him before he smashed his phone.

Weldon hunched over the laptop and began typing. Pecking at it like some animal. Miles began to get angry.

He didn't wake at 4:30 a.m., maintain a perfect physique, and do deep work for the hell of it. Everything was done in service of his company. And his company was the direct expression of his vision. He ate and drank and breathed Avalon. When he slept, he dreamed about Avalon. Miles wasn't about to forfeit his life's work.

He was so angry he almost missed his opening. Weldon's gun lay on the desk, momentarily forgotten.

Miles slowly pulled his legs closer and planted his feet. He loosened his muscles and took three deep, quiet breaths. He visualized his outcome.

There was no time like the present.

CHAPTER 21

WITHIN SECONDS, A verification code popped up on Gillen's laptop. Chase typed it in as the CEO sat impatiently.

Suddenly, folder after folder telescoped on Gillen's desktop, blooming like electronic flowers, opening almost too fast for the eye to see, until the screen froze on a dashboard. It was an Avalon account, and the time stamp showed a transaction from a minute before. The account's total had lowered by $200 million. More folders bloomed.

"What are you doing?" asked Gillen.

Chase was staring at the screen as if in a trance. He hadn't touched the laptop since typing in the verification code.

The computer was operating of its own accord. As if it had a mind of its own.

"I'm not sure..."

The screen froze again, revealing another account, this one unlabeled. He looked at the transaction history. One minute ago, the account had risen by $200 million.

Of course. That's why there had been no evidence of an outside hack to the Avalon/Techtronics system. And why Madison had been tossed from the manufacturing plant before she would have discovered the same thing—or rather, the same nothing. There *was* no penetration.

You don't need to hack your own system.

Chase realized it just as he saw movement in his peripheral vision. Fast movement.

Gillen launched himself from the couch, covering the distance between them in an instant. Chase reflexively protected the laptop instead of his 9-millimeter.

Which was now pointed directly at him.

CHAPTER 22

"YOU IDIOT," SAID Gillen, beaming. "You perfectly golden fucking idiot."

"It's you..." said Chase, stunned. He raised his hands. "*You're* the Voice, aren't you?"

Gillen shook his head. It was a gesture of supreme frustration.

"*No*," said the CEO as if speaking to a child, "of course I'm not the Voice, Weldon."

"Then why does it look like you just paid yourself the $200 million ransom? I don't understand..."

Gillen smiled briefly, but it looked more like an animal baring its teeth.

"Of course you don't understand! It's like showing a dog a card trick. I'm on the cusp of transforming the world but privacy advocates and grandstanding congressmen who still think the Internet is made of tubes are holding me back. Do you have any idea how maddening that is? It's like Prometheus stealing fire and giving it to humanity, but man punishing him for it. It's a scary world out there, but I'm making it a better place. Avalon will be pushing software updates and the next generation of Ava devices to keep our users safe."

"Let me guess. With additional monitoring capabilities."

Gillen shrugged. "People will cede some autonomy for convenience, but they'll cede it all for security. All I needed to do was put some fear into them, and they'll willingly hand over anything."

Chase narrowed his eyes. "I thought you said you weren't the Voice."

"I'm not." Gillen grinned. "But the Voice speaks for me."

"Just tell me why," pleaded Chase. "Why didn't you just hire some damn lobbyists to blow past your roadblocks? Why all this? The stadium? The plant? The Metro? *My family*? *Why*?"

Gillen sidestepped the questions. "After two decades, Avalon is finally on track to be the top dog. We can withstand a lot, but not an antitrust investigation. Not right now. I wasn't lying to you when I told you I had the utmost respect for your wife. But she accessed...a tranche of private investments. Shay Summers was a ticking time bomb. We had to act decisively before she filed a whistleblower complaint. Or worse."

"Oh, God," said Chase, bending over. "I feel sick."

"You know, I ran my own risk analysis on you, Chase. I'll give you this—you're nothing if not persistent. You would have caused too many problems unless I made you culpable."

"You're insane," said Chase, tears in his eyes.

"No, Chase, *you're* insane. That's the point! My executive assistant and two security guards will testify to your aggressive tactics and wild conspiracy theories. Your wife must have discovered your harebrained scheme and the shame was too overwhelming. You couldn't stand the look in her eyes, in your children's eyes, so you murdered your entire family. Finally, broke and with nothing left to lose, you kidnapped me. But I got the drop on you.

"It's such a perfect plan, Weldon, and Avalon products are

nothing if not elegant. Don't feel too bad. I'm a futurist. I was always going to get the drop on you."

Chase looked around, stymied. He squeezed his eyes shut and balled his fists.

"I know it's cold comfort," Gillen continued, "but I really am sorry about your family. I just couldn't let Shay ruin what I've spent my life building. Sometimes sacrifices have to be made."

"Can't make an omelet without breaking some eggs?" said Chase, his teeth gritted.

"In fairness, it's going to be one hell of an omelet."

Gillen pulled the trigger and kept squeezing until the slide locked to the rear. Once the deafening sound faded, Chase, still on his feet, opened one eye.

"*Damn, that was loud,*" said a voice in his ear.

Chase touched his hidden earpiece. "Sorry about that, kiddo."

"*Just punch this douchebag in the face already.*"

"Roger that."

"Who the hell are you talking to?" asked Gillen, incredulous.

"My family," said Chase, advancing. He cracked his knuckles. "Did I not mention they were still alive?"

CHAPTER 23

SHAY CHECKED HER watch, took a slow, deliberate sip of her coffee, then looked at the man across from her. He wore a sour look.

"Should be any time now," she said.

Seated at his kitchen table, Captain Townsend Wade stared back at the woman who had turned it into an impromptu OPCEN and, Shay guessed, his normally quiet evening into a royal headache. The Weldons were imposing on him, but Shay didn't care.

It was the least he could do, she thought.

Beside Shay was Madison, hovering over her laptop. In the corner was Luke, scratching Titus's belly. Though the massive cane corso weighed more than her son, he was kicking at the air with his hind legs and scooting along the floor on his back, eyes wide and tongue lolling, as happy as a manic puppy.

"Must he do that?" asked Wade, making a face.

"He's happy," said Shay.

"Who?"

"*Both of them.*"

"Making a damn fool of yourself, Titus," he grumbled, but

that was that. Luke scratched, Wade seethed, and Shay drank her coffee and watched everyone until Madison said, "They're in the office."

"Finally," said Shay, blowing out a breath.

"Tell me again who came up with this insane plan?" said Wade.

"Chase," Shay said evenly.

"Hey!" said Luke.

"Sorry, honey. You helped."

Titus paused his gyrations momentarily, then continued bicycling with his hind legs.

"We megged him," said Luke.

"I have no earthly idea what that means, young man."

"Here, I'll show you. Stand up."

Luke sprang to his feet. Wade cast another glance at Shay, but stood warily and faced Luke. Luke rolled a rubber ball he'd brought for Titus between them with his toe.

"Don't let me get it past you," said Luke.

"Please," said Wade, towering over the young boy.

Luke juked left, then right, and when Wade widened his stance in response, Luke drilled the ball right between his legs. Luke darted around him and ran down a long hallway, the dog bounding behind him, barking like mad.

"It's called a nutmeg," said Shay, smiling.

Wade grunted, then leaned against his kitchen sink.

"So your grand plan was to kick a ball between the legs of one of the most powerful men on the planet?"

"The key to a nutmeg is to do it so quickly and seamlessly that your opponent only realizes it after the fact."

Wade folded his arms.

"It's reckless. You should have come to me first. We could have come up with a better plan."

"Chase did come to you. You didn't give him a chance. You never did."

"I gave him the same chance as everyone else."

"Bullshit," she spat. Shay looked over at her daughter. Madison hadn't noticed the outburst. She tapped away on her keyboard, headphones on, concentrating on the conversation at Avalon Headquarters.

Wade leveled a finger at his former executive officer.

"You could have done so much better for yourself than that...that snake-oil salesman."

Shay raised her eyebrow. It usually silenced Chase. It didn't work quite as effectively on Wade. "Chase didn't bat an eye at torpedoing his business and professional reputation to protect us. Say what you want, but the man has flair."

"Too much flair for my taste," muttered Wade. "I just never understood it, is all. Damn it, Summers, you could have been a general! You were the finest officer I ever worked with. You could have gone all the way. I'm talking commandant material." Wade blew out a long breath, looked off to the side. "It's not what I wanted for you."

"It's what I wanted for me."

Shay was no stranger to combat. Once upon a time she had also been Wade's second in command, JSIVA-9's executive officer. She had led a unit of terrorist-operations experts, security op specialists, engineers, emergency managers...all culled from special operations, the finest the different services had to offer.

And she had been in charge.

If Ginger Rogers did everything Fred Astaire did, but backward and in high heels, Shay did the same with JSIVA—with an M16 slung over her shoulder. Everyone in the unit respected her. Some feared her. Only one had dared to love her, and she married him.

"You know he delights in pushing my goddamn buttons..."

"Maybe. But when the chips were down, where did he go?"

Wade allowed himself a small smile. "I was surprised to read his letter and this harebrained plan of yours. Too much flair."

"Maybe. But I'll say this: Chase loves me and the kids with everything he has. And right now, he's risking it all."

"He did it!" Madison interrupted. "He's in! I'm in! Rubber Duckie, you're the one!"

"What?" asked Wade. Luke ran back into the room, Titus on his heels, one ear up, the other inside out, like a pig's.

Madison cocked her headphones back and her hands flew across her keyboard. "I have control of Gillen's terminal and I'm rummaging through his financial closet."

"What's happening in the room?" asked Shay.

"The guy is monologuing Dad to death. So lame. He's, like, one step away from threatening the world with a weather machine. Now everyone shush."

Minutes passed, and Shay fought the urge to pepper Madison with questions. She knew her daughter was hard at work, infiltrating as deeply into Gillen's personal network as she could. But it sounded like Chase had actually managed a confession and Mads was collecting information.

Suddenly, Madison threw her headphones down. Even as they clattered across the Formica top, the sound of repeated

204 • JAMES PATTERSON

gunfire coming through them was unmistakable. Everyone fell silent.

Madison put her headphones back on. "Damn, that was loud..."

A low, visceral rumbling filled the kitchen. Titus was growling.

A moment later, light flooded Wade's yard.

CHAPTER 24

CHASE WALKED OVER to the CEO, plucked the pistol from his grasp, and smashed the shocked man in the nose. The blow sent him sprawling.

But Gillen did not collapse. Instead, the man rolled into a reverse somersault, kicking his legs high up. He snapped at the waist and was on his feet again, facing Chase. Gillen's muscles were engaged, his upper lip peeling back in an angry sneer. Blood streamed from his nose.

Gillen charged, coming low.

Chase pulled the Glock tucked at the small of his back and whipped it around in front of him. Gillen halved the distance between them but stopped short before his forehead kissed the Glock's muzzle.

The CEO's eyes went wide.

"The last one fired blanks," said Chase, "but I'm guessing this one that I took off your security detail works just fine. They're zip-tied to your fence, by the way. Try not to hold it against them. They've had a bad enough night as it is."

Chase waved Gillen back and ordered him to sit on the floor. Gillen crouched, still ready to pounce, but Chase said, "Uh-uh. Crisscross applesauce. Pretend it's yoga."

Gillen stared daggers at Chase but complied. As he settled into position, he wiped his nose with his sleeve.

"Sleight of hand," said Gillen as he daubed his nose. "Cute."

"More sleight of foot. It's called a nutmeg."

"It's going to take more than a little misdirection and a punch in the nose to stop me, Chase," Gillen said.

Suddenly, a disembodied voice came from everywhere and nowhere. The ubiquitous voice of Ava, feminine and soothing, filled the suite, announcing *"Protocol, calling."*

Before Chase could stop him, Gillen said "Answer" in a firm voice.

Chase glimpsed the ceiling. Like FIRST's conference room, Gillen's ceiling—the entire suite—was likely embedded with invisible speakers and microphones, more sophisticated than FIRST's budget would allow.

"Mr. Gillen, we have a problem."

Digitized and distorted, the familiar voice hovered in the room without a source. The Voice was calm, not taunting, which made it sound even more inhuman.

"Yes, we do," said the CEO.

"It appears the Weldon family is still active; however, I have a team sitting on them. We tracked Weldon's phone yesterday to a ranch an hour west of the District. Very isolated. Say the word and we'll put this matter to bed."

Chase took three steps closer and pointed the pistol at Gillen's face.

"Do *not* 'say the word.'"

"Is that you, Weldon?" A slight chuckle oozed from the embedded speakers and echoed around the suite. It sounded like feedback.

"Stand down," ordered Chase. "I have a Glock in your boss's face."

"Mr. Gillen, Weldon is bluffing. He's not going to kill you. It's not too late to fix this."

Chase pressed the Glock to Gillen's forehead. "I wouldn't take that bet if I were you, Miles."

He jerked his chin toward Gillen's computer. Protruding from it was a flash drive with a Rubber Duckie logo, which at that very moment was installing malware, delivering payloads, exfiltrating documents, and stealing passwords. Full system penetration. All at lightning speed. And all visible to Madison.

"A very pissed off nineteen-year-old currently has command and control of Avalon," Chase said. Gillen's face fell. "It's over."

"Not necessarily, Mr. Gillen. There's just one thing though," the mercenary added. "My team and I are more than happy to get our hands a little dirty, but it's going to require an additional $50 million. With all this money flying around, it doesn't really seem like that's going to be a problem for you."

Chase dug the muzzle into Gillen's flesh. The CEO said nothing.

"Tell you what, Mr. Gillen," said the Voice. "It sounds like the cat's got your tongue. But I'm going to go ahead and take care of this for you. See that you take care of us. Or else."

"Tell him no," ordered Chase through gritted teeth.

"No . . ." said Gillen.

Chase relaxed, took a step back.

". . . *witnesses!*"

Chase fired the Glock.

Gillen's left foot exploded. The CEO screamed and rolled to his side. He bent into the fetal position and rocked back and forth, spattering blood and flesh, his scream replaced by a high keening. Tears streamed from his eyes. He clenched his teeth.

Chase turned from the writhing CEO and spoke to the room, to whatever hidden speaker was closest.

"Gillen is going down. You do not have to do this. Walk away while you still can."

The Voice didn't answer, but Gillen was muttering to himself. Chase didn't care. But in straining to listen for a reply from the Voice, Chase caught something from Gillen's mumbling. The man hadn't been muttering prayers or even curses, but a string of numbers.

"*Confirm transfer?*" asked Ava suddenly.

"Confirm—"

Chase straddled Gillen and put the barrel of the pistol beneath the man's eye.

"What was that?"

"Einstein's phone number," said Gillen. It took great effort, but the CEO smiled.

Chase cut him off with the butt of his pistol to Gillen's mouth, but it was too late.

"*Transfer complete,*" said Ava.

"Sorry, Weldon." The mercenary's voice filled the room. "I'm afraid that Mr. Gillen just wired me $50 million to finish the job. I'm a professional with a reputation to protect. How would it look if I didn't follow through?"

CHAPTER 25

"MOTION SENSOR," BEGAN Wade, as the window above the kitchen sink exploded and the captain went down. Shay tackled Luke, covering his body. When she looked up, Madison was beside her, protecting her laptop the same way.

They heard several muffled *pops* and the yard plunged back into darkness.

Titus was going nuts, barking and running in circles, knocking the table and spilling coffee. Wade was on the floor in front of the sink, clutching his right shoulder. Blood seeped through his fingers. He didn't make a sound.

"Captain," said Shay.

"Alive," he said, teeth gritted.

Shay gathered Luke and shoved him and Madison into the hallway, which led deeper into the house, out of the line of fire. "Stay low," she ordered, then looked at Madison. "Go."

One hitter or a team? Titus was still barking like mad.

"Captain. Your piece."

With his good arm, Wade tugged a Colt 1911 from his rig. He slid it across the kitchen floor to her. Shay squeezed three rounds of covering fire through the shattered window as she darted toward Wade. She cupped him under his left arm and dragged him into the hallway, firing again over her shoulder.

"Now what?" she said.

He grimaced in pain, his forehead already beaded with sweat. "Basement," he grunted.

The door was off the kitchen. Shay crept down the stairs, but Titus bowled past her. He whipped around the space, satisfied the level was unoccupied. She returned to the main level and called to Luke and Madison. Together, they hauled Wade downstairs. He tugged on a light switch and a bright halo appeared over a long workbench. Madison set her laptop on it, then gasped. Along the wall behind it, hung from brackets, were at least a dozen weapons.

"Whoa."

Captain Wade's personal arsenal.

Shay moved to the wall as the kids helped Wade sit on the floor, his back against the bench. She grabbed an AR-15 set up for night work and slung it over her shoulder.

Firing back would have given the assaulters a moment of pause—but just a moment. They would still proceed. And though the basement gave them a few precious seconds to collect their breath and gear up, they were cornered here.

She spotted a Goodman Special Operations Combat Knife and tucked it into her waistband. "Which way?" she asked.

With his left arm, Wade pointed to a swath of darkness in the corner, deeper than the shadows pooling outside their nimbus of light.

"Connects to the root cellar fifty yards off. They likely spotted the cellar, but wouldn't know it connects."

You boys and your secret tunnels.

Shay turned to her children and took one last look at them

in the light. Luke's eyes were wide, alive with questions, but too overwhelmed to ask. Madison's lips were quivering. They were terrified, but keeping it together. Shay had never been prouder of them. Had never loved them more.

In that moment, both her love and her fury bloomed like an expanding mushroom cloud, almost more than she could process. But if they were to survive, she was going to have to corral her anger. Her children didn't need a forest fire, they needed a laser.

Her kids wanted their mother, but right now, they needed Lieutenant Colonel Shay Summers.

When she spoke, Shay's voice was low but authoritative.

"Listen up," she said, "it's time to go. I'm going to lead you through the tunnel to the root cellar. Stay there. No light, no sound. Do not emerge unless you hear my voice and the word *nutmeg*. Repeat the word."

"Nutmeg," said Luke and Madison.

"Captain?" She looked at Wade, seated with his back against his workbench, weapons arranged in a semicircle around his body, a rag pressed to his shoulder. She didn't need to explain the plan and he didn't need to hear it. If they were to have any chance at all, Shay needed to get outside.

"Titus and I'll keep them busy. *Go.*"

Shay nodded and led her children into the darkness.

CHAPTER 26

SHAY LOOKED BACK at the pool of deep shadow where her children hid, nodded once, and said a silent prayer that Wade hadn't gotten lazy in retirement.

The door to his root cellar opened quietly on well-oiled hinges.

Good man, she thought.

The door was built into a mound of earth, a small protrusion in the terrain of Wade's property, fifty yards from his home. It was far enough away from the captain's house that one would be forgiven for thinking it was unconnected.

She crept along the bottom of the mound in bare feet, having shed her boots before emerging to remain silent. It had drizzled earlier and she felt the cold, wet grass beneath her feet, sensitive to the smallest twig snap. Around the side of the mound, facing the house, was a single man, clad in black, rifle raised, murmuring.

Overwatch.

She didn't know how many attackers were skulking around the perimeter of the house, but on a quiet night across the expansive lawn they would surely hear her weapon, even suppressed for sound and flash.

She approached the man from behind and plunged the Goodman into the mercenary's neck. She drove it to the hilt. With her other hand, she grabbed the top of his head and bent it forward, keeping him from making a sound. The mercenary spasmed, then crumpled as she released the blade. She grabbed his rifle and radio to prevent them from clattering to the ground.

Overwatch down.

She retreated to the top of the mound, proned out over her AR-15, and sighted on the house. She didn't have to wait long. A silhouette rounded the corner low and crept beneath a window.

It had been a while since she'd fired one of these. She took a breath, let it halfway out, and took the slack out of the trigger. When the round leapt from the rifle it was almost a surprise.

But a pleasant one. *Just like riding a bike.*

The crouching mercenary dropped, his figure dark and still.

She donned the earpiece from the overwatch's radio and listened.

"Do you copy? Simpson?"

She didn't know if Simpson was overwatch or the dead man beneath the window. But there were two down now, she hadn't heard the boom of Wade's shotgun yet, and she could hear the uncertainty in the voice over the radio. A mercenary, confident in the infallibility of his unit and their element of surprise, suddenly alone in the dark. If her children hadn't been cowering below her in the root cellar, Shay might've smiled.

Instead, she keyed the radio. In her deepest voice, she said, *"Abort."*

She doubted they'd buy it. But it would cause more confusion, and they'd know their channel had been compromised. And with two of their men not answering hails, they were likely to fall back. They were mercenaries, paid to take out a mother, two children, and an old man. They weren't expecting opponents who fought back.

Shay waited several moments, and strained her ears. The root cellar was behind the house, between it and the woods. The road they had come in on was on the other side of the house. She didn't want to leave the cover of the mound, but it was time to press whatever momentary advantage she had.

She ran for the house.

Crossing the wide lawn felt vulnerable, waiting for bullets to rip into her at any moment, but after what felt like an eternity, she made it to the nearest wall of the house and its deep shadow. She crept around the dead man and was about to clear the corner when she thought better of it. She turned back to the dead man and took his impact helmet. There was a night optical device affixed to it. She put it on, lowered the NODs over her eyes, and saw the night awash in crisp green detail.

She spied around the corner. Two figures, far apart, advancing on the house. Shay yanked her head back as one took aim.

CHAPTER 27

"MADISON?" YELLED CHASE. He pressed his earpiece, willing it to transmit a sound from his daughter. Willing her to be alive. "Mads!"

Finally, he heard a low whisper, barely audible. Her words made the hair on his neck stand on end.

"Mom said not to make a sound."

"Copy," he said. "Don't talk. Just tap once for yes, twice for no. Is everyone okay?"

A muffled thump.

Good. Chase exhaled but knew that wasn't an answer likely to last.

"Are Mom and Wade taking care of things?"

There was a long pause before the next muffled thump. Madison had to think about it.

Not good.

Chase needed to be there. But at least there was a way he could see what was going on.

"You're doing great, kiddo. Do you have your bag?"

An instant tap.

"Is your tablet inside?"

Tap.

"Power it up. I left an extra set of eyes outside Wade's gate just in case. Tap once you're up and running."

Tap.

Chase pulled out his smartphone and opened an app. His screen became a controller.

"Good girl. Just one more thing: Deactivate the obstacle avoidance."

CHAPTER 28

SHAY HEARD THE crack of a supersonic round in the air-space her head had occupied a second earlier.

There were two of them. And they were going to flank her.

She considered running back to the mound, but she needed to lead them away from the children at all costs. She weighed her other options. It didn't take long.

There weren't any.

She was heading toward the other corner of the house when she heard a grunt and the sound of someone dropping.

"The fuck?" someone shouted.

Then she heard running.

It could have been a trick to draw her out, but she peered around the corner through her NODs.

There was a figure on the ground, not moving. The other figure was in a full sprint toward the road. He was at the edge of property, about to disappear into the trees.

She ripped the NODs off and stepped away from the house.

She raised the rifle, brought the scope to her eye, and tried to lead him.

There was no time to get into a good firing position. She could only pray she hit him before he vanished.

There was a blur at the edge of her vison. She whirled to meet it. Through the rifle's night optic, she saw a dark torpedo streaking across the lawn. Moving too fast to keep in her scope.

Titus.

Wade had let slip the dogs of war.

Head low, the dog charged soundlessly. The mercenary sprinted, unaware of the one hundred and twenty pounds of tooth and claw and muscle hot on his trail. The dog halved the distance between them in the space of two heartbeats. Shay regained the merc in her scope just in time to see Titus leap.

Then the two silhouettes merged into one writhing mass. Shay could no longer make sense of what she was seeing, but the sounds told the tale: Titus's growls, an impossibly loud vibration that carried across the lawn, like the throaty idling of a muscle car. And the shrieks punctuating the growls as the dog savaged him.

Suddenly, there was an awful tearing sound. The shrieking stopped.

She heard the sibilant sound of tires on gravel.

A getaway vehicle, parked somewhere down the road. She sprinted toward it, traversing the front lawn.

She glanced at the first body as she ran past. Beside him, a drone that had seen better days.

Air FIRST One.

The stupid drone Chase absolutely had to buy for the firm. Telling her it was an *unmanned aerial system* for overhead capture of client facilities...

Now he'd turned the two-thousand-dollar titanium alloy quadcopter into a missile and had flown it into a man's face at thirty miles per hour.

Love you too, baby.

"Titus!" she called as she drew closer. The animal's blood was up, and she wanted him to hear her voice, recognize that the figure now running across the lawn was a friendly. He lifted his head, ears up.

"Come on boy!"

Chasing the vehicle along the road would be fruitless, so she angled for the woods. Titus waited for her as she approached, hopping in place by the ravaged mercenary, a big puppy again.

She hoped.

The dog charged off ahead of her. He seemed to know where he was going.

Who am I to argue? she thought.

She followed.

One moment, Titus was approaching the tree line, the next he vanished. Shay aimed for the spot where she'd last seen him, finding a well-worn trail, probably one Titus and his master walked daily.

Ahead, Titus barked.

Branches snagged at her clothes and stones bit her bare feet. But Shay felt none of it. She picked up speed as her eyes adjusted to the full dark. She knew the dirt lane to Wade's ranch intersected the road somewhere. It was thin and wound through the woods, but she plowed on.

"Please," she said aloud. It was all the prayer she had breath for. A tiny burning flare launched into the cosmos. She wasn't picky. She would accept help from any being taking requests.

Ahead, she detected a slight change in the light. A break in the relentless trees. She heard a vehicle racing.

An SUV roared past just as she burst through the trees. Titus in pursuit. She planted her feet and raised the rifle.

She led the vehicle's driver side window, careful to avoid the bounding dog, and let fly.

She wasn't sure whether her shot had found purchase until the SUV lurched, taillights tracing red back and forth in the night. Then they pitched suddenly as the nose plowed into a small gulley along the dirt lane. Metal and fiberglass impacted earth, followed by the steady blare of a horn. Titus barked over and over. Shay shushed him. She dropped the rifle and leapt into the gulley, Colt raised. She crouched, grabbed the door handle and jerked, stepping aside.

No shots followed.

A bloody man was slumped over the steering column. She lifted her foot and shoved him off the wheel. The blaring stopped and silence rushed in. The man fell down into the passenger side footwell. No protest, dead as can be.

Satisfied, she leaned against the side of the car and exhaled. She stared up into the trees for a moment. The taillights, pointing skyward, painted the branches an eerie red. To anyone else, it would have seemed like a hellish landscape.

Not to Shay.

She climbed from the gulley to find Titus waiting for her, tongue lolling, tail wagging.

"Good boy," she said and headed for the house.

CHAPTER 29

"IT'S OVER," SAID Chase.

He held out his hand for the wounded CEO.

"I'll decide when it's over," said Gillen.

"Don't you understand?" asked Chase. "You think you're in control, but you're not. Despite all your towers, all your devices, all your money, it didn't even come close."

Chase grabbed Gillen by the forearm and hauled him onto his good foot, then pivoted, and seized the man around his wrist and the meat of his upper arm. He would help the CEO move, but it wouldn't be painless.

"Time to go," said Chase. "I wonder if they have free Wi-Fi in prison…"

"I'm not going to prison, you ape," said the CEO. "I'm Miles Gil—"

Chase heard the tinkling of glass. Gillen pitched forward.

Chase let go of the falling CEO and spun. His brain registered what was happening without conscious thought. He knew the sound of a sniper's work. He dove for Gillen's desk and pulled all of his limbs under its massive slab. His eyes found the CEO on the floor.

Miles Gillen was right. He wasn't going to prison after all.

Half of his head was missing.

"Change of plans," said the disembodied voice.

The Voice wasn't with the assault team on his family. He was somewhere near here, staying close to Gillen. Judging by the bullet's trajectory, Chase placed the shooter on the roof of the adjacent high rise. In a sniper's nest.

Chase's thoughts fell into place. The Voice could've killed him easily but chose Gillen instead. The plan changed because the math changed. Which meant...

"My family just kicked your ass," said Chase.

"My ass?" That grinding laugh, like copper wire dragged across a chalkboard. "My ass is fifty million dollars richer. There's no one left to split it with. My ass is sitting pretty."

"Not for long," said Chase. "You came for my family. You don't get to walk away. I will hunt you down."

"Don't make this personal, Weldon. Unlike Gillen over there, I learn from my mistakes. My plan is to vanish into a life of island luxury. But if I feel you over my shoulder, I'll have to get back in the game. Besides, I'll always have an eye on you."

"How so?" Chase said, stalling. The electronic voice was coming in little, rhythmic punches. *He was running, probably down stairs.* Chase darted for the door to the office suite, keeping low just in case. With one hand, he grabbed his bag and with the other, snatched the Avalon ID badge from the dead CEO's body.

"Because you and every other idiot on the planet allow it. Phones in your pocket. Tablets in your bedrooms. Laptops with cameras and facial recognition. All linked to your identity. To say nothing of our dear little Ava..."

"How may I assist you?" chimed Ava.

The mercenary laughed. "Nothing, darling. Go back to

sleep. The grown-ups are talking. See, Mr. Weldon? An all-knowing, ever-growing artificial intelligence that you tell your preferences and cede responsibility to. And you lemmings pay for the privilege."

As he exited the suite, Chase heard the Voice say, "I just did the world a favor. Take the win, Weldon. Or I'll see you around."

Chase plowed through the doors, past Ashley's empty desk to the elevator bank. Gillen's private elevator opened immediately and he rode it to the ground floor. He sprinted for the street, startling the after-hours security guard in the lobby.

"Call the police!" ordered Chase as he ran past. "Miles Gillen's been murdered!"

Chase wasn't about to shed a tear over the CEO's death, but he knew it would get the police on scene quickly.

He burst onto the street with his Glock pushed in front of him, sweeping three hundred and sixty degrees.

But the street was empty. No pedestrians, no cars.

"Shit," muttered Chase.

He walked back to the lobby and past the flummoxed security guard.

"Sir, wait, you can't—"

"Quiet," said Chase. He did not bother to conceal the Glock. "Send the police to Gillen's suite."

When he returned to the top floor, he used Gillen's ID badge to get back into the suite. Thwarted and furious, he glared at the CEO's body. Chase had wanted Gillen to face justice. And failing that, to kill him himself. He needed to talk to Shay, to his kids, but there was still unfinished business.

He already knew the answer, but he had to be sure.

"Ava," he said, "trace the last call."

CHAPTER 30

IT WAS ALEX Teague.

Chase told the police that Avalon's chief security officer was also Gillen's personal fixer—until he double-crossed his boss, tendering his resignation with a high velocity round.

The Arlington Police were the first on scene, but the responding officers weren't apt to believe the man standing over the corpse of one of the richest men in the world. They burst in with weapons drawn.

Chase had anticipated that. He greeted them with his hands up, fingers spread wide, concealing nothing.

"It's not what it looks like," he said.

There was shouting and shoving to the floor. They cuffed him and cinched his wrists tight, but Chase didn't care. He had spoken with Shay moments before they arrived. His wife was alive. His kids were alive. Wade was alive—in pain but alive. The grumpy bastard came through in the end.

The officers yanked Chase to his feet and read him his rights.

"The bullet that took Gillen out came from a sniper's rifle," Chase persisted. "Opposite roof." He jerked his chin toward the shattered circle in the window. "The man you want is named Alex Teague. He's Avalon Communications' chief security officer. *And he's getting away right now.*"

A senior officer surveyed the body on the floor. Then he got in Chase's face, all smiles.

"And the bullet in the foot?"

Chase was about to answer but thought better of it.

"Lawyer," he said, and sighed.

Shit, Shay's normally my lawyer. It's going to be a long night...

From inside a cell at Arlington County Police Headquarters, there was nothing left to do but wait and reflect on the last few days.

From the night of Avalon Park, Chase had known something was off. He had gone straight to Shay. They'd hoped Madison could get to the bottom of it when she examined the Echelon, but when he received the second text and the phone call that put his family under threat, Shay had led him outside. They'd sat on their front stoop—without their devices—and she'd revealed she had found evidence of price fixing and payoffs at Avalon. She had been mulling how to proceed, but now she agreed with her husband that something was awry at the company.

"So you discovered dirty dealings—" began Chase.

"At the same time someone threatens you to extort money from my boss," finished Shay. "It's not a coincidence."

They decided Chase ought to play along. It gave him an excuse to see Gillen. Look him in the eye and see what he knew.

But the man was hard to read.

Chase drove to Wade's ranch to talk to him and, failing that, deliver a letter summarizing what they suspected and a request for safe haven if the time came. He knew their old commanding officer would never refuse. Meanwhile, Shay visited the FBI Washington Field Office, turning over evidence in a classified space. The special agents assured her she would be safe, but Avalon was a twenty-first-century tech giant and the FBI was a twentieth-century bureaucracy. Things were moving too fast for the feds.

Chase needed to get creative.

With the train collision, Teague overplayed his hand. Until then, it had been about the money. When the Voice demanded the deaths of his wife and kids, it was too much of a swerve. Chase realized then it had never really been about the money at all—it was about silencing Shay. For good.

The concern was that if Chase didn't appear to comply, a "clean team" would do it anyway and make him look responsible. So Chase and Shay had pulled the kids into the tunnel and told them everything.

"We have to meg them," Luke had said.

Chase and Shay were stunned, but their twelve-year-old was right.

Chase concocted an elaborate ruse they'd all play out for the benefit of Ava, their home's electronic informer. Afterward, the entire family would flee through the tunnel. Shay and the kids would make their way to Wade's ranch.

Once everyone knew their roles, Chase canvassed the neighborhood for a van or a tail or anything out of place. He spotted nothing, but it did little to settle him. He kept walking until it was time to go home.

And go through with it.

The Academy Award for Best Actor goes to . . . Chase Weldon, he thought ruefully.

Except he hadn't been acting. Not completely. Aiming a

gun—even one loaded with blanks—at his wife and children took a toll on him. The whole episode sickened and enraged him. It had taken all of his willpower not to put a bullet in Gillen's head the moment he saw him.

He was still angry, but the adrenaline of the evening had long since faded by the time an Arlington police officer arrived at dawn to unlock his cell. The officer was accompanied by two clean-cut men in suits. *FBI*, thought Chase.

"Took you long enough."

They introduced themselves as the special agents Shay had met with the day before. Most agents Chase had known over the years presented as unflappable, but these two looked sheepish. Which meant they were really freaking out on the inside. Yesterday, Shay had given them evidence of corruption by Avalon Communications. A day later, a hit squad tried to execute the whistleblower and her family, and Avalon's CEO was murdered via sniper.

Not the Bureau's finest hour.

"Where's Teague?" demanded Chase.

The special agents looked at each other. One cleared his throat and said, "In the wind, I'm afraid."

The other spoke up. "Mr. Weldon, it took us a few hours to sort out—"

"Save it," snapped Chase as he strode past them. "Take me to my family."

CHAPTER 31

ALEX TEAGUE WAS still out there, but Chase's family was alive. So tonight they were celebrating at a pizzeria near Dupont Circle. Chase was still unsettled—they all were—but they laughed and toasted each other and were more raucous than any of the other tables.

They didn't care.

Chase hoisted a beer. "To my children, the cleverest, bravest kids ever..."

Madison and Luke's cheeks grew red, but they raised their glasses in return.

"And to my bride..." said Chase, but his throat caught.

Shay rubbed his back. He had been trying to keep it light and breezy, but his emotions betrayed him. The dark thoughts still came for Chase when he stopped moving. He remembered the Voice, mocking him: *Women and children first.* As if it were a slight. But in the Weldon family, "women and children" was a superlative.

As Chase tried to recover, swallowing the lump in his throat, Luke raised his glass.

"To Dad, who landed his first big client...and then killed him."

Madison did a spit take, spraying her soda across the table. Shay threw her head back and laughed.

"Hey," said Chase, pointing at his son. "Technically, I only shot him in the foot..."

His family howled. The table next to them left abruptly. They laughed harder.

On the walk home from the pizzeria, Shay and Luke strolled ahead. Chase hung back with Madison.

"Mads," he said quietly, "how goes the hunt?"

The FBI had raided Avalon's offices the morning following Gillen's death, confiscating workstations and files, but that wasn't a problem for Madison. Thanks to a backdoor she installed, FIRST still had full access to Gillen's files, accounts, and shell corporations. "Teague mentioned islands," Chase had told her. "There will be a boat, I'm sure of it."

Sure enough, one of Gillen's shell corporations had purchased a Sea Ray 500 Sundancer in Miami, Florida. High-end and roomy, but not flashy enough to draw too much attention. A perfect boat to get lost on.

If Madison didn't already have his scent.

"My friend at FinCEN says the boat was spotted refueling in Aruba a few hours ago," said Madison. The Financial Crimes Enforcement Network, a bureau of the Department of the Treasury, specialized in analyzing financial transactions to combat money laundering and terrorist financing. Between blowing up a manufacturing plant, causing a train collision, and murdering a prominent CEO—even if he was the same one financing the operation—the United States government was more than happy to label Teague a terrorist.

"The net is tightening, Dad. It's just a matter of time. The Coast Guard is patrolling the area. And if he somehow slips past them and lands in another Egmont Group country," continued Madison, referring to the association of the 164 Financial Intelligence Units around the world that shared FinCEN's mission, "we'll know. Then we can alert the FBI."

Or Shay and I can take a little trip to the islands and handle it ourselves.

Plus, Shay looked great in a bikini. Two birds...

"What do you need?" he asked.

"It's just a matter of time. But if I had the big office, maybe it would go faster..."

"Here we go."

"And tacos. Every day for lunch. Delivered to my desk in the big office."

Chase was laughing as they mounted the stairs to their townhouse but stopped short as soon as they walked inside.

"Oh, my God," said Shay.

The floor shook as their houseguest bounded toward them, swinging his entire hindquarters and sweeping the contents from the entryway table. There were feathers in his jowls, and knickknack debris on the foyer floor.

Titus was happy to see them. With his owner still in the hospital after shoulder reconstruction, the dog needed a temporary place to stay. Luke was delighted. Chase less so.

Luke dropped to his knees and the dog began to lick him furiously. Feathers stuck to his cheeks.

Chase looked at his wife.

"Are you sure they don't allow dogs in the hospital?"

Her answer was an arched eyebrow.

"I'll get the broom," he muttered.

Later, when Madison was in her room, headphones on and

lost in a digital world, and Luke was in bed with Titus curled at his feet, Chase and Shay spoke privately in their bedroom.

"I'm sorry," said Chase.

"For what?" On the other side of the bed, Shay unbuttoned her blouse.

"For all of it. If I hadn't been so preoccupied with FIRST, I could have seen things earlier, more clearly . . ."

"Chase, Gillen was one of the smartest men in the world and we beat him. End of story."

"Exactly. *We*. I need you watching my six full time. If FIRST is to become what I know it can be, I need you. Without you, I'm just a guy. But together, we're unstoppable."

They had put off talking about the future this week, but Chase could not imagine her returning to Avalon. Avalon was Miles Gillen, and Miles Gillen had tried to murder her family.

"Wade," said Shay.

"What about him?"

"I don't like him out there all by himself. He needs purpose again. And he came through for our family."

Chase sighed. Their old commanding officer, who hated his guts, at FIRST? "Fine. Any other outrageous demands?"

"Just one," she said, her eyebrow raised. In the good way. "Am I president or CEO?"

Chase smiled and met her on the bed.

"Let the negotiations begin . . ."

THE HOUSEKEEPERS

*James Patterson and
Julie Margaret Hogben*

CHAPTER 1

MASHA POPLOV COULD kill a live chicken by snapping its neck, but she liked to do it in Jimmy Choos. Chanel, Vuitton, Prada, Gucci, spider-leg lashes and acrylic nails, so what if she had to work hard for a living? She did it in style.

Cleaning houses.

Stealing from them.

It was two o'clock and sunny when she and her cousin, Sophie Poplov, both Russian beauties, both approaching their thirty-third birthdays, pushed their carts down the Sumners' drive in Hancock Park.

The carts were filled with brooms and rags, plus cleaning supplies that Masha stole from the Sumners' pantry that afternoon; all the expensive Whole Foods brands. Organic, natural. Method, Honest. Blah-blah. The stuff the LA housewives liked. Masha refused to pay for that crap. Not when ammonia from the 99 Cent Store did the same job at twice the speed. And Mrs. Sumner would never notice.

She wouldn't notice the missing diamond either.

Masha had swiped a two-carat ring.

"It's wrong," Sophie said of her cousin's never-ending schemes. She didn't approve. Especially now, after what happened at the Bel Air house with Dr. Parks. They had to be careful. They shouldn't be doing anything sketchy. The people they worked for trusted them; allowed them into their refuges.

"What's wrong is her hiding this beautiful ring. This rock lives in shadow. In the dark. In a box. It's time for this rock to see the sun," Masha argued.

"It's stealing."

Sophie would not steal like Masha. At the grocery store once, she popped a loose grape into her mouth. After feeling guilty for days, she finally went back and paid the cashier 25 cents and told him she'd stolen some fruit. He thought she was nuts.

"I'm giving this ring its freedom," Masha said. "This diamond would thank me if it could. And cubic zirconia shines bright, too!"

The ring was stamped. A Tiffany's classic. Platinum, with a pavé setting. New it was maybe worth thirty grand.

But Masha only wanted the diamond.

She'd drive to Glendale right then and there and give it to Gor, a jeweler on North Brand Boulevard. Gor, an Armenian, ran a "diamond downgrade" business.

He'd swipe the stone out, set a fake, give Masha a third of the after-market cash, all in the time of a legal cleaning. About an hour. In the morning, Masha would go to the Sumners', put the ring back, and Ellen Sumner would never be the wiser.

"It's Lent," Sophie said. It was. It was March. They had survived the pandemic. People were opening their houses again and letting in the cleaning crews. They should be grateful. "Try to control yourself. Ask God to help."

Sophie preferred to clean houses in Adidas, and she was concerned for her cousin's soul. "Try to steal nothing for forty days. Can't you try?"

"No," said Masha. "I can't do nothing about my habit." She laughed. She loved to steal. "I don't do drugs. I don't sleep around. This is how I ease my demons. What can I do?"

"You can stop," Sophie said, and then she froze. Something down the street caught her eye. Her face fell, concerned.

Masha turned to see what it was.

Down at the Stop sign, two blocks away, three men in suits climbed from a big black Escalade. They all turned and looked toward the cousins.

"What is this?" Masha said, a rhetorical question.

The four men studied them, too, but not in the way the cousins were normally ogled. The men were focused. Serious. Fast. In tandem, they started walking toward them.

"They're coming to us?" Sophie wondered.

"We should go," Masha said. "We should go now."

Sophie agreed. Masha rounded the old Chevy, popped the trunk, threw in the buckets, and collapsed the cart as fast as she could.

Sophie clumsily lunged for the door, knocked her cart over, and all her supplies spilled to the curb.

"No, no, no," she whispered, panicked, and gripped the door handle. She flung the door open, turned, and bent down to fetch the bottles and brushes, tossing them into the back one-by-one, feeling stupid and terrified.

The men seemed to notice and quickened their pace.

"Mrs. Poplov!" the tallest one called from across the street, a block down, on the sidewalk.

Masha and Sophie looked up and froze like rabbits scenting the breeze.

Missus? he had said. That meant Sophie.

All three men were tall and broad shouldered. Russian?

Maybe. American officials or police? Possible. They all wore suits, shiny shoes, and aviator glasses, and headed toward the cousins in long, swift, quickening strides.

"Mrs. Poplov, please wait a moment for us," the tall one called again, this time louder.

He held a briefcase, the second gripped the car keys, and the third, a blond, looked too baby-faced to be in this company, a college boy playing at tough.

"Hurry, hurry," Masha chided her cousin. "Sophie! Leave it! Get in the car!"

Sophie shoved her collapsed cart into the back seat and slammed the door shut while Masha slipped behind the wheel and started the engine.

"Mrs. Poplov! Don't leave!" the tallest one shouted. They were now crossing the street at an angle from Masha's Chevy.

"Sophie! Get in!" Masha yelled.

But heart pounding and stomach clenched, Sophie froze, stuck between the passenger door and inside. She slipped her right hand into her purse, the messenger bag across her shoulder, and felt for the gun she kept at the bottom amid the crumpled-up tissues, latex gloves, and hand sanitizer.

Would she have to use it again? In broad daylight? Never again, she had told herself.

She'd promised God.

"Sophie!" said Masha. "Run! Run away! They're coming for you!"

CHAPTER 2

"MRS. PARKS, YOUR client is dead."

Elizabeth Parks blinked in surprise at the two detectives who sat in her study across from her desk. She said nothing. They were from Beverly Hills.

Of course, Stanley Lewis was dead, she thought. Lewis was in his nineties, with advanced pancreatic cancer. Of course. He had days to live the last time she checked. Two weeks, at most.

He was a lovely, charming man, white-haired, handsome, and always good humored, even when he was weak and struggling with terrible pain. He'd survived the pandemic, only to receive a cancer diagnosis six months later, the day before Christmas.

"First of all, he's not my *client*," the doctor corrected the detectives. "He's my patient. And second, I'm not *Mrs.* Parks, officers, I'm *Doctor* Parks. Before I became a CEO, I had a surgery practice for sixteen years."

The detectives glanced at each other. The shorter one, Will Hernandez, leaned in.

"*Doctor* Parks," he said respectfully, "Stanley Lewis did not die of cancer. He was murdered with a hammer to his head in his home. In his bedroom. In his pajamas."

Dr. Parks's eyes widened. "You're kidding me," she said, and took a moment to absorb the news. "Why am I only hearing this now? When? When did this happen?"

"Two nights ago."

"My God, that's horrible." She couldn't believe it. Poor Mr. Lewis had served in Korea, then in the Middle East, in the air force. He had survived three wars. Four decades of military service, then to be murdered in his own home? In bed? How? How could this be? The news shook Dr. Parks to her core. It belied the singular myth she believed: that a person's home exists as a safe haven from the world, a sanctuary and refuge from danger.

Hernandez continued.

"We have reason to believe the persons who killed him wanted his morphine. Not his life. It's possible that Mr. Lewis woke up and fought them off."

"Where—where was his nurse?" said Parks, as she reached for her laptop to pull up Mr. Lewis's file. "The nurses aren't mine, you know that, right? I contract out. Various agencies. I get them from all over the place." She felt horrified. Was she to blame? Was that why the detectives were here?

"His nurse was asleep two floors down, in the TV room," the second detective said. Morse. Neither gentleman wore a nametag, but this one had said his name was Morse when they came through the door and into her house. "She checked on him at five in the morning, but he had been dead for several hours. She called 911."

A whirring sound then came from the hall and drowned Morse out. Dr. Parks rose from her desk to shut the door. But before she could, Masha, her housekeeper, pushed the vacuum around the corner and into the room, her eyes fixed blindly on the floor.

She didn't see them.

"Masha," the doctor said over the whir, but Masha couldn't hear. "Masha!" she said again, raising her voice with a nervous laugh.

"Oh!" Masha said, and startled. "Sorry!" She yelled and pulled out her earbuds. "I didn't know you were in here!"

"We are." Dr. Parks sighed, and asked Masha if she might start upstairs in the bedrooms. She was having a meeting and needed the privacy and quiet downstairs.

Masha said, "Sure. Yes, Mrs. Parks. Hello." She smiled at the gentlemen, lifted the vacuum, and walked out.

Dr. Parks closed the study door, moved to the desk, and sat back down. Morse looked amused, and she knew why.

"She looks great, right? She cleans in high heels," she said to the men. Her housekeeper always cleaned in stilettos, with a full face of makeup, in a matching outfit, jewelry, and elbow-high silicone gloves. She always wore gloves to protect her nails. "Cocktail casual. It's impressive."

The officers smiled.

"Well," said Hernandez, moving on, "whoever murdered Mr. Lewis, Dr. Parks, they got in and out and no one saw them except Mr. Lewis. We have very few leads."

The doctor shook her head and exhaled slowly. This was a terrible and sad event on so many levels. Poor Mr. Lewis, his poor family, and the police showing up at her house like this, sitting inside her home. She'd never had trouble with the law before. Not once in her life.

"So why are you here?" she asked the officers. "Am I a

suspect?" She gestured around the decorated study with its imported wallpaper, chesterfield sofas, Queen Anne chairs, walls lined with built-ins and leather books. "Do you think I need to steal morphine? I still write prescriptions. I can still practice."

Parks had started the private hospice after her aging mother had died, after she'd seen the terrible job the care facility did in her mother's final months. She contracted out with St. John's and Cedars, and was doing well. She had worked hard to afford her life, her home especially: the purchase of the house, the expansion, two renovations five years apart; her home was her hobby, obsession, and escape. She'd paid it off and owed nothing, except for the annual property tax. She'd live and die there. No old nursing home for her. She'd promised herself.

Morse opened a file on his lap.

"Over the last few months, Dr. Parks, we've seen a pattern of residential burglaries. A string," he said, "in upscale neighborhoods: Bel Air. Beverly Hills. Hancock Park. Entrance gained through unlocked doors. No damage. No broken windows or locks. And no one hurt, until Mr. Lewis. The perps—whoever they are—they're not there to kill. They come to lift tramadol, lithium, fentanyl, Oxy, codeine..."

"Oh, drugs," the doctor said. "I see." Prescription drugs were a hot commodity. She knew that.

"And all of the homes have two things in common. A person inside is sick or dying..."

"That makes sense."

"And they're being cared for by City of Angels Healthcare and Hospice...Incorporated."

Dr. Parks blanched. She hated the way he gave her this

news. Morse said the word "incorporated" with some kind of edge, some kind of attitude she couldn't read, as if she were committing some kind of crime by profiting from sickness and death. Then he paused, and in case she hadn't followed his point, he said:

"Dr. Parks, all of the victims are your clients."

CHAPTER 3

THIS WAREHOUSE SMELLS like death, Sophie thought, as she handed Boris the envelope. Five thousand dollars for her son. That was the offer. That was the deal she'd made with the Odessa brothers and their LA lackeys.

Boris was solid and mean looking, with ink that covered over his bald head and down his neck, and across his chest there were tattooed stars and snarling tigers in front of the Kremlin.

Sophie was Russian, too, after all. Born and raised. Why should they extort a Russian? She had done nothing to her ex, Andre. Knew nothing. And Ivan, her elder son, was only a boy. Still a child. He knew nothing of his father's crimes. Sophie and her sons had not laid eyes on Andre in seven years, since Ivan was nine and Nikolai six. Was this revenge for leaving him? Abandoning him to jail in New York?

The envelope hid the hundred-dollar bills, all from Masha; sweet and sassy cousin Masha, who always found a way to come up with money. No matter how much, she could always provide. And it was dollars, as they asked, not rubles. She had followed their directions, so now it was time to give Ivan back.

Ivan had been gone now for weeks, her baby and first born,

sixteen last year, and somehow in trouble with the gang from back east: the Odessa brothers, all friends of Andre's, all from Uglich, with ties to Moscow.

Bad things and worse went down in New York, in Brighton Beach, where Andre's family had set up shop. Protection and prostitution rackets. Drugs. Smuggling.

Sophie refused to speak to her ex. She and Masha bought the old Chevy, which Masha fixed up. Masha was a mechanic at heart, and replaced the fuel system, then spread her legs for a new rear axle. Car up and running, they made the drive, Masha, Sophie, Ivan and Nikolai, to the West Coast.

Sophie wanted an honest life. A life in service of her Lord, Jesus. That was it. She was still young. She could work hard. Get married. Start over. Be good. She wanted so badly to be good. To do the Lord's will.

She watched in the dark as Boris slipped out the cash and counted.

"One thousand four, one thousand five..." They were clean and crisp, fresh from the bank. "One thousand eight..."

She looked around the warehouse. The smell was death, she thought. How could anyone live in this place? How could anyone make this a home, even a gang of criminals? The smell was the rot of rodents, she thought. Dead rats and mice. It was different from mold or mildew, or stink. Mold smelled earthy, like soil from the orchards back home in spring. And mold didn't make her nauseous like this. Mildew smelled like wet socks or newspapers left in the rain. And stink was years of microwaved fish, coffee and cigarettes, dog breath and diapers, dirt and oil tracked in from outside.

Death, on the other hand, did not leave a smell. It left a stench. The smell of bacteria breaking down flesh, of methane gas, too many cows trapped and steeped in their own manure. It was rot, decay, a sickening odor that turned the stomach of any good housekeeper or good mother.

And Sophie was both.

"It's all here," Boris said. "Better be real."

Sophie's anger rose in her chest.

"Where would I get counterfeit? Huh? Me? Where do you think?"

"I don't know," Boris said, and lifted his brows.

"I make an honest living. Cleaning homes. Making homes pretty and clean and shiny. Not like you."

"Mom," whispered Nikolai. "Stop," he begged.

"I'm a *Christian*," she spat. "And so is my son here, and Ivan, too. Now bring him to me, and let us go on and live our own lives. We want nothing to do with you people."

Boris wore sunglasses on his bald head. "People?" he said with disdain. "We are your family." Since this was Hollywood— well, North Hollywood—even inside a dark warehouse, Boris felt he had to wear shades. Five gold chains, Rolex, loafers by Gucci, no socks.

"Family?" Sophie said. "Family?" She turned her head and spat on the concrete floor. "You are not family. This is not what family does. How family treats its members. No."

Boris stared coldly at her and turned, clenching the envelope as he walked off toward a steel door with an Exit sign.

"Calm down, Mama," Nikolai pleaded. "Please. Please."

"I'm sorry," she whispered, and looked around. She knew she was asking for trouble. She was an exquisitely beautiful woman, svelte and blond, and Ivan and Nikolai were beautiful boys. They attracted the wrong kind of attention.

Ivan had tagged the wrong wall in North Hollywood, and

gangbangers jumped him and dragged him away. They stuffed him into a van, said Nikolai, and drove him away. Nikolai thought it was MS-13. The men looked Mexican. But Sophie later got word that the Russians and MS-13 had a deal. They worked together on various streets. Maybe it wasn't about the graffiti. Maybe the jump was because of Andre. Andre's revenge. He had threatened revenge over and over. "Someday," he'd said. "You cannot hide."

For weeks in church, she'd sunk to her knees and prayed to the saints, begged God and Mary to bring Ivan home. He was an innocent.

She'd searched the Valley and learned all about the LA streets. The Latin gangs owned north LA. The Armenians ruled Glendale and Burbank. South of downtown, the blocks belonged to the Bloods and the Crips. But the Russians, the Russians were everywhere. Ruling over everything. Making deals. Forging alliances.

Who could keep track?

She begged the priest and parish to help. Taped her son's photo to telephone poles, like a lost puppy. She couldn't call the LAPD. She didn't have papers. They would deport her. Hand her to ICE.

Then one day Boris found her in Crenshaw and made her an offer.

"Five thousand cash by Sunday," he said. "Meet us with cash, or your other son is next." So now they waited in the vacant warehouse.

Sophie turned when she heard a noise from inside the doorway where Boris had walked off and disappeared. It was the sound of rolling wheels. Over the floor.

Boris and another man stepped in again. The other man,

younger and slight, wore all black; a black T-shirt, black jeans and boots, and dragged behind him a black four-wheel suitcase.

Heavy. It had weight.

What was it? Sophie wondered. Her eyes widened as they approached, her heart started pounding, and Nikolai looked at his mother, confused. Where was his brother? Where was Ivan? They paid the money.

What could this be? His things? What things?

"Here you go," Boris said, and stopped in front of them.

The second man righted the suitcase, turned, and walked back toward the Exit sign.

Sophie stared for a moment in silence. The suitcase handle slowly retracted.

"What is it?" she said, and looked up at Boris.

"Your son," he said.

Sophie looked down. Liquid dripped from the bottom zipper to the warehouse floor. It formed a puddle the size of a quarter. It was dark. It was blood.

"What are you saying?" she said softly and sunk to her knees. "You're monsters." She reached out and touched the nylon. "You're monsters! This is not him! This is not my son!"

Tears cascaded down Nikolai's cheeks.

CHAPTER 4

THE DOCTOR FELT like her life was ending; her entire purpose, her precious patients who relied on her company to care for them, to protect them in their final weeks, in their final days, were now exposed to a vicious new threat.

And it was her fault. The company's files were not secure.

Hernandez and Morse left their cards and she walked them out, reeling.

A stranger, or strangers, had hacked in and stolen her patients' files? Either that, or someone in her office? From the inside? Someone she trusted? To sell the information or use it themselves?

She felt faint and sick to her stomach.

Back in her study, she sat at her desk and logged onto Axis, the software system that stored the appointments, billing, and files. Her fingertips flew over the keyboard, changing usernames, passwords, security questions, and codes.

The detectives advised her to lock out everyone. Even the people she trusted, they said, as soon as she could.

As she did, she made a call.

"Elena, it's Dr. Parks," she said, when Elena picked up the phone in the office.

Elena Gomez, the doctor's secretary, handled calls and scheduling. For a year, she'd arrived to work early daily, without fail, and left the office well after five. She ate at her desk. She had been the doctor's first hire and only employee who showed up throughout the whole pandemic, despite the doctor's pleas to stay home. Elena insisted that patients needed caring hospice more than ever. They had to stay open. They had to serve the dying at home.

"We have a problem," the doctor started. "I need you to shut the office down now. And go home."

"Now?" said Elena. "It's only two."

"Leave for the weekend, and call me tonight. I'll explain."

"Is everything okay?" Elena said, worried.

"No, not really. Call me when you get home. And Elena?"

"Yes?"

"Make sure you shut the computers down and lock the front office door today, from the waiting room. Cancel all appointments for tomorrow."

"Okay," she said.

"I'll explain later."

"Speak to you then."

Lane Jones was the discharge manager. Dr. Parks had created the position when she realized the importance of a well-timed exit; how crucial it was to fight the hospitals to get the elderly out and into their homes before death. To kiss loved ones goodbye. To see their own beds for the last time and surround themselves with things they loved.

Lane, she could be abrasive, true, but the doctor needed a brazen fighter. Could she be capable of something like this? Stealing? Murder?

And why? The doctor wondered if any of her staff were

struggling somehow or needed a loan. The downturn meant they all took cuts, but she couldn't be sure.

Either way, she had to furlough the whole team until the investigation was over. She called Lane and told her so.

"Dr. Parks, I have bills," Lane said, a few minutes later, over the phone.

The doctor took a deep breath. "I'm going to wire you six months' pay. I'm wiring everyone six months' pay."

She had done this before. She'd paid her employees six months upfront during the first pandemic shutdown. She felt as if it were the least she could do. She had the savings, her staff did not. She went on the hospital visits herself, sometimes ten or eleven a day. She'd do the same now. She'd take over for a few weeks or a couple of months.

Thirty minutes later, she'd secured the software, and her mobile phone rang. The area code was 818, so maybe the Valley? Josh's school? She hung up the landline and picked up her mobile.

"Mrs. Parks?" said the voice. On the line, a girl was sobbing. "This is Lulu Belmont from Buckley?"

"Lulu?" said the doctor.

"Do you remember me?"

Remember Lulu? The doctor sat back. Was this kid kidding? Dr. Parks had seen this girl naked. In bed. In her house. Lulu had broken stay-at-home orders, sneaked from her house in Calabasas, driven across town, and somehow broken into the doctor's house. They had no idea how. She got through the gate, past the alarms, and climbed right into Josh's bed.

It was a careless and lethal move that neither Parks parent could abide or forgive. And like Romeo's parents, they forbade Josh from contacting Lulu again.

"Dr. Parks?"

The doctor startled. "Lulu, hold on." The housekeeper, Masha, stood in the doorway. "Masha, you need me?"

"No. I don't."

"How can I help?"

"I'm going to the stores. I won't be back until late tonight. What can I get you?"

"Nothing. Thank you," said Dr. Parks. "I'm great. We're fine. I don't need a thing."

Masha nodded, turned, and left, and Dr. Parks went back to her call. Masha was part of the household, yes, but she didn't need to know everything.

Back on the phone, she said, "Lulu, of course I remember you. Are you all right?"

"It's Josh," Lulu said. "The people at that place are torturing him!"

CHAPTER 5

MASHA KEPT HER rusty Chevy behind the wall of privacy hedges at the bottom of Dr. Parks's drive near the gate—out of sight from guests and the family. She supposed if she drove a nicer car, Dr. Parks might let her park near the house.

But maybe not.

She drove to East Crenshaw to pick up Sophie.

Boris had found Sophie's number. He said he was headed to Crenshaw to find her. He had a few questions, he said, about Andre, Sophie's ex.

In the motel room, Masha and Sophie packed up the toiletries, clothes, and dishes. Everything Sophie and Nikolai owned. They had to leave. It was time. Sophie, of course, would lose her deposit of six hundred dollars on the motel room, but she didn't care. Running was better than sticking around and having some way to defend herself. And her son. From murderous thugs who knew no God.

She refused to take Masha's gun.

"It's perfect for you! I bought it for you!" Masha insisted. Masha had bought the gun off a Tinder date; some guy she'd met for a couple of drinks. He gave it to her for a French kiss and a hundred dollars. He sold them illegally, pre-owned, no papers.

Sophie grabbed Nikolai's briefs and stuffed them into a trash bag.

"I don't want the gun."

"Only in case," Masha said.

"No," Sophie said, and she scooped up T-shirts. Everything was ironed and folded, how she liked. "I wouldn't use it. I couldn't do it. Not to no one."

"Yes, if you had to."

"We're going away. They won't find us."

"Where?"

"I don't know. Away, I said. Anywhere else."

"But where?" Masha asked.

"They murdered my son. What more do they want?" She paused and looked up at the ceiling, then down. She bowed her head and took a deep breath. "I honestly think they're all possessed. I'll pray for them. If they come for Niko, I'll drop to my knees and pray. I won't kill. Not like them."

Masha sighed.

"You know how they work. It's not about you. It's about Andre. To get back at him. For whatever he did. You need the gun, wherever you go. Listen to me."

"Fold the jackets," Sophie said. "Then go to the kitchen and pack up my pots."

Masha ignored her. "This gun is tiny. Perfect for us. For tiny hands. Only six shots. Use it to scare. Don't even load it."

"Don't load it?"

"Put it in your purse. For a rainy day."

She took Sophie's hand and gave her the gun.

"Here. Feel it. It feels good."

Sophie held it flat on her palm, without curling her fingers around it. Refusing it.

"Feels good, no? Not too heavy. Not too light."

She handed it back to her cousin. It gave her the chills. She'd seen Andre bust a man's teeth from his mouth with the butt of a pistol like that.

"Where will we go?" Sophie said. "It's a good question."

"You'll come stay with me. With Dr. Parks."

"Yes, for a couple of nights, okay. But then?"

"Until you decide. But only if we can make an agreement. Can we? Can we make an agreement?"

Sophie turned and glared at her cousin. What agreement? She was holding back tears. She wouldn't cry. She'd been crying since the night in the warehouse. She couldn't stop.

Her heart was broken.

"You take this gun. Learn to shoot it. Teach Niko."

"He already knows how to shoot a gun. Ivan taught him. Andre taught Ivan." Sophie was worried about Bel Air. "Dr. Parks, and her husband and son? Did you ask them already if we could stay?"

"The husband is gone," Masha said, and shook her head. She turned and pulled her purse to her lap and fished for a cigarette.

"Because of you?"

"No, no," Masha said in a singsong way, finding her pack. "We had our fun, but that was for Christmas. For holiday tip. He had one special girl from the bank. Young. Twenty-three. Last month, he moved to Westwood. And the boy is away at a place for drugs. To get clean. All she has left is the dog and me."

"You didn't ask?"

"No."

"But what if the doctor uses the pool? She'll see us in the pool house."

"No. She never uses it. She never goes back there. Only the front. Only the gardeners go back there. And sometimes the dog."

Masha took out her lighter and flicked it. Lit up her menthol.

"But how will we get in if you don't ask?"

Masha paused. That was the question. She thought a moment. She had an idea.

"We put your things in the back of the Chevy." She indicated the plastic bags. "And stuff you and Niko into the trunk."

The trunk?

But Sophie didn't have time to respond. From down the hall, she heard her son:

"Mama! Open the door! The door!"

Sophie and Masha ran to the door and flung it open. Niko-lai burst in, out of breath. He turned, shut the door again, locked the deadbolt, and strung the chain.

"What's wrong? What happened?" Sophie said, looking him over.

Someone had beaten him up.

"They chased me! They followed me!"

"Who?"

"Boris!" Nikolai shouted. His cheek was scraped pink and bleeding, with bits of embedded asphalt, his hair was a mess, T-shirt ripped where a thug had grabbed it and held on tight. "They followed me here!"

Boris and his men waited until three o'clock that day, and then chased Nikolai into an alley behind the school.

They laid him out with a backhanded *thwack* that twisted his neck and sent him soaring to the pavement.

Then they attacked him with boots and fists, three against one.

Men versus boy.

But Nikolai knew, Ivan had taught him, to guard his groin, cover his stomach, protect his head, and he curled his body up like a worm, facing the ground.

He managed to press to his hands and knees down, like a starting sprinter, then thrashed and kicked like a horse from behind, and took off running.

"My backpack is gone," he said to Sophie, ashamed to have dropped it and left it behind.

"It doesn't matter. It's only books," Sophie said. She turned to Masha. "Fine, the gun. Give me the gun. And fine, the trunk. We leave right now for Dr. Parks's."

CHAPTER 6

AN HOUR LATER, the three snuck out through the motel back door that led to an alley. They loaded the garbage bags into the Chevy and climbed in front, Sophie in the middle. There was no divider.

Masha pulled onto Pinafore Street to South La Brea, to take the surface streets north through Mid-Wilshire. They were sure no one had seen them leave.

But Boris, with his lackeys, was in his van waiting, and had seen them through his rearview.

At Sunset Boulevard, Masha went left, and Boris followed. They headed west toward the beach, and then at Bellagio, when Masha went right, Boris waited, and a few cars behind them, he took a right, too, up into the hills of Bel Air.

By six, the sun had all but set, and golden light flooded the car windows. It pierced through the trees and dappled the streets.

It was quieter here. Less traffic. Less grit. More green.

Masha pulled into a vacant driveway on Stone Canyon Road, behind a thicket of eucalyptus and old-growth pine. Down the hill and around a bend, Boris pulled over and stopped to watch. He could see the tail of Masha's Nova.

She rounded the car, popped the trunk, and Sophie and Nikolai got out, too, and followed her around.

"As soon as it's dark, and as soon as I can, I'll get you out," Masha said, and propped the trunk open with one hand. She reached with the other, tipped the spare tire, rolled it out, and lifted it over the bumper.

Nikolai carried it to the back seat.

"I'll go first," Sophie said, and stepped up and over the back bumper and into the trunk.

It was more spacious than she imagined.

"We'll be like this." She crouched, then tipped her body over and lay on her side, facing back, in the shape of a C.

Nikolai climbed over the bumper after her and did the same in front of his mother. Sophie wrapped her arms around him. They'd slept this way sometimes when he was little.

"We'll close our eyes and sleep," she said. "Get in a nap."

Nikolai did as he was told. He shifted around, made himself comfortable, and closed his eyes.

Sophie looked up.

The trees behind Masha haloed her head in lush green, gray, and silver-blue leaves. Sophie thought of her thatched house in Uglich, surrounded by birch trees and farmland.

The streets of Crenshaw, like most of LA, were hard and gray; cement sidewalks, dirty thoroughfares, low-built buildings, and no green at all.

No grass. No smells. No stars at night.

You have to have money for trees here, she thought as she gazed at the glorious reaching tall branches. Shade is a luxury. You have to have funds. Back home, they were poor, but they had the woods and the Volga River. But here, a person must pay for the nature that should come for free.

"Here we go," Masha said.

Nikolai opened his eyes.

They watched the window of light collapse as Masha lowered the lid of the trunk until it was perfectly dark inside.

The chill of the hillside breezes ceased, and mother and son were suddenly lulled by the dark moist warmth and sweet smell of cleaning products and brown paper bags.

"Whatever you do," they heard Masha say from outside the Chevy, "do not panic."

As she said this, she heard the approach of a car from behind, from down the hill. She turned her head as Boris pulled up and stopped the van. He gazed at her through the driver's side window. His eyes narrowed, and he nodded and smiled a stupid fake smile. A mean smile.

Masha had never seen him before, but she knew the look. Had he seen her put Sophie and Nikolai in the trunk? She rounded to the front, climbed back in, locked the doors, and started the engine.

This thug might tail her, she thought, so she circled the turnout and headed back down the hill toward the flats, the opposite direction from Dr. Parks's house.

But Boris did follow Masha down.

He stayed out of sight, seven cars behind, and trailed her for miles through Beverly Hills. An hour later, he climbed in the back and let his friend drive. They followed her back up to Dr. Parks's. They drove right by as she pulled through the gate, then turned and drove a mile down, pulled over, and parked.

Boris was good at being patient. He was happy to wait until later that night to climb the gate and get inside. He called New York.

"I've got them," he told his boss in Russian. "We're good. By morning, the boy will be dead."

CHAPTER 7

"THEY MADE HIM wear a diaper," cried Lulu into the phone.

"A diaper? What?" Dr. Parks frowned.

"His proctor made him put a diaper on, over his jeans! For a week! Because he cried in group therapy."

"Come on. That's impossible." Dr. Parks looked up at the ceiling. Was it impossible? Would they, could they do this at Wellborn?

"And they locked him in a closet!"

"Honey. That cannot be true. It's not a torture house. It's not a cult."

"But that's what he told me." Lulu was now fully sobbing.

"Who told you? Who did you speak to?"

"Um," she said hesitantly, with her Valley girl lilt, "Josh? He—he called me last night? Did he call you?"

Call his mother from rehab? No. Josh hadn't called Dr. Parks. There were no phones at Wellborn Ranch. Not for the kids.

"Josh? Called you?" the doctor said for confirmation. She was stunned.

"Yes. From a computer. He bribed the chef. He gave the chef money to borrow his laptop. Or maybe the line cook?"

Great. The doctor picked up a pen. She jotted the words *chef* and *money* into her Filofax and underlined them three times. At Wellborn Ranch, the rules were clear: no calls and no cash. Josh had managed to come by both? She'd call Adam Shaw, Wellborn's director, first thing tomorrow. About the chef. They'd left Josh at Wellborn with empty pockets. How did he find money? He was like a magician, Steven said. Josh bought his way out of everything—with Steven's money. So Steven had frozen Josh's accounts, canceled his allowance, and, despite her disagreement, written Josh out of their trusts. Not for forever. But as a scare. To wake him up. His therapist had said: "Love can't conquer Josh's addiction. You have to cut off his cash."

"Lulu," the doctor gently explained, "he's not supposed to be making calls."

The doctor wanted to like this girl. She wanted to like all her son's friends. But she was trained as a neurosurgeon and understood teenage cognition. Neurologically speaking, her son was literally insane right now. His brain was sixteen. Its capacity to assess risk and reward was deeply affected by emotional arousal—meaning it was affected by girls.

And Lulu was nothing if not arousing.

"He needs to come home," Lulu whined like a four-year-old. "You need to go get him. Pick him up. Please, Mrs. Parks."

This girl had been in their lives for years. She and Josh had gone to Buckley together. Then, in ninth grade, her dad shipped her off to boarding school on the East Coast. But three months in, Northfield Mount Hermon expelled Lulu for hacking into their security systems and hiding chardonnay in her dorm room. She was good with computers and liked to party. For this combination, the school sent her packing to Calabasas by Christmas vacation, and she called Josh, rejoicing.

"Adderall for exams," she'd said, "and wine for the weekends to celebrate my grades!" She'd been making straight Cs! How dare they send her back to LA! Josh had been glad to see his friend home.

This was the last thing the doctor needed. "Lulu," she said, resting her forehead in her hand, "I spoke to the staff at Wellborn this week. Josh is having some up days and down."

"But—"

"He must've called you on a down day."

"He was totally down. Super down. And Steven won't go get him either. I tried."

Steven? This girl was calling Josh's dad by his first name?

"Lulu. Please. Please stop crying," the doctor said, trying her best to console the teen. "Wellborn Ranch is highly respected. It's the best there is. In the whole country. I promise you. We wouldn't send him away from home if we didn't think he was somewhere safe. Somewhere he can get real help." The Ranch was famous in medical circles for sending kids home sober for good, with only a 10 percent recidivism rate. Success was practically guaranteed.

Lulu paused and her voice grew soft. "You left him alone all last year. All last year, he was all alone, and then you came back and sent him away."

It wasn't all year, the doctor thought. Yes, it was true, she'd flown to New York to help out colleagues at NewYork-Presbyterian hospital during the Covid pandemic. She'd put her life on the line to assist. It was her duty; what she signed up for in medical school. Josh was home with his father, and sure, okay, Steven was a distracted father—money, the bank, and who knows what else—that was true—but everyone was alone last year. Everyone had to hunker down and fend for themselves. It wasn't a punishment.

"Honey," the doctor said gently. "He really has to stay in Montana for the full three months. That's how long the program is. Maybe longer."

"And they took away his boots, so he can't run away."

"His boots?"

"He walks around barefoot."

Run away? Why would Josh run away? And where would he run? Into the forest? Down a mountain? In the snow?

"Listen, Lulu. I do appreciate your concern. I truly do, and I'm glad you called, but Josh is not going anywhere. He's not. My son has serious mental health issues, on top of the drugs—"

"You think I don't know that?" Lulu said. "I know your son. I know him better than anyone."

"Maybe. Maybe you do."

"What if, what if he hangs himself there? Don't you love him?"

"Of course, I love him. I'm his mother."

"Then go get him!"

"He'll be back in sixty days. Sixty-one. Two more months. It's not that long."

Lulu stopped crying. Her voice grew lower and serious. "He's right, you know."

The doctor sighed. Right about what? Did she really want to ask? Did she want to pursue this conversation? She finally did and girded herself.

"About what?"

"Your husband only cares about money. And you only care about your patients. You only love strangers."

"Lulu."

"That's what he says. That's how he feels. Did you know that?" She was like Jekyll and Hyde. One moment she was sweet and crying, the next moment she was spewing hate. "You spend all your time caring for strangers when he's the one who needs your attention. He's your son. You're supposed to love him."

"I do love him."

"No, you don't. That's why he hangs out with us. Because we love Josh for who he is—for all his, like, problems—and not for who we want him to be."

"All we want is for Josh to be healthy. Healthy and safe."

"We're his family. Not you. No wonder he hates you."

"Listen, Lulu. I won't have you speaking to me like—"

But it was too late. The line went dead. Lulu hung up.

CHAPTER 8

DR. PARKS WAS in the pool house, snooping through Masha's things, while on the phone with her ex-husband. "What if Lulu is right?" said the doctor, pulling open the bedroom drawers.

They'd built the cottage as a playroom for Josh, when he turned twelve. It was his hangout, until it wasn't—until they discovered his stash of weed and powdered Ritalin hidden inside. Then it was converted for guests or, in Masha's case, permanent staff: a tiny two-bedroom, with kitchen and bath, an arcade Pac-Man, a foosball table, a pullout couch, and a flat-screen TV.

"What if she's right, and Wellborn is weird? What if they're abusive?"

The truth was she'd had her doubts about the Ranch. She would never admit it to Lulu, of course, but Josh had a double diagnosis: brain injury and addiction. Did he really need to be chopping wood? Knitting? Learning to bake? When his therapist first brought up the idea, Dr. Parks had called HSBC, their bank in New York, and asked them to run some numbers on the place. HSBC said Wellborn Ranch reported a profit every year of $30 million. That was a lot, and it bothered her. Hospitals didn't make money like that, if at all.

But, at Steven's insistence, and despite her doubts, they flew to Billings with Josh in February. A van met them at the airport and they all rode together on the four-hour drive, ascending through snow and a sugar pine woods up to the Ranch.

It looked like a ski lodge surrounded by tepees and strange round huts. Proctors, not doctors, ran the place, and all of the adults wore Timberlands and flannel, and smiled a lot. Too much smiling, Dr. Parks thought, and way too much tie-dye and L.L. Bean. She wondered why the grown-ups all looked so cheerful when the children didn't. They all looked, what? Resigned? Subdued? Sleepy? Bitter?

"She's probably making the whole thing up," Steven insisted. "Lulu's a liar."

Takes one to know one, the doctor thought but didn't say.

"And she's a thief. She's bad news."

"A thief? Why?"

"Last year."

"What about it?"

"You don't remember?"

"No," said the doctor, as she opened up Masha's closet. She started to sift through her housekeeper's clothes.

"Lulu and that girl, Amory Banks. Four or five kids, can't remember—all got caught in the Greenbergs' house. David's parents?"

The doctor had no idea what he meant, and she was distracted by Masha's shoes. They were all designer, expensive shoes. How did she afford them, eBay?

"During the quarantine. The Greenbergs rented a place in Hawaii. To ride out the shutdown."

"Okay."

"David was stupidly posting brags on his Instagram account, saying they'd be gone for months, surfing, eating coconuts—"

"Right, right—"

"So the girls broke in. Lulu and her weird gang of Valley girl Heathers broke into the house while they were away."

"Seriously?" The doctor was shocked. They formed a new Bling Ring, but pretty. Like *Mean Girls* meets *Ocean's Eleven*, Steven said, but the doctor had never seen those movies, so she had no idea what he meant. The house was decked out with cameras, and on their way out with purses and shoes, the girls were greeted first by security, and then by the police.

"Lulu's dad paid some bond, the charges were dropped, and the girls were given community service."

"How did I miss this?" the doctor said.

"I guess you were away. In New York," said Steven.

What else had she missed? She could hardly believe it. Shoplifting, maybe, was one thing. That was almost a rite of passage. Pocketing a lipstick from Walgreens or bottled water from Starbucks. But breaking and entering?

"Where are you?" said Steven, "You're going in and out."

Dr. Parks looked around. "I'm in the pool house. Speaking of stealing, do you think Masha is honest with us? Do you think she'd ever steal from us?"

There was a silence on the line. Before the divorce, Steven had slept with Masha more than once while Dr. Parks was away in New York City, but Dr. Parks had no idea.

"Uh," he said, thinking about it.

"Do you?" said the doctor, and moved from Masha's bedroom closet, into the hall, and to the kitchen, but Steven suddenly said he had to take another call.

CHAPTER 9

AT THE FRONT of the house, at the base of the driveway, Masha stood next to her car, looking up. The garage door was open and Dr. Parks's Audi convertible sat inside—and that meant the doctor was still at home.

She usually left at five o'clock and stayed out at least until seven or later, to go and sweat at her Bar Method class, or SoulCycle. Or Pilates.

She would leave in sneakers, half-dirty T-shirts and pilled leggings, her greasy blond hair pulled into a messy bun, or worse, in a ponytail under a hat. A baseball cap. Like a boy.

Masha hated this look.

The real LA housewives were grubby, she thought. Not like the ones on the TV shows. Dr. Parks looked way too natural, too boyish, and too skinny. She never dressed up. No makeup. Not even a stroke of mascara in the morning. No lip gloss. And she had plenty of bling to wear. Tons of it. But she never wore it. Like Ellen Sumner, Dr. Parks's jewelry sat in a box in her bedroom closet, next to the drawer with the linty gray sports bras. These wives, she thought, took too much for granted. No wonder their husbands eventually left.

Dr. Parks was not at Pilates. It was eight o'clock, night had fallen, and she was still in the pool house out back.

"The one night. The one night she's not going out," she whisper-yelled into the trunk. "She's usually gone by five or six."

"We're okay," Sophie called.

"Fuck it," said Masha. She scanned the windows, but didn't see a single shadow. No movement. So she popped the trunk to give them some air.

Sophie and Nikolai opened their eyes and sat up straight.

"What is it?" said Sophie.

"She's home, but I can't tell where she is. Stay until I come get you, okay?"

"Okay," Sophie said, as Masha gently closed the trunk, but not all the way. She left it open an inch.

The driveway was dark as she took off up the hill toward the house. She circled the garage to the herb garden and went down the path toward the pool.

The light from Masha's bedroom was on, but the rest of the pool house was dark. The front door was closed. She had definitely locked it when she left. But she could see that the screen door was open. It rested on its hinge, open an inch.

Someone was there. Or had been there.

Masha ran up the steps, opened the screen door, pushed through the main door, and stepped inside. There in the dark, Dr. Parks dropped her phone and screamed. Masha screamed.

"Masha!" The doctor put her hand on her heart. "I thought you were out!"

"I was," Masha said carefully, calm. "Now I am back."

CHAPTER 10

"I SEE THAT you're back," the doctor said. "I'm so sorry."

Embarrassed, she scrambled to find a light. But Masha found a lamp first and turned it on. Of course. Why not? This was her home. She flipped the kitchen switch near the door, and the overhead pendant lit up the rooms.

"I'm sorry. I was looking for something," the doctor said.

"In the dark?"

"Yes."

"Looking around?" Masha raised her brows. "You should've turned on a light to see. To see better."

"Yes, I could have. But I was snooping," the doctor admitted. "And I'm so sorry, but those men today, they were from the police department."

"Really?" said Masha, and moved from the door and put down her purse.

"Something happened. It's kind of a mess. Can we sit for a second and talk? Please? I was robbed."

Masha nodded, moved to the kitchen, and put down a takeout bag from Chipotle. They sat at the table.

"It was some kind of hacking thing," said Dr. Parks. "Pretty widespread. I have to let go of all my employees. The police insist. At least for a while. Until they investigate. A man was murdered. An elderly man. For his drugs. One of my patients."

"You think it was me?" Masha asked, the same way the doctor had asked the detectives.

"No," Dr. Parks said, assuring her. She really didn't. "No, Masha, please. You know me. We're friends. I know it wasn't you. But it could have been. That's the point. It could be anyone, anyone at all, with access to my computers."

"Oh."

"Here at home. Or in my office. Most likely my office. Or maybe not. Maybe anywhere. Maybe China, if it was hackers. Maybe anywhere. Idaho!"

"Terrible," Masha said. "I'm sorry this happened to you." She didn't sound sorry. She sounded annoyed. She sounded pissed off.

"Me too. After the time we've all had. I thought we'd all get a break from the drama. I thought we could all relax for a second, but I guess people are feeling desperate."

"I guess."

"Understandably."

"Right. No peace for the wicked, I guess."

The doctor nodded. But then, who was the wicked in this scenario? Was she? Still, she appreciated Masha's concern. "But I will…make this totally easy. Just like the shutdown. I'll give you your wages for three months. Find a place to live, get other work, or not, your choice. I'll pay your way. Until the police figure it out."

Masha nodded.

"Is that fair?" the doctor asked rhetorically, thinking it was more than fair. "Then, when it's over, the investigation, you can come back."

"Okay," said Masha, and nodded.

The doctor studied her housekeeper's face. It was poker. No expression whatsoever.

"Think of it as a paid vacation."

"Okay. Thanks."

Dr. Parks sighed and rose. "And I'm sorry for, you know—being in your space and looking around. With you not home. But I am allowed. As your landlord and your boss. This is my house. I mean, it's your house right now, sort of—but mine officially. Legally. So . . ."

"Sure," said Masha, and looked around. "There's nothing to hide." Except for her cousin and nephew in the trunk of her car in the driveway. And a gun.

"I know there isn't," Dr. Parks said, and moved toward the door. This was awkward. "That's what I told the police today. That you would never steal from us. But they said I have to wipe the slate clean."

"Let me know when you need me out," Masha said, and the doctor detected an edge in her voice. Finally. Masha was offended, for sure, she was angry, the doctor could tell, but what could she do? She had no choice.

"I don't know," she said, and thought. "In a couple of days, or a week? A week. As soon as you can. I'll get you the money in the morning."

CHAPTER 11

DR. PARKS LEFT the pool house. She wondered how Josh would react to this news. If Masha left and stayed away for another two months. Josh and Masha liked each other. They were pals, and over the years had forged a bond. Maybe Masha got his life-world, the doctor thought. They shared the same interests and sense of humor. She liked his TV shows, they liked the same kind of music, and all the TikTok and online crap.

The doctor tried to respect their friendship. She tried to respect Masha's boundaries. She'd never gone into the pool house before, but there, now she had, and it was her right. The day had been hellish and couldn't get worse. Except that it could.

"Mrs. Parks?"

Lulu was standing in Dr. Parks's kitchen.

"Lulu?" said the doctor, as she walked in. "What are you doing in here?"

"I was on Melrose buying sneakers. I wanted to stop by and say I'm sorry."

Dr. Parks shook her head in dismay. "How did you—how did you get through my gate?"

"I used the code," Lulu said, and took a sip from a glass of water. She'd helped herself to the contents of the fridge.

"You know my gate code?" the doctor said, and turned and closed the mudroom door.

"Josh gave it to me. Your birthday, right?"

"He's not supposed to give you that. He's not supposed to— give anyone that."

"I rang the bell," Lulu said, eyes wide, feigning innocence. "From the front. Didn't you hear me? Didn't you hear me drive up? I'm in the circle."

"No," said the doctor, "I was out back. Down by the pool."

"That's what I thought. So I came around and the back door was open."

"Fine, but please. Please. Call first next time. Where's Bandit?"

"I wanted to say I'm sorry, though," Lulu said. "For what I said and hanging up."

"Have you seen the dog?"

Lulu didn't seem to hear the doctor. "I know—I know we both love your son, and Josh loves us, too."

The doctor nodded and rounded the girl, taking in her miniskirt, bracelets, boots, the choppy layers of platinum hair. Lulu had pierced her eyebrows and nose since the doctor last saw her, and tattooed one arm with a haloed cherub. The cherub held a submachine gun.

Lulu tucked her butt on a bar stool, as if she had sat there a hundred times, and felt at home, as if she were going to stay for dinner.

"Lulu," said the doctor, "Josh ended this thing last year. No? I thought he ended this thing with you?"

"Thing?" Lulu seemed offended. She placed her water glass down on the island. "Do you mean relationship?"

"Yes," said the doctor. "No? I mean, not your friendship, but—"

"He only told you that. We're still together. We never broke up."

"Okay, fine. So maybe he lied. But you need to know, we asked him to, and his doctor thought that it would be best, while he gets clean, that he not date. It's not about you. It's not personal. No one should date when they first begin a twelve-step program. So . . ."

"So what?"

"So. If you care about Josh, I hope you'll try to give him space. And not take his calls. If he calls. Can I walk you out?"

But Lulu didn't move. "He doesn't need space from me. He needs space from you and Steven. From here."

"Okay, fine. We'll just agree to disagree, but then you'll force us to step in."

Lulu cocked her head right. "How?"

"I don't know. Like something legal."

"Legal? Like what?"

"I don't know, like a restraining order or something," the doctor said. "My son's health has to come first."

"Seriously?" Lulu said. "Because of last year?"

"Because Josh needs to stay focused."

"You shouldn't believe the things you hear. Like, people and gossip. I had nothing to do with that night."

"I don't care what happened last year. It's not about that. I only care about my son."

"So do I."

"And Josh needs to stay out of trouble right now, so I have to do what I have to do—if you cannot respect our wishes."

"Fine," Lulu said, and slipped from the barstool to her feet.

"Fine," she said again glibly and turned. "I'll let myself out. Don't get up."

The doctor didn't plan to, but watched her fly out into the mudroom. "Move, Bandit," Lulu snapped on her way out as the dog trotted in, and she slammed the door. "I was only trying to be nice!" She yelled, from over her shoulder.

The doctor stood frozen, heart beating wildly. Why did this girl freak her out so much? She waited a moment, moved to the hall, and crossed the length of the house to the front. She slipped into the living room, crossed to the window, and hid in the dark behind the drapes.

Out in the circle, a black Range Rover sat waiting. Lulu trudged to it, climbed in, slammed the door shut, turned on the engine, and peeled out over the gravel. She sped down the driveway and disappeared from sight. She had buzzed herself in, she could buzz herself out, the doctor thought. Forever, she hoped.

At the base of the driveway, next to the Chevy, Lulu quickly keyed in the code. The gate slowly opened, and Lulu screeched right, down the hill.

The gate then rested open a moment, then started to close as Boris slipped through it.

He was on foot.

CHAPTER 12

IN DR. PARKS'S driveway, Nikolai had fallen fast asleep. Ten minutes later, Sophie did, too. It was warm in the trunk and dark outside as Lulu peeled past them, waking Sophie out of a dream. She forgot where she was, went to sit up, bumped her head, and then dropped down uncomfortably.

"Mama?" said Nikolai.

"Where is Masha?"

"She'll be back."

"O, Holy Angel of God," Sophie whispered, "guardian protector of my soul..." Then she heard footsteps on the gravel. Someone was passing right by the Chevy and heading up the drive. Was it her cousin? Was it the doctor?

The footsteps came and the footsteps left, and two minutes later, Sophie heard, "I'm coming, I'm coming. I'm here." It was Masha making her way back down.

"Oh, thank God," Sophie whispered. Her leg was starting to cramp. Masha finally flew the trunk open.

"You didn't suffocate? You didn't die?"

Mother and son sat up and breathed in the cold, fragrant air. The driveway was surrounded by trees, and the house was shrouded in darkness: with its whitewashed brick and exposed timber, the English Tudor looked like something out of a fairy tale, the prettiest Sophie had ever seen.

"Snap out of it," Masha barked at her cousin.

"I'm coming, I'm coming," Sophie whispered.

"Something bad happened. I'll tell you later. Let's go, let's go. She's back inside." Sophie and Nikolai climbed from the trunk, opened up the back, grabbed a few bags, and shut the doors gently. Inside the house, the dog started barking.

They ran up the drive and circled left at the side of the house. When they reached the back, they dodged through the hydrangeas and made their way along a stone wall and up the hill. This way they'd avoid the back patio and the back windows.

Minutes later, they wove down the hillside, sight unseen, through the orange grove to the pool house.

CHAPTER 13

LATER THAT NIGHT, around nine, Masha opened the Cuervo to drink with the tacos she bought from the Chipotle in Westwood. After the tequila, she switched to vodka. The old country Stoli. The gold. Her favorite.

"I'm going to get her back for this. She's going to pay." She was angry at Dr. Parks.

Sophie, on the other hand, was quietly cleaning the pool house kitchen, its marble counters, a shiny fireclay farmhouse sink, and a stainless fridge with an icemaker. A perfect kitchen. The whole cottage, she thought, was designed with care, with kindness even—a stark change from the Crenshaw motel room, with its peeling paint, mildew, grime, and roaches. She would sleep well here. She would sleep deep.

"She doesn't know who she's messing with," Masha said. "We're more dangerous than the Sicilians. Worse than the Mexicans. We have brains. Business degrees!"

"So?" Sophie said.

"Other gangs beg to work with us. Beg to know our Russian tradecraft."

"And we should be proud?"

Sophie wiped down the table, took a deep breath, and

studied her cousin. Masha was drunk, and maybe Sophie could get a confession.

She picked up one of the cut-crystal glasses and dried it off with a dish towel. The glass was thick and heavy. The towel was pretty. She wiped the glass and gently, casually asked her cousin:

"Did you do it? Steal her patients' information? For Mikhailov?"

Jorge Mikhailov was Masha and Sophie's oldest uncle. He lived in Las Vegas, a brother-in-law to their fathers back home. Married to an aunt.

Masha looked up and blinked, but said nothing. Then she looked down at her magazine again, *Town and Country*. She turned a page and took a sip.

"Did you?" Sophie pressed again. But she already knew the answer, or thought she did. "Fine," she said. "Don't admit it. I already know. Nobody else could be so brutal. Murder an old man in his bed, so close to death. It had to be him."

Mikhailov now had a hundred Russians working under him in Las Vegas. He was laundering cash, Sophie knew, for bigger, more powerful gang members, and running a ring called Girls Unlimited out of Reno. She knew he'd started to traffic drugs, too: cocaine from Mexico into Texas, then across the I-10 into Miami, and across the Atlantic and into Marseille, where the French paid a premium. And he was spreading out into LA.

Masha blinked slowly with bloodshot eyes.

"I wish I had thought of it. It was smart."

Sophie turned and cleared the Chipotle wrappers and bowls.

Nikolai was watching TV in the living room, half asleep,

and Sophie was sure he had overheard nothing. Fine. They were safe in the pool house for now. At least for one night.

"New Russia, but old poverty..." Masha rained the last of the Stoli into her lowball. "An old iron's bargain: capitalism with no law...capitalism run by criminals. That's Russia now."

Sophie turned. What was Masha talking about? She always talked this crap when she drank.

"It's no different here. The Hollywood people and Silicon Valley. They're as cruel as Mikhailov. All that money in off-shore accounts and thousands of people sleeping with rats on the sidewalks, under the bridges."

"No," Sophie said. "It's not true. It's not the same. They don't murder. They don't torture."

"They do," Masha said. "Think about it. All that money. They could help us, but they don't; people like us, a bad day away from the street. What happened last year—all the poor people died. No one rich..." She closed the magazine and rose. Picked up the bottle.

"That's not true," Sophie said.

"What do you know? You know nothing. You only believe in a fantasy tale about some God. There's no God! God won't save you. He didn't save Ivan. Only money." She turned dramatically and smashed the bottle into the sink. Sophie jumped back and hid her face.

CHAPTER 14

MASHA, DRUNK, STUMBLED and fell. She reached to the counter, righted herself, lumbered down the hall into the bedroom, and slammed the door.

Nikolai looked up from the TV.

He glanced at his mother, and Sophie slowly shook her head. She whispered, "Jesus, help my cousin." Then louder she said, "She'll be better tomorrow. She's just sad." She went to pick up the shattered glass in the sink. Nikolai then appeared from behind. Sophie jumped.

"It's only me." He put a hand on his mother's shoulder.

"I'll help."

"Be careful."

They'd done this before. Masha would drink, and she loved nothing more than to smash a bottle into a bathtub, onto the street, or against a wall, and watch it shatter.

The house was now lit by a low kitchen lamp and the flicker of TV. The alarm was set, and Boris sat outside, in the dark, watching through a low window.

He watched as they picked the shards of glass from the sink and counter. Sophie placed them, some small and sharp, others larger with dull edges, into a brown paper grocery bag.

Watching this gentle, determined cleanup, Boris felt nothing. Sophie was pretty, and so was the boy, but he had killed prettier, and this was his job. There was a time, back in Moscow, when he had to murder a person a day. At age twelve, he had started to work for the gang, stealing fur coats, and he killed for the first time at Nikolai's age. He had no mother, and no father. He became an enforcer, part of the death squad, trained as a sniper in Chechnya. Contract killing became his living. Andre had paid him fifty grand for the boys, all in an effort to punish his wife for running away. It was just a job. Like cleaning homes.

The pool house alarm was clearly connected to the main house alarm, and this was a problem, Boris thought, as he moved from window to window. Could they get in, murder a boy, and get out of Bel Air in time? If the alarm tripped, the police would take at least seven minutes, but a Bel Air private security patrol might get there sooner and spot the van.

He moved back to the hedges to think it through.

Meanwhile, Sophie knelt and wiped the floor with a wet paper towel to pick up the glass. A grain of glass is like sin, she mused. Sometimes she'd feel an invisible shard stuck in her foot and have to dig it out with a blade. It had to be removed and only then would the tiny wound heal. Just like sin. She wished she could make Masha see this.

She finished the job, turned off the light, and moved into the living room to pull out the sofa bed for Nikolai. Together they peeled off the sofa cushions. Then something started to cry from outside. High-pitched, distressed, it sounded like some kind of forlorn monster crying for help. In pain or in horror. They looked at each other and froze.

CHAPTER 15

THE COYOTES WERE up in the hillside again.

Their cries were a terrible mournful sound, and the doctor sat there and shivered in fright. It was base, existential, like grief sobbing, a terrible warble that seemed to get closer by the week.

They started that night around ten o'clock. The doctor was sitting at the kitchen island, poring over files, trying to figure out which of her patients might be at risk.

The poor dogs were howling because of that golf course, she thought. Builders had raised an entire ravine on Stradella Road. They probably dug up a whole coyote den without knowing. Without caring. Displaced the whole pack.

She rose and moved to the mudroom door, checking that it was shut tight. Bandit, she knew, would want to head out. If the pack breached the grove wall, Bandit would head out to put up a fight, to defend his turf. Recently, she'd heard, a pack had jumped an eight-foot gate at the Stoneridge Estates. They dragged a house cat into the woods, never, of course, to be seen again. Her privacy gate in the front was nine feet high, but the property wall in the back was six.

Bandit would stay indoors tonight.

An hour later, the hillside fell silent.

In the backyard, Boris turned away from the pool house and snuck through a divide in the bushes. He headed left into a thicket, reached for the chaparral, hand over fist, and pulled himself through. It was prickly and dark, but he knew where he was. He was headed up the hill along the periphery of the grove. At the top, he descended through a wood and walked the street back to the van.

Twenty minutes later, he pulled a baseball cap over his head, pulled on a jacket, and pushed a shopping cart into the Ralphs on Weyburn Street.

A fully cooked rotisserie chicken, or maybe two, would buy them a full fifteen minutes, but the bones might shred the dog's internals, its bowels and belly, and bleed it out.

Boris had a soft spot for dogs. So tonight, as he looked around the brightly lit market, scanning all corners for security cameras, he decided to use only nonlethal methods. No slug pellets. No poison. He chose two watermelons, perfectly ripe, raw T-bone steaks, a deli tray of cooked hamburger patties, which he'd sprinkle with a stinky blue cheese for good measure, twelve jars of peanut butter, and six bags of pretzel nibs stuffed with fake cheese.

This was the kind of dog with a nose.

They'd scatter treats around the yard, and this handsome mutt would seek and peck like an Easter egg hunt for half an hour. Boris knew this. With the right temptations strewn on the grass, the dog would eat until it vomited and then eat again.

Boris chose aisle three, away from the exit, where his brim would obscure his face from the cameras, and started to unload his cart.

"Having a party?" the cashier asked through a polka-dotted mask as she scanned the heavy white parcels of meat. "Whoa. This is a ton of burger. It's like a baby!"

Boris nodded, pulled cash from his wallet, all real fifties, and handed them over.

"Birthday?" she asked. He shook his head no. "Anniversary?"

Was she flirting? My, she was chirpy. He shook his head a second time and forced a smile while she scanned the jars of Skippy and Jif.

"Somebody likes peanut butter..."

Boris didn't hear her yammering. He wasn't paying attention. He was wondering about the two cameras perched on the patio over the doctor's back side door. Did they have the paint pistol in the van? He thanked the cashier, loaded the shopping bags into the cart, and headed out to the parking lot.

A nineteen-year-old, ex light-welterweight boxing champ climbed from the van and helped Boris. The gang called him Shev.

"You didn't get fish?" Shev said.

"No, this is a red-meat dog."

"I thought I said salmon. Cooked salmon. Bone out."

"And I said steak. Steak works best."

Shev let it go, and back in Bel Air, Boris's driver pulled the van to the side of the road. Shev followed Boris off the pavement and into a ravine filled with bay laurel scrub. They slogged through the thorns, each with duffle bags, ascended through the wood, weaving between the white spotted sycamore and eucalyptus with long hanging shreds of ghostly white bark. "Tinder," thought Boris as they wound toward the property's highest peak. Back home in Uglich, the woods never burned like they did in LA.

From the top of the hill, they gazed at the doctor's house below. The orange grove thinned at the base of the hill and dispersed a dozen trees through her yard. The pool sparkled, the sprinklers hummed, and crickets sang, but the houses were dark and seemed asleep.

In the main house, one room was lit, second floor, warm and gold, but neither Boris or Shev saw movement. The driveway was empty except for the Chevy at the bottom by the gate, and the Audi sedan in the open garage. No new car had arrived since they'd left. The sky was unusually clear, dark and cloudless, and a smattering of stars blinked at each other across the expanse.

A nice quiet night and nice quiet place to finish the job.

What could go wrong?

But first, the dog.

CHAPTER 16

IT WOULD BE easy to strangle the blond inside the big house. What was she, forties? What did she weigh, 110, max? Shev would creep in. He'd approach from behind, wrap his elbow around her neck, and put a choke on her carotid artery. In seven seconds, she'd pass out cold, and one minute later, she'd die in his arms. Then they'd be free to take what they wanted and head to the pool house to kill the kid.

The steel box that housed the cables hung on the outer wall near the garage. It was, of course, locked. Normally Boris would jimmy it open or pick the lock, but that would be noisy and the lock would take time. And anyway, now, with some alarms, cut cables alert the service. They had to go in gentle and soft.

Boris led Shev down the hill. Midway, he cut right to get to the house from its west-facing side. They moved from the bushes and made a run.

Shev followed as they hugged the side wall and crept toward the back, toward the patio door, approaching the cameras from behind.

From deep in the house, the dog barked, as they knew it would.

Good boy, thought Boris, come down and get us.

Dr. Parks was asleep in the master bedroom, and Bandit lay sprawled at her feet. He jumped from the bed and beelined downstairs.

The next two minutes, they had to work quickly. Boris pulled a ski mask over his head, crouched below the camera, took a step forward, pivoted back, aimed a paintball gun at the lens, and fired. The paint pellet hit the lens dead center and exploded on the concave glass, obscuring its view.

Boris nodded. His aim was perfect, and this was good. Better than burning out the lens with a laser or cutting the cables. This was old-school, streamlined, clean.

Just as they thought, the dog raced downstairs and entered the kitchen. Shev moved in, crouched at the doggy door, and stretched his arm through it. In his gloved hand he clutched a raw T-bone slathered with stinky nuggets of cheese.

Bandit latched on and whined with relief and anticipation. Shev held tight and pulled the dog right through the plastic flap to the outside mat and his knees.

"Good boy," he whispered. "Eat up good."

Boris grabbed the dog by the collar and led him by the steak out to the yard while Shev cocked his head and slid his frame sideways through the flap of the large pet escape. Twenty-three by fourteen inches wide, this was no problem. On his knees, he angled his shoulders, tucked his chin, and shoved himself through. He righted himself to face the floor and plank-slid his torso across the floor.

He was in.

The alarm panel, one of two, sat on the counter next to the fridge. Boris had spotted it through the window earlier that evening.

Shev crossed the kitchen, flipped the panel, and dislodged three double-As from the bottom; the backup battery was now dead. Then he yanked the plug from its socket. He left it all there, moved to the hall, and sailed through the first floor to the front hall where he'd do the same with the second panel.

In the backyard, Bandit swallowed what was left of the meat on the bone. He lay on the grass and got to work gnawing, but then he froze. On a Santa Ana breeze, he picked up a scent.

He lifted his head, hackles raised, rose, and held still. He dropped the bone, nose to the wind, and lurched toward the pool.

Bandit growled as Boris strengthened his grip on the collar. Bandit swung around and snapped at Boris's face. Boris flinched and Bandit squirmed backward. He nodded and squeezed his head from his collar, backed right out of it, and ran off with a low-pitched bark that echoed up into the doctor's bedroom.

"Fuck," muttered Boris. He looked at the one lit room in the house.

Had Shev gone upstairs and dealt with the bitch?

CHAPTER 17

OUT IN THE pool house, Nikolai sat at the living room window, staring out. The room was dark. The garden was dark. His mother was asleep in the second bedroom, and Masha had passed out earlier that night.

He'd never seen anything like these dogs. Skinny, he thought, like foxes but taller, with longer legs. It was a pack, six of them, and they scared and darted, scampered and fed right there on the grass and deck. They were sniffing and eating the bits of hamburger and cheese-filled pretzels that Boris had scattered through the grass.

Nikolai's eyes popped open wide when the black dog bounded over the bushes.

Strong and lean, he had spots of white and a black patch around his eye like a pirate. This must be Bandit, he thought, the dog Masha walked and watched when the family went on vacation.

Bandit galloped along the pool deck, barking and striking out at the coyotes. Nikolai watched as the animals scattered.

Seconds later, they all doubled back and formed a circle around Bandit, darting in, then darting back out, scratching, biting, crying.

Earlier that night, Dr. Parks had opened the windows in her bedroom. They looked out over the backyard. It was orange blossom season, the time of year when her backyard erupted with the scent, sweet and thick, and she wanted to let the smell waft in. The snarling and wailing woke her up.

"Bandit?" she said, rolling from bed. She scurried to the window and saw the canines out by the pool.

Downstairs near the door, Shev stood quietly, prying batteries out of the second alarm panel.

"Bandit!" he heard, and looked upstairs. What the hell was Boris doing? He needed to shut the fucking dog up. Now.

Dr. Parks ran down the hall, toward the stairs. *Dammit, Bandit,* she thought. *When did you learn to pry open doors? And how did you get through the mudroom door?*

Shev bent over, unplugged the panel, looked left and right, and moved past the stairs and into the living room. He slipped behind a large potted tree in the corner next to the door. The doctor ran down.

"Bandit! Dammit!"

Clearly, she was alone in the house.

He could kill her right there, from behind, before she reached the backyard. This was his chance, as good as any, but bedrooms were always the better choice, and, unlike Boris, he'd only ever killed once. He emerged from behind the plant, left the living room, and craned his neck past the stairs, catching a glimpse of the doctor's nightshirt as she ran to the kitchen. He was too late. Would she stop to disarm the alarm first? He hated when plans got fucked up.

The doctor burst through the patio door, into the brisk night air. Barefoot and frightened, she veered to the right, onto the garden path, screaming.

"Shoo!" she shrieked, waving her hands. "Shoo! Shoo!"

When she got to the pool deck, three of the coyotes scurried away, but one jumped at Bandit, and a fourth and fifth hovered nearby. They were much smaller than she thought they'd be, and skeletally thin, so with every pathetic jump attack, Bandit mounted a gruesome defense, his poundage and teeth no match for these pups.

"Shoo!" she cried, waving her arms. She ran right into the fray. "Go! Shoo! Shoo! Shoo!"

Then, overhead, shots rang out.

Pop-pop-pop!

The doctor screamed and fell to her knees.

"Oh, my God!" she cried to no one, as five of the coyotes bolted up the hill and disappeared into the grove.

One was left. Injured, it lay on the grass, dying or already dead, shot in the head and in the belly. Bandit circled her warily, sniffing and whimpering, limping.

The doctor looked up and around the yard.

"Oh, my God," she said again. "What was that? Where are you?" She'd never heard live gunshots before. Where had they come from? She didn't see a soul.

"Who's there?" she cried. "Where are you?"

And then her gaze landed on a twelve-year-old boy. She figured he was twelve or thirteen. In the dark, he stood alone on the deck, in T-shirt and sweatpants, barefoot like she was. He was impossibly handsome and pale as a ghost, with a swath of sandy-blond bangs in his eyes.

Intelligent eyes. Calm. Reassuring.

"Did I scare you, sorry," he calmly said. "Are you all right?"

In his hand, at his side, he held a gun.

CHAPTER 18

"WHO ARE YOU?" the doctor said to the boy.

Suddenly, Masha ran from the pool house. She was disheveled—hair a mess, makeup smudged—still in the clothes she'd worn that day.

"Nikolai!" she said. "What happened? What happened?" She swayed and stumbled, half asleep, and still drunk.

"He belongs to you?" said Dr. Parks.

"This is my nephew," Masha cried. "What did you do?"

"He saved my dog," the doctor said, tears streaming down her cheeks. "He saved Bandit's life!"

Nikolai and Masha exchanged a glance. He wasn't in trouble? They weren't in trouble? He'd done the right thing?

The doctor rose and looked around. Some kind of nuggets and hamburger meat were scattered in chunks all over the grass.

"What happened? What is this? There's—food trash all over..."

"I don't know," Masha said. She turned to Nikolai. "Did you—did you bring food out here?"

He shook his head.

"What is this stuff? Did a garbage bag break? I have to—I have to—go call the vet. Look at Bandit's leg."

Bandit was sniffing the dead coyote.

"Bandit, no," the doctor said, and turned to the boy. "I'm so sorry. What's your name?"

"Nikolai," the boy said.

"Nikolai? Okay. And Masha, where did—Masha—why do you have a gun?"

Masha could only shake her head. "I'm sorry, Mrs. Parks. The gun is mine. No one I know does not have a gun."

The doctor paused. No one she knew did *not* have a gun? How to parse this double negative? Then, she exhaled. "Okay, okay." She looked at the boy. "Thank you so much. I'll be right back. I'll find you guys later—I have to call the vet."

The doctor turned and grabbed the dog and led him off, toward the main house. She called to them over her shoulder.

"Is it—is it legal?" she said.

"What?"

"The gun. Do you have a license and permit?"

Of course, she didn't. Masha said nothing, but watched the doctor cross the patio and disappear around the side of the house. Masha looked over at Nikolai, then at the spilled pretzels. She asked him again:

"You're sure you didn't do this?"

He shook his head again, and held out the gun to her. She took it and pointed it toward the ground.

"Bullets in here?"

He shook his head. "I loaded three. I used them all."

"I didn't buy this for play, you know. But Dr. Parks loves that dog. He's all she has left."

"Where's my mom?" Nikolai asked, and glanced at the pool house.

"Your mother sleeps like the dead."

CHAPTER 19

"WE BETTER CLEAN up this food," Masha said. "That's why they came." She looked at the thin dead coyote. "Very good aim. Ivan taught you to shoot?"

Nikolai nodded.

"He taught you good."

"Thanks," said Nikolai, with a sigh. It was nights like this one, with scary noises, when he missed Ivan the most.

Across the pool, in a dark shadow between two hedges, Boris crouched. He held close the duffle bags and watched as the doctor entered the house under the paint-splattered camera. The paint was black, the lens was black, and in the dark, it looked no different. But in seconds, she'd flip the kitchen light on and find the alarm transformer unplugged.

And she'd find Shev. Or she'd never see him coming.

Nikolai gathered the pretzel nubs from the deck. Masha disappeared into the pool house and walked out moments later with two plastic bags and wearing thick yellow dishwashing gloves. She helped the boy pick up the scattered banquet. This was perfect. If Shev could get out of the house unseen, Boris could snipe the boy dead from there.

But suddenly someone appeared from the bushes from

behind the pool house. It was too dark to see her face, but she was hysterical.

"Elizabeth?" she yelled. "Hello! Dr. Parks!"

"Veronica, wait! Call her! Stop!" A man behind her yelled. He, too, appeared from out of the bushes, trying to calm down his wife.

"I am calling her!" said the woman. "I'm on my phone! She's not picking up!" She stopped short when she saw Masha and the boy on the deck.

"You can't barge in on her like this!" the man called.

"Oh, I can't?" the woman said, and turned her head with disdain toward the man. "Go home, you pussy."

In the kitchen, Dr. Parks flipped on the overhead light. Bandit was limping. His right leg was either bitten or scratched. She picked up the landline to call her vet and, despite Shev's fears, she moved right past the unplugged alarm.

He stood in the hall and peered through the gap in the kitchen door, holding his breath.

Jeanine was the doctor's concierge vet, and she lived two miles down in the flats. It would take her ten minutes to get up the hill. The doctor thanked her and rang off.

"Dr. Parks?" said a voice from behind, and the doctor jumped.

"Veronica!" she said, hanging up on the vet.

Veronica Burns, her next-door neighbor, had walked past Boris and let herself in through the mudroom door.

Veronica, braless, in sweats, held her phone. "Drake thought he heard gunshots. Is everything okay? Did you hear them?"

The doctor nodded.

Drake was Veronica's husband or boyfriend. Partner? They

both starred on cable TV shows the doctor didn't watch, and were constantly calling with kind complaints: The Bel Air water was poisoning them. The pools attracted West Nile mosquitoes. The gas-powered leaf blowers were deafening their pets.

"I'm so sorry," Dr. Parks said. "A pack of coyotes came down the hill and attacked Bandit. I shot at them to break them up."

"What? No," Veronica said. "Is Bandit okay?"

"He is. I just got off with his vet. She's coming right now."

"At two in the morning?"

"Isn't she amazing? She's concierge, 24/7."

"So good to know." Veronica and Drake kept pot-bellied pigs and a family of bunnies that roamed their house, leaving poop pellets on the floor where their toddlers crawled. But at least they were attentive neighbors. At least they cared. People in Bel Air were strangely private in an ill-mannered way, the doctor thought, and at least the Burnses called and came over after hearing the shots. It made the doctor feel less alone.

"Oh, thank God," Veronica said. "As long as he doesn't get rabies or something."

"Let's hope not."

"You have a gun?" Veronica said. "You shot in the air to scare them away, and it worked?"

"No," lied the doctor. "And yes, I have a gun. I shot right at them. I killed one. It's awful."

"Oh," said Veronica, running her hand through her hair. "Tragic." And then she sighed. "Poor little pups. It's our faults, you know. Pushing the wildlife around like we do. All the construction. And then with the Covid, they all came out, and then they had to go straight back in. I'm sure it's been a confusing year for...you know, wildlife."

"For everyone," the doctor agreed.

"Yeah."

"I hope I didn't wake the twins," Dr. Parks said.

"No, you didn't," Veronica said. "But Drake was up, and he called the police. He wasn't sure if it was, you know, a murderer, or a...domestic thing..." Her voice trailed off uncomfortably.

"And you came over? That was brave," the doctor said.

"Yeah, well, yeah. I live for this shit."

"Wait, the police are coming?" They would ask about the gun.

In the house, Shev shook his head. The police? On the way? Now?

"Drake called them. Is that okay? Believe me, he knows gunfire when he hears it. He plays a cop on TV, in Chicago. You know. Chicago. But still."

"Right," said the doctor, suddenly stricken. She'd never actually asked Masha...if Masha was working legally...or even living in the US legally. The accent was thick, and Masha only took cash, off the books. "Can you watch Bandit for one second?" the doctor said. "I'll be right back."

"Uh," said Veronica, and watched the doctor run through the kitchen and out the back door. "Sure."

Boris watched from the bushes as Dr. Parks ran out and down the garden path toward the pool.

This was a strangely busy night. Where was Shev?

But Masha and Nikolai were nowhere in sight. They'd gone back inside. The doctor took the pool house steps, and barreled in, startling them all.

"My neighbor called the police," she announced.

"No," Masha said, and rose from her chair, suddenly looking much more sober. Dr. Parks didn't recognize Sophie, who stood there in her bedclothes, looking upset. "The police are coming? Here?"

"They're on the way. Who are you?" the doctor asked.

"Mrs. Parks, this is my cousin, " said Masha. "Her name is Sophie. She's Nikolai's mother."

"Hi," said the doctor. Sophie looked frightened and said hello. But this wasn't the time for introductions.

"Go down the steps on the side of the house to the basement door. I'll unlock it from inside. Hide there and don't come out until I tell you. Turn off the lights here and lock the door. We don't have a minute to spare."

CHAPTER 20

THE DOCTOR TURNED to flee the pool house, but stopped on the step and turned back around. "Who has the gun?" she said. "Bring that gun. Don't leave it here."

Inside, Masha turned. She grabbed the gun from the kitchen counter as Sophie turned off the lights and grabbed a jacket for her son. They followed the doctor out to the deck.

Back up the path, past the hot tub, the doctor headed straight to the patio door, while Masha veered left, toward the cement steps that led down to a basement door. Sophie and Nikolai followed her.

It was then that Boris straightened up. He couldn't see the stairs on the side of the house, so where was the Russian trio running off to now? And why, at two in the morning?

He crouched back down, at a loss, and waited in the brush. Maybe it was time to hit the woods again, retreat to the van. Shev might have to fend for himself. The stupid kid got himself trapped in the house, and now they had two blondes in pj's to kill.

Dr. Parks sailed past Veronica, who was patiently sitting with Bandit, and raced toward the basement stairs. The kitchen door swung open, temporarily pinning Shev in the corner behind it. He ducked and held his breath.

The doctor flew down the steps to the basement and crossed the vast space, pulling a cord to turn on a single light bulb on the way to the side door. She flipped open the lock and let the stowaways in from the cold.

"Lock up behind you," she said. "Find a place to hide and kill the light." She was gone in a flash, taking the stairs two at a time. "They might not come in. They probably won't. Stay and be quiet."

"We will," Masha said.

Just as the doctor shut the door at the top of the stairs, the front gate buzzer buzzed. Shev was crouching behind the door to the kitchen as she blew past and answered the intercom next to the fridge. "Hello?"

Through the intercom, an officer spoke.

"Good evening, ma'am. My name is Officer John McKay. From the Beverly Hills Police Department."

Fuck, thought Shev, *that was fast.* The police were at the gate already?

"Hi," said the doctor curtly. "Hello."

"We received a call from your neighbor about a disturbance. Is everything all right inside?"

"Yes, I'm fine."

"Your neighbor said he heard possible gunshots from your property. If you have a problem you cannot discuss, please say the words, I am okay."

"Yes," said the doctor. "No. Thank you. I was the one who used the gun—I shot at some coyotes in my backyard."

"Is everything okay?"

"Yes. My dog got out. I'm sorry."

"What's your name, ma'am?"

"Elizabeth Parks. I own this house. There were coyotes in my backyard."

"Can you buzz us in?"

"Really, officers. It's not a good time. It's late, and my neighbor's here. The same one who called you. We're fine. Do you want to speak to her?"

"Ma'am. Please. Open the gate. We'd like to make a quick house check."

"Okay." The doctor rolled her eyes. "But I'd like to get to bed soon..." She looked at Veronica, then buzzed the buzzer that opened the gate at the bottom of the drive. It led to the street. "Um," she said, into the intercom, "head left as you come up the driveway. Park in the circle. I'll meet you there."

"Thank you, ma'am," said Officer McKay.

Dr. Parks released the intercom. Veronica headed toward the mudroom door.

"I'm out," she said. "You good? You feel safe?"

"Thank you so much," the doctor said.

"I'll call you in the morning," Veronica called over her shoulder, as Dr. Parks turned and scurried from the kitchen, past Shev again.

"Thanks!" she called. "'Night!"

"'Night!" called the actress.

Shev listened as Dr. Parks went down the hall, past the basement door, and entered her study.

After several seconds, when all was quiet, Shev slipped from behind the door and entered the kitchen.

Bandit lay on his doggy bed, whimpering and licking his wounded leg. He looked up and started barking, so Shev grabbed a few pretzels from inside his pocket and tossed them on the floor before heading out through the mudroom.

But they were wrong about the dog. Bandit made no move toward the snacks. He was smarter than they thought, and had had enough to eat. Plus, the bite on his leg cut deep, and he was in pain.

In her study closet, Dr. Parks knelt in front of a black steel safe. She turned the dial lock once around right, then right again, and landed on number thirty-one.

"Come on, come on…"

The safe could be finicky. It was at least a hundred years old and held their old jewelry, the deed to the house, stock certificates, and copies of their wills and trusts. Hack-proof, this old mule, she thought. No one could ever access it. The thing was fire and ballistic proof, and weighed almost a thousand pounds. It was deep and secure in safes like these that doctors used to hide their files.

"All the way left and around to twelve. Stop. And back again…to almost, almost…twenty-nine."

Tires spun on the gravel outside. The police car's headlights shone through the shutters, but then went dark. The engine stopped, and there was silence.

Maybe they were talking for a minute, she thought. The police? Inside the car? Getting ready? But for what? She heard car doors open and shut, and the safe finally popped open.

Just in time.

She reached in and grabbed her ex-husband's gun. The Beretta M9 he bought for the house to keep them safe. This was before she had rescued Bandit, and she'd been wildly, totally against it.

But now, it was coming in handy.

She grabbed the envelope underneath, now yellowed, with registration, permit, certificates: all she needed to prove her lie. She'd show them the gun and tell them she was the one who used it. The only one home. There was no one else there. She was the one who shot the coyote.

The doorbell rang.

CHAPTER 21

IN THE BASEMENT, Sophie stacked two cardboard boxes and crouched behind them in a corner. Nikolai tucked himself safely in a crawl space behind a giant freezer. Masha tugged on the string to the light bulb and found her way through the darkened room to the washing machine and sat on the floor behind it.

They heard Bandit bark a few times, then stop. They heard the front doorbell.

Out back, in the bushes, Boris waited.

This had turned into a circus, he thought. A comic but tragic Chekhov play. Doors opening, doors closing. In and out. Then Shev burst from the mudroom into the side yard, looking as scared as a jackrabbit. Headlights were shining bright from the drive.

"Shev!" Boris called. Shev turned and followed his boss's voice toward the brush. Boris rose from between bushes, turned on his heel, and calmly said, "Let's call it." They hiked back up and into the woods. "What happened?"

"The neighbor called the police. The fucking police came."

"Shit. What'd you get?"

"Just the alarms. You?"

"Nothing. Fucking coyotes. The dog went nuts."

From inside her study, Dr. Parks heard the doorbell ring a second time. Her heart froze. She'd never had contact with the police. And here they were in her home again? Twice? In one day?

But now she was actually breaking the law. She was harboring Russians in her basement; hiding this threesome she hardly knew. Why? Maybe a year saving lives made it a habit? So many months high on adrenaline and fight-or-flight instinct in New York City.

She left the study, went down the hall, unlocked the door, and opened it wide. She decided to play the harried hostess. A lady scared of the wild coyotes. Alone. Innocent. Grateful.

"Thank you for coming," she said to the officers, feigning relief.

"Good evening," said McKay as he stepped inside, and they all shook hands and traded names. The front gate buzzed again from the kitchen.

"Oh, that's my vet," the doctor said. "Follow me." She left the front door and headed toward the kitchen. The officers followed. "She makes house calls. Only in LA, right? My dog got out and fought the coyotes before I got there to chase them away."

The officers followed her past the study and then past the basement door. They stepped into the kitchen, and Bandit barked as the doctor hit the intercom. "Jeanine?" she said.

"Dr. Parks? Is Bandit okay?"

"I'm buzzing you in. The police are here. There were coyotes. Don't be alarmed."

"Okay," she chirped. "See you shortly."

Dr. Parks buzzed the gate open and turned to look at Steven's gun. She'd put it on the counter under the paperwork.

"That's the gun I used," she said. "It's empty now. And there's the paperwork. What do I do with the dead coyote?"

"Animal Control," McKay said, "and we'd like to see it. And perform a house check."

This again? What even was that? The doctor's heart sank. Why did they want to check her house? Did this have something to do with her files? With Morse and Hernandez?

"This was perfectly legal, right? To shoot a coyote in my own yard?"

"Yes, ma'am," the second officer said. His pin read MOY. "Coyotes have the same rights as rats. Which is basically none."

"Phew."

"The county and state laws differ a little, but you can shoot them if they're aggressive and posing a threat."

The doctor put her hand on her heart. "All right, great. And yes, feel free to look around. There's nothing to see. I live here alone."

"No one else lives here?" McKay said.

"Not right now. My son's away at school," she lied. "My husband's away on a business trip." The doorbell rang. "That's my vet. Excuse me, please." And she left them to let Jeanine inside.

A minute later, and back in the kitchen, Jeanine crossed to Bandit as Dr. Parks led the police outside, but stopped in the middle of the kitchen floor.

"He's still bleeding," she said to Jeanine, staring down at the pretzel nuggets that scattered her floor. What the hell? She reached down and picked one up. This was nothing she'd ever buy, these things. Where did they come from? Distracted, she said, "We're headed out back…to, um…to see the coyote." She suddenly felt light-headed. Where had all this food garbage come from? What the hell was going on? What were these called?

"You're not giving Bandit Combos, are you?" Jeanine said. "These are disgusting. They'll make him sick. They're full of gluten."

"No," said Dr. Parks absently. "Masha must've bought them."

"And doctor?" said Moy, as he looked around the kitchen. "You know your alarm is off its charge?"

The doctor turned and looked at Moy. Then she looked at the alarm panel on the kitchen counter. Indeed, the transformer sat unplugged.

"Did you mean to unplug it?"

"No," she said, and suddenly felt uncertain and breathless. "No, I didn't. Maybe—maybe my housekeeper...Maybe she knocked it out by...mistake? She was here earlier...this afternoon."

CHAPTER 22

ON THE GARDEN path, the doctor led the officers through the backyard to the pool. They wielded Stinger tactical flashlights that lit up the dark wherever they pointed. The poor coyote lay dead in the grass.

"Small guy," said Moy.

"There were six altogether," the doctor said. "They ran off up there." She pointed up the hill, and Moy aimed his flashlight into the grove.

"There's a wood that leads to a ravine back there and only a wall. Stone. Six feet. They hop right over."

"They're jumpers," said McKay. "We'll give you the number for Animal Control. They'll come get him and send us the bullets."

"The bullets?" the doctor asked, and turned. "Why?"

"Sometimes we check them for prints," he said. "Casings, too. But revolvers don't lose them. It's for ballistics matching reports."

"Oh."

"You know. We match the bullet to the gun."

That made sense. She didn't know that. She had no idea. How would she? The doctor nodded. "Smart," she said, and hoped this would not be one of those times. But what could she do or say to stop them? She looked around and changed the subject.

"Man, it's freezing. Can we go back in?"

"Sure," said Moy.

"I was asleep. Sorry for the bare feet and bedhead." She led the officers back around the pool, away from the pool house.

"Got something here," McKay said, and stopped. "Is this scat? No…" He knelt and shined his light into the grass. It was a hamburger patty. And another and a third. And more pretzels. "Someone dropped a couple of burgers. There's about four or five them here…"

"Really?" The doctor crossed to look.

"You guys barbecue out here today?"

She was at a loss and shook her head. "Um, no. But maybe the gardeners? They eat lunch on the job sometimes."

"Yeah, these are fresh."

"I guess that's why the coyotes came. I'll call them in the morning. Make sure they come back and do a quick sweep. I don't want any more critters back here." The doctor felt confused and tired. She was done with this visit, and hoped they were, too. It was almost two in the morning.

She led them back in, through the kitchen, and past Bandit, who stood at the basement door barking, cone on his head.

The doctor panicked. Where was Jeanine? She was nowhere in sight. Where had she gone? She had already bandaged his leg.

"Bandit," she said to him. "Back in the kitchen."

"What's in here?" Moy stopped and asked.

"The basement."

"I'd like to check it."

"Sure," said the doctor, trying her best to remain calm. "Bandit, back. Back, back." She opened the door. "Watch your step," she said a little loudly, trying to warn the three below. "The steps are steep and the light is—the light is sometimes out. There's only one bulb. Sometimes I need to change the bulb. I'll stay up here. I never go down. It bothers my allergies." Another random lie.

The stairs and the basement itself were pitch black.

Please be hiding well, she thought. There were places to hide. Behind the freezer or moving boxes. Behind the washing machine and dryer. There was even a closet.

At the bottom of the stairs, Moy aimed his flashlight in every corner. The doctor held her breath and waited.

Bandit kept barking.

"Shut it, Bandit. Enough," she whispered, losing patience and holding the dog by the scruff of its neck. "Where's your collar?" How had Bandit lost his collar?

"Maybe mold?" Moy said, turning, and heading back up. "Have you checked for mold?"

Dr. Parks sighed with relief. "Um..." she said, grasping for lies and conversation, casual, easy. "Yes. We had a bleach thing done. Didn't work. Maybe it's dust. Mildew. Who knows." She closed the door and led them down the hall and out.

In the circle, Moy and McKay climbed into the cruiser as the doctor walked down the hill to the gate pad and buzzed them through.

"Thanks!" she called, and waved. "Thanks again!"

CHAPTER 23

WHEN BANDIT STARTED barking at the basement stairs, the street-smart Poplovs slipped back outside, closed the door, climbed the steps, and scattered like the wind throughout the backyard. Dogs were not to be trifled with. Dogs can smell, hear, and sense things that humans cannot. The Poplovs knew this, and they knew the police knew this, too.

Once the police car had cleared the gate, Dr. Parks backtracked into the house, went back to the basement, and tugged on the light. She looked around. They'd hidden well.

"They're gone," she announced to the luggage and skis, thinking the Poplovs still hid. She crossed to the outer door and found it unlocked. She locked it again and went back upstairs. Clearly, they'd sneaked back out, but when?

Jeanine was packing her bag in the kitchen.

"Where did you go? You disappeared," Dr. Parks said.

"Oh, the bathroom," Jeanine said. "Sorry." And then she continued: "Coyotes aren't vectors for rabies."

"Oh, that's good."

"But they can carry parasites."

"All right. Yuck."

"Right. Amoxicillin for ten days, in case." She placed a bottle of pills on the counter. "Wrap it in turkey."

"What about his leg?"

"Neosporin. Change the bandage. Keep the cone on. You know the drill."

Dr. Parks walked Jeanine out. Then she headed to the backyard again to find the Russians. She stood on the pool deck and looked around.

"Hello?" she called out, and then gazed at the dead coyote. Would it attract other animals? Raccoons? Crows? Should she cover it with something? Probably . . . Or maybe she should bury it. Would Animal Control retrieve the bullets for the police? What were the odds? The officers, she thought, suspected nothing, but she decided not to chance it. She'd bury the coyote herself, deep.

"Hello?" she called out again. "Everyone left. My neighbors, the police." No one responded. "Anyone here?"

A moment later, Nikolai crawled out from behind a bush, brushing the dirt from the palms of his hands, and Masha appeared from the back of the pool house.

"That was close," Masha said.

But none of them saw Nikolai's mother.

A few minutes later, they found her sitting in the grass in the grove, her back against a tree, trying her best to sob as quietly as she could. Masha and Nikolai gently approached, but Dr. Parks hung back.

From the ground, Sophie looked up at the doctor. "Please don't make us go," she said. "Please let us stay."

CHAPTER 24

"WE GO BACK in two hours," Boris said. He and Shev trudged through the woods, back out onto Bellagio Road. They'll all be asleep and the dog knows us now."

"I'm hungry," Shev said. "I need a burger. It all made me hungry. We didn't have lunch."

Boris said nothing. He was too angry. "You should've killed the lady."

"She was too fast," Shev said. "You should've killed the dog.".

"I wasn't hired to kill the dog."

"I wasn't hired to kill the lady. And you should've used a cooked fish. Salmon or tuna. A dog would not leave a fish behind. I know this."

Boris stayed silent the rest of the hike. Shev had a mouth that needed shutting and an attitude that needed a readjustment. He cleared the brush, stopped walking, and looked up the hill, and then back down. Where was the van? It was nowhere in sight.

"Fuck," he muttered. "Where's Vad?" He listened, heard nothing, then took off down the hill toward the city. Shev followed six feet back. They didn't carry phones on these jobs. Too risky. Phones could be traced. They walked about a quarter mile, then Boris rounded a tight bend and stopped.

He sidestepped right, off of the pavement and into the shadows behind some trees. Shev followed and stood behind him.

Down the hill, the van was stopped on the side of the road and blocked in by cop cars, one in front and one behind, with red flashing lights.

Vad was pulled out onto the pavement, feet spread, and hands on the hood. Two of the cops were frisking him. The van doors were splayed, and two other officers searched the inside. They found the bags from Ralphs, all the receipts, paint guns, machetes, Glocks, a gram of cocaine, and duct tape.

"What a night," Boris mumbled, and turned on his heel, heading back up the hill, into the mist, and straight into the headlights of Moy and McKay.

Moy and McKay had taken their time outside the gate at Dr. Parks's house, finishing up the "loud noise" report. McKay hit the brakes and screeched to a stop, as Boris and Shev bolted into the brush.

"Aw, man," McKay said, as they both swung out of their seats to give chase. "Here we go." He pulled out his radio: "George-32, foot pursuit, foot pursuit, George-32!" He called to the Russians. "Hey! Hey!"

Boris ran through the twisted sagebrush, pulled out his Glock, turned, and opened fire: *Pop! Pop!*

"Shots fired! Shots fired!" Moy yelled, gaining on him, ten feet behind. He drew his gun and returned fire.

"Any units!" McKay yelled. "Two white males on foot! On foot! We're in the woods!"

Shev and Boris parted ways. Boris veered right uphill, and Shev veered left downhill, through the bramble. His boot caught a snare, and he pitched forward and fell.

"Stay on the ground! Stay on the ground!" McKay yelled as he caught up.

"Do you have a gun? Do you have a gun!"

"No, no!" Shev said, as McKay pulled a Taser and hit him hard with it under his ribs. Shev cried out, feeling the sting of searing pain and a wave of hot cramping that spread through his torso and down all four limbs.

"What're you running for? Give me your hands!" McKay said, and knelt at his side. "Give me your hands! I need your hands! My cuffs are out!" He grabbed Shev's wrists, slapped them in cuffs, and held them there. "William-355," he said. "We need an am for a man who's been tased." He turned to Shev. "Why, kid? Why did you run?"

"To get away . . ." Shev murmured.

McKay shook his head. Maybe his was a dumb question. "Yeah, that makes sense." Then he sighed. "Just relax. Ambulance coming . . ." He looked at the treetops and looked back down. "Did you try to hit a house tonight? Up the street? Did you hit a house?"

Weaving through the eucalyptus, Moy gained on Boris, and Boris reached back and fired again. *Pop! Pop!*

Moy returned, and a bullet pierced Boris in the bottom of his left buttock. He seized and yelled—he hated pain—and his left knee buckled into the dewy cold leaves and underbrush. He was out of ammo.

Moy closed in, aiming, two-handed, and yelled, "Man down! Man! Down!"

CHAPTER 25

FOR THE NEXT two hours, the three women talked until the sun rose while Nikolai slept in one of the bedrooms. Masha confirmed they were there illegally and had overstayed their visas; and Sophie explained she'd fled her husband, Andre, in Uglich, north of Moscow in western Russia.

"Where Ivan the Terrible's son got his throat slit," Masha added.

The doctor frowned, and Sophie continued, explaining she'd hidden in Brooklyn with friends, but then Andre found her and forced them back into his family. Then, thank God, he got into trouble.

"ICE," she said, "marked him for deportation. Once he's released from prison in New York, he goes back. In about two months."

But she was worried he'd find a way—that he'd stay stateside and track her down. She only needed a place to hide for a few weeks more, enough time to save a little more cash and buy a used van. She and her son would live in the van and use it to drive out of California. To disappear. She left out the part about Andre's friends and how their orders were to kill both Ivan and Nikolai on Andre's behalf.

At five in the morning, the doctor decided she'd let them stay for a few more weeks. All was settled until late that morning, when Moy and McKay called from the West LA Community Station.

The food detritus had matched the receipts in Boris's bags, and broken bramble and tracks in the hillside matched the men's boots. The doctor called Masha into the kitchen, and Sophie, too. The doctor was scared.

"You think it was us?" Masha said. "You think it was me, don't you? Do you?"

The doctor had never seen her like this, on the defense in such a manner. She was deeply hungover, eyes at half mast, and staring daggers. A switch had flipped.

"Masha," said Sophie, trying to calm her cousin down.

Dr. Parks shook her head and sighed. She didn't know what to think. She leaned against the kitchen counter. "Three men tried to break into my house. This is the report from the police who came here last night. Thank God. Thank God they came and scared these men off. They arrested them two miles down the road. There was a shootout. These people were armed."

"So?!" said Masha.

"So they were Russian."

"So?"

The doctor sighed, frustrated. "How can that be a coincidence? Tell me how that's a coincidence."

"I don't know."

"After what you told me last night?"

"I don't know!" Masha said, raising and raising her voice. "You don't trust me. You think I stole your files to steal drugs, and murdered a man. What can I do? What can I say to that?"

"I didn't say that. That's not what I'm saying."

"You don't have to. I can see it in your eyes."

The doctor was losing her patience. "What am I supposed to think? Someone hacked into my files, and then someone else entirely, randomly, tried to rob me last night, or murder me, or who knows what? That these two events had nothing to do with each other at all? And these—these burglars and my housekeeper both happen to be Russian? I mean, what am I supposed to think?"

"Think what you want," Masha said, and stood from the barstool. "I quarantined in your backyard—for you. I moved to the backyard for you—to make things easy. For your home. I let go of my place. I did the shopping. Risked my life to go to the markets."

"Masha," said the doctor.

"I did the cleaning while you were gone. Took care of your dog, your son, your husband..."

Sophie's eyes shifted to her knees.

"And I paid you for all of that, and paid well," said the doctor, "and I've been grateful—never asked you a single question or pried, nothing—and I protected you last night. You and your family. I haven't said a single word yet to the police."

"Oh, *yet*? Yet? No," said Masha. "Fine, I'm gone for good then, fine."

"I said you can both have a couple more weeks, and I stand by that."

"No. I'm out," Masha insisted. I'm happy to go somewhere else to live. I will not be insulted in this way. Sophie can stay. She can clean. Do all your bullshit."

"Masha," said Sophie.

"What?" Masha turned and snapped at her cousin. "What do you want? Stay. I want you to. You'll be safe. I should've moved out months ago."

"Fine," said the doctor. "Do what you want."

"I will," said Masha, and turned and walked out. "I don't need your fucking permission."

CHAPTER 26

TWO MONTHS LATER

DETECTIVE MORSE AND Detective Hernandez called the doctor with news every week for eight long weeks. That afternoon, as they spoke on the phone, the doctor stood at the patio doors and gazed out onto the sunny backyard.

Nikolai and Bandit played and roughhoused. Nikolai tossed a tennis ball high, and Bandit caught it in midair in his mouth and ran away, but only to tease. The boy then tackled him and pried the ball from the dog's strong jaws, and the whole charade started over again.

Happily.

It was so nice to see a boy laugh, having fun in the sun, in her yard, with her dog. Sober.

Nikolai had won the doctor's affection over the months, digging into his weekend chores while Sophie slept in or drank her coffee on the pool house porch like a backyard queen.

When the doctor asked her how she got her son shining, scouring, sweeping, Sophie said Russian sons always do chores.

"It's how we train them to be a good husband," she said

with a laugh. Unlike her own ex, Andre, she said, who was finally released from prison that week and on a plane to Moscow.

The doctor felt sick with shame hearing this, imagining how her own son, Josh, would respond to spending a Saturday mopping floors.

Not well.

Masha used to make his bed for him, tidy his school books, do his laundry, cook his meals. Steven insisted. Josh was to be free from chores to study. The doctor even made his school lunch at night, a bagel and cream cheese, Ziploc of almonds, chocolate pudding, carrots. He could have done that himself. But he'd never held a broom in his life, and rarely, if ever, played with the dog. Would Josh and Nikolai get along? Masha had moved out, but they'd made up. Or at least, the doctor thought they had. Masha visited sometimes to help Sophie out with certain big cleans, like the basement and attic, to pick up some cash. That day they'd cleaned out the doctor's garage.

Over the phone, Morse had good news: none of her patients had suffered a break-in since Mr. Lewis eight weeks before.

This was a relief. She had secured her company's systems. This had worked, or the perp (or perps) had maybe moved on. She had also upgraded and secured the house. No more wired alarms. The doctor's system was top of the line, with HD night vision, digital smart locks, and nothing wired that could be splattered or cut.

The other news, Morse said: "There was no match between the files and the Russian guys." All three men had ties to the Russian mob, but alibis that checked out the night of the

Stanley Lewis murder and the nights of the other robberies, too. "We haven't found another lead."

"No one?" said Parks. "Even with forensics?"

"No blood, no hair. We haven't lifted a single print."

Elena, Laticia, all of the doctor's hospice employees had checked out fine, and business could resume as usual.

The doctor sighed. "That's so weird. It must have been a random hacking. Maybe it was."

"Easily," said Morse. "These guys could be anywhere. China. Korea. Wisconsin. Iran. Information is hard to secure."

Dr. Parks nodded. The truth was she wanted it all behind her. She could only handle so much at once, and Josh was coming home in three days. That alone—he alone—was enough to manage.

She was nervous about it. Dreading it, actually. He'd been away now for three whole months.

Steven would fly to Billings in the morning, attend a few meetings at Wellborn Ranch, and then fly Josh home two days later. Josh would spend a week at his dad's, in the condo in Westwood, and then move back to the Bel Air house. He'd live there with his mom, except on weekends, all summer long and for the upcoming school year. Junior year would be a tough one, she thought, with SATs, college visits, and AP exams. She wondered how Josh would get through it. She hoped Wellborn worked, and that her son would come home clean and sober, well-mannered, sane, and stay that way in his outpatient program in Beverly Hills.

"Thanks," she said to Morse, and sighed. "For the update."

"You're welcome. We'll be in touch if we get any leads."

"I appreciate it."

The doctor hung up her mobile and turned to the landline, which was ringing on the counter. She looked around to find the handset, sure it was Steven calling about tomorrow. She found the receiver and picked it up.

"Hi, Steve," she said. But it wasn't Steven.

It was Adam Shaw from Wellborn Ranch.

CHAPTER 27

"WE'RE MISSING JOSH," said Adam Shaw. He sounded too calm. "As of this morning." Shaw was Wellborn Ranch's director.

Dr. Parks had never liked him.

He didn't have a medical degree. That she knew. But he called himself a doctor. She'd asked him about it, point blank, when they all met at the intake meeting. Shaw had mumbled, "PhD," but in what exactly he never said, nor did he specify a school.

The doctor sank onto a barstool. She needed the ballast. Missing? Her son was missing?

"What do you mean?" She felt as if she'd been punched in the stomach.

"He's gone," Shaw said. "We've searched the mansion. And the grounds. All the camera feeds. No one has seen him since last night at sleep-check. After lights out, when he was in bed."

The doctor's thoughts spun. How could Josh leave Wellborn Ranch? It was smack in the middle of the Montana wilderness. There was a single one-lane road that led through the woods and up a big mountain to the damn place. It was totally remote, a hundred miles or more from Billings.

"So…you're saying…he escaped?" she said, for clarification.

"Escaped?" Shaw said. "No, we'd never use that word."

What word would they use?

"He escaped," she said again, to herself but loud enough for Shaw to hear.

"No," said Shaw. "But he did leave. We cannot find him."

Dr. Parks shook her head. Maybe Lulu had been right all along. Her son busted loose. He broke out of Dodge. She was almost proud of him for a moment as she leaned forward and slid her elbow onto the bar. She placed her forehead into her hand, closed her eyes, and kept them closed.

"He was coming home Wednesday," she whispered. "He was supposed to be back here in three days."

"This rarely happens, Mrs. Parks."

Now Josh was a runaway, too? A drug-addicted, bipolar runaway?

"What do we do?" she said barely, almost to herself and the placemat.

"Excuse me?"

"What do we do?" she asked again, raising her voice with a dangerous snap. "You're the expert!"

Shaw paused. Then he said, "Well. First. We take a deep breath."

He was so condescending.

"Are you fucking kidding me?" Dr. Parks asked. "Are you? Take a deep breath? What the fuck?" She could hardly believe the man's gall, trying to calm her, to placate her with his New Age crap. Then she heard the door slam and she whipped around—and froze.

Sophie stood in the mudroom doorway.

"My fault," Sophie said, and turned to leave the way she came in. "I'm not here."

Dr. Parks did not try to stop her. She watched her go, then took a deep breath, like Shaw said, and composed herself.

"What do we do?" she asked again, this time with phony, exaggerated calm.

Shaw continued. "Well, first we respond, Mrs. Parks. We do not react. We respond."

This? Again? From this poser? Seriously? Was he actually using the royal we? After she'd paid sixty-two grand, and her son escaped? She looked up at the clock on the range. It was just after noon.

If Josh had sneaked out—if he had been missing for twelve hours now—he could be anywhere. On foot, he could've gone to Wyoming. The Dakotas even. If he'd hopped a ride, hitchhiked, he could be in Canada by now. If he'd hopped a flight, New York or Florida. Mexico even. He could be halfway around the globe.

He could be injured.

He could be dead.

She thought of Lulu. "I thought you took his boots away."

"Excuse me?" said Shaw.

"Josh's girlfriend...she stopped by, concerned, a couple months ago. She said you took his boots away and hid them at night, so he couldn't escape."

"We do that sometimes," Shaw said. "With the rare child we consider a flight risk, but no. Not Josh. In the meantime, Mrs. Parks, we've contacted local police. You'll be hearing from them soon."

"The police are looking for him?"

"Yes."

"Trying to trace his steps? How?"

"They have a photo. This is protocol," Shaw said. "We've

registered him with the National Center for Missing & Exploited Children."

"What? When?"

"Excuse me?"

"When did you do that?"

"This morning," said Shaw.

Dr. Parks paused. Seriously? Josh's face on a milk carton? On TV? "Can you even do that without our permission?"

"Yes, we have to. There's no waiting. There's no hold time for children. Ever. Under eighteen."

Missing? Exploited?

Children? The word hung in her brain.

Josh was a child. He was still a child, at least legally. It didn't matter that he towered over her, that he'd had sex or taken drugs, that he cursed like his dad.

Legally, her son was still a child, and she had failed him as his mother and as a physician. She couldn't help him, she couldn't cure him, she couldn't save him.

"The Billings police have issued a BOLO," Shaw said. "Helena, Missoula, Butte, Spokane."

"Okay."

"I'm sorry, Mrs. Parks. We all thought he was making progress. We all thought..." Dr. Shaw's voice trailed off.

"You all thought what?"

"We all thought he was doing well."

Clearly, they were dead wrong.

CHAPTER 28

AFTER THE DOCTOR hung up on Shaw, she called Steven.
They agreed he should book a flight to Billings and leave right
away, that afternoon. He'd deal with the police and with Wellborn. The doctor would stay put and hold down the fort in
case Josh came home.

Who knew, they thought.

Maybe Josh was headed home.

As they spoke, the doctor was overcome by a nausea, a
wave of dread. The year had been an amusement park ride,
like the kind she rode at Playland Park when she was little.
On the Dragon Coaster, she'd adjust her seatbelt and instantly
regret she ever got on. The ride would take off, and all she
could do was grip the seat bar and suffer the terrifying dips
and turns, completely and utterly out of control.

The rest of the morning and all afternoon, she waited and
waited, and heard not a word from Wellborn Ranch or the
police. She called a few times and no one picked up. She could
not get through. She'd leave it to Steven to deal with Wellborn
Ranch in person.

What else could she do?

In the evening, she retreated upstairs, went to the bathroom, and scrambled through the cabinets and drawers. What did she need and what did she have? Ativan and Ambien. The magic A's. One for nerves and one for sleep. Maybe a double dose of each. For a moment, she paused over the sink, water glass in hand, and wondered if she should go to sleep forever. It would be easy, a great relief, but it would be wrong. A huge betrayal to her life's work, the Hippocratic Oath she'd once sworn. First, do no harm. Even to herself. Maybe, she thought, maybe Josh was on his way home. Maybe he was sober. Maybe he was finally sane. Maybe. Either way, there was no way to sleep without the drugs, so she took them both.

But neither worked.

The coyotes were back on the hillside again, wailing their sad and mournful cries. And sometime later, in the middle of the night, the doctor woke with a frightened start, anxious as hell, and saw only white.

She knew it was blood. She knew that she had blood in her eyes, she knew it was hers, and knew she was no longer in her own bed where she'd fallen asleep.

She woke up face down on her bathroom floor.

CHAPTER 29

THE DOCTOR'S EYEBALLS were soaking wet, the sockets brimming, the sickening liquid filling her ears and hot in her mouth. Blood had already soaked through her cotton nightshirt.

Shit, she thought. What the hell happened?

The floor felt freezing against her cheek, and the grout would stain from all the blood, and maybe the tile. She and Steven had fought about it. They should have gone with the porcelain, she thought. It was far less porous than marble. Wine, coffee, and now, tonight, copious blood would never clean up. Sophie could scrub it for weeks, or Masha, the better scrubber, but the tile would be ruined. She'd have to redo the bathroom floors.

If she survived whatever this was.

That was her first thought. Not for her health, but for the house. She was going to die here, after all, and maybe tonight.

Her cheek was stuck to the cold marble. Clearly, she had suffered a head wound. The amount of blood told her that. Her scalp must be split open, she thought, its millions of tiny vessels ruptured, and her right ear burned.

Had she tripped? Had she gotten up, fallen, and busted her

head open wide? This was, of course, how old people died. For sure she'd concussed, but was coming to. She was thinking, breathing, and part of her mind was assessing her state:

She was alive, yes, check. She hadn't bled out. At least not yet.

With her ear to the floor, she could hear Bandit barking from deep in the house. Somewhere, but where?

He sounded alarmed, and was most likely trapped, wherever he was—otherwise he would be by her side. This she knew. At bedtime, she'd left the windows open, and Bandit, she knew, smelled her blood in the air. She could tell by his bark that he was concerned. It was his job, of course, to keep her safe.

She flattened her palms against the floor and pushed to her knees.

As she did, her head throbbed as if her brain was about to implode: a horrible pressure she'd never felt before, as bad and as fierce as a birth contraction, but inside her skull. Her palms were sticky, some blood had dried, and suddenly she was hearing voices.

There were voices behind the bathroom door, inside her bedroom.

Voices arguing.

She couldn't see yet, but she could listen. She bowed her head and swore one was Josh. But she barely heard them. Or maybe, maybe she was dreaming.

Had Josh come home?

Whoever it was, they were whisper-shouting. But maybe it was Josh. She was his mother, after all. Like penguins, maybe she could pick up his voice from out of thousands? Josh's larynx hadn't caught up to his six-foot frame, and his voice always cracked when he was upset, like this voice did.

He was only a child.

But who was he fighting? The doctor couldn't be sure.

She realized her head was still gushing. She needed a towel, to apply pressure on her wound. She blindly clambered to her feet and groped in the darkness for something soft, a towel, the shower curtain, something, anything, to wipe her eyes, unplug her ears, and stop the flow.

She found a hand towel on the sink, wiped her eyes, then cheeks and jaw, but still blood poured. She had been whacked.

The room was dark, and as her eyes opened and her vision adjusted, she saw herself in the bathroom mirror. She looked like the star of a horror movie. Her white nightshirt had turned black-red. It was drenched and clung to every curve. Her cheeks, clavicle, shoulders and elbows dripped with blood.

On the sink counter, too, a hammer sat. Someone had left a huge, bloody hammer? That was stupid. That was poor judgment. What the hell? Why would they leave it?

Part of the doctor wanted to cry, to vomit and collapse, and call out for help. But another voice, calm and collected—her doctor voice—told her to go; to stay quiet and slip away, into the other bedroom, and fast. The dual master bedrooms with one shared bath were a last-ditch effort to save her marriage, but tonight they might save her life. She had to flee. Get out of the house and away from the voices inside her bedroom. She had to find help before she fainted a second time. Or died.

Whichever came first.

CHAPTER 30

THE DOCTOR, PRESSING the towel to her head, slipped from the master and looked both ways up and down the hall.

All the bedroom doors were shut, and she could still hear the fighting.

She headed left, away from the voices, down the hall toward the hidden stairs in the front of the house.

With a blood-soaked grip, she grabbed the banister and paused for a moment to catch her breath.

This, she thought. This was what happens to other people. People in the news who court or invite misfortune, who make bad choices. What had she done to deserve this wretched, wretched year? She took a step down but again paused.

The second set of stairs, narrow and steep, were finally coming to use. They were the secret service stairs from a bygone era of what architects called "the age of separation," stairs and corridors, secret rooms and hidden closets built to keep families from staff and vice versa.

Breathe, stay calm, the doctor told herself, like Dr. Shaw said. Slow. Breathe. Respond, don't react. Don't pitch forward down the steps. Hold the banister tight. Grip. Feeling dizzy, she closed her eyes to regain her balance.

She had to secure herself heading down, step by step, but move fast. Whatever this was, whatever had happened, someone might find her missing soon and follow her trail of blood like breadcrumbs.

Halfway down, she missed a step, pitched forward, and caught the banister two-handed. She rolled her right ankle, winced in silence, and straightened back up to listen again.

Downstairs, there were more voices.

Who the hell were all these people?

It wasn't Josh. They weren't boys, not down here. Not men. These were two female voices. Sophie and Masha? The voices came from the doctor's study, below her downstairs and to the right.

She had changed the gate and alarm passcodes. She'd changed the locks. Only the housekeepers knew the codes and where she had hidden the new spare keys. But someone got in and now she had to escape her own home. But which way?

Right, toward the study, toward the voices, into the kitchen, and out the back? Left, toward the front and out to the driveway? Right, to the basement, down, and back up into the side yard?

From inside the study, the voices grew louder. More heated argument. Suddenly the doctor's heart froze. Was it, could one voice be Lulu Belmont's?

CHAPTER 31

FURY SENT THE doctor off the last step, down the hall, and into the shadow of the living room doorway. She stood and listened.

"Move it out," she heard Lulu say.

"What? No way," a second girl said.

"It's too dark in there."

"I can't move it," the second girl scolded.

Dr. Parks knew the second voice too. It was Amory Banks.

"It weighs a ton," Amory said. "That's the point of having a safe. You can't, like, just lift it and, just, like, leave. They make them heavy for a reason."

They were trying to open the doctor's safe? To get what? And how did they come by the combination? She crept closer.

"I can't hold the flashlight and turn the thing. Come here and help."

"Seriously?" Lulu scoffed.

"What's the combo?"

"You don't remember?"

"What's it again? Just tell me. Hurry!" Amory laughed.

"Thirty-one, twelve, twenty-nine," Lulu said. "But Josh said you have to go around right four or five times, and then for twelve, on the way back, you have to skip it the first time around, and then keeping going and land on the twelve."

"Huh?" said Amory. "I can't remember all of that."

"Fine. Hold my phone. I'll do it."

"Why?"

"I'll do it."

"Oh, now, see! You can't see either. I told you it's too dark in here."

"Hold the flashlight, nerd," Lulu said.

Amory whined. "Why do we even need a watch? Who wears a watch?"

"Josh says it's worth ninety grand. It's solid gold and French or something."

"Why don't the Parkses keep their rich shit in offshore accounts like normal people? Who has a watch?"

"Because. This is how old money does it."

"They're not old."

"Old *money*," Lulu said. "Classy people."

"But who wears a watch anymore? Like, no one."

"It's not for wearing. We'll sell it. Pawn it. There's a guy in Venice Beach. No questions asked." The girls then fell silent as Lulu attempted the dial lock again under the glare of an iPhone flashlight.

Out in the hall, Dr. Parks felt yet another surge of fury and sidled closer to the study. She peeked inside, and her hand gripped the doorframe and left a stain of sticky red. She was leaving a blood path like one of those zombies on TV.

"Dammit. Is that a three or an eight?" Lulu asked.

"Is it smudged?"

"Maybe." The girls were bent over a sticky note, squinting.

"He has the worst handwriting ever."

"It looks like an eight, but maybe a three."

"Let's forget it and get the laptops."

"No, we need the gun," said Lulu.

"I'm getting nervous. Where is Josh?"

"Upstairs, finishing off his mom," Lulu said, and looked up and out toward the hallway, annoyed. "I wish that goddamn dog would shut up."

CHAPTER 32

BANDIT KEPT BARKING and wouldn't stop.

Someone had locked him in the basement. Josh, most likely, the doctor thought. Behind the door, Bandit was on the top step, barking his head off and pawing at the frame.

Beyond him, in the kitchen, the doctor could hear that the bedroom argument moved downstairs. Someone was chasing somebody else. Someone was yelling. But these two were boys.

Lulu and Amory heard them, too, and sailed from the study right past the doctor's prints on the wall. Lulu had pocketed the watch and was loading the doctor's handgun.

"Who's yelling?" Amory whispered as they moved off, six feet away from the blood-covered doctor. She wished they would turn around and see her there. She looked like a ghoul escaped from hell. Instead, she hid behind the fiddle-leaf fig, a tree she had raised and that now towered at ten feet high, its leaves wide and dark. She peered from behind it. Her house, she decided, and everything in it was on her side. Stanley Lewis flashed through her mind. His sparkling eyes. This was how poor Mr. Lewis felt when he woke to find someone slicing his drip. He must've been terrified, but also irate. No wonder he put up a fight, even at ninety-six.

She slipped from the plant and peeked around the corner. Lulu was heading for the kitchen but Amory doubled back for the stairs.

"Where are you going?" Lulu called.

"I want to see her shoes! If she has good shoes!"

"Doubt it," said Lulu, and disappeared into the kitchen.

Dr. Parks waited until Amory made it up the stairs, then followed Lulu toward the kitchen. It was then that she felt her fingers turn cold. They were practically blue, and her palms were growing clammy. The dizziness was coming in waves at that point, every thirty seconds, and the towel on her head had soaked through. Was she headed into hypovolemic shock? She wondered. Had she already lost two liters of blood? Maybe, possibly. How long, she wondered, had she been passed out on the bathroom floor?

Adrenaline made her thoughts fire. She was weakening, for sure, but that voice inside kept diagnosing and kept barking orders. Could 10 percent of her blood be gone? Fifteen percent? By 20 percent, she'd be in real trouble. She had to get better control of her gash. What had it been? Four minutes? Six? Since she awoke? If she wanted to live, she told herself, she had to stop stalking Lulu. She had to think. She had to stop acting like a crazy person and take control of the situation. She had to escape and call 911.

She needed a plan.

From there in the hall, she could turn left and head out through the front door to the driveway, or she could head down into the basement if, only if, she could get by Bandit.

The basement was safer. Once she got in and shut the door, no one would hear her head down the steps, not in bare feet.

But could she get up the outside stairwell? She had to keep her heart rate low. The harder her heart pumped, the more blood she'd lose.

A cry rang out from the kitchen, and that voice she knew.

It was Nikolai's.

CHAPTER 33

"DON'T SHOOT ME!" Nikolai cried from inside the kitchen.

Down the hall, the doctor sneaked closer. At the end of the hall, the kitchen door was left open a crack.

Lulu stood near the patio doors, beyond the island. She'd pulled the gun and pointed it straight at the boy's face.

"Shut up, dumb ass."

Nikolai raised his hands in surrender. He looked calm but his voice sounded weak.

"Okay. But don't. Please don't."

"Yeah, don't shoot," Josh said, coming to the young boy's defense. "Someone will hear you. Listen, Lulu—"

"What?" Lulu snapped.

"A month ago, before I left, I flushed two g's of tar in the basement. Maybe it's still in the pipes down there. Let's all look for a drain snake thing and we can relax. Okay? We did this. It's over. My mom's gone. We're good."

Lulu frowned and looked at Nikolai. "Fine. Do you want to get high with us?"

Nikolai shook his head slowly no.

"See!" she said. "Let's take him out. What is he even doing here?"

Behind the patio doors it was dark, and the doors caught splashes of light from the range clock and the icemaker. Impossible to see through the windows to the yard.

"My mother's here," Nikolai begged. "In the pool house."

"I'll shoot her, too," Lulu said. "It's no problem."

"Wait, where's Masha?" Josh said.

"She moved out," replied Nikolai. "She's my aunt."

"Masha? Masha's your aunt?"

"We've been staying here now."

"Shit," Josh said, and turned and looked at Lulu. "I didn't know."

"Exactly, so let's just take them all out."

"No, we can't. It's Masha's family." Josh stepped between Lulu and Nikolai. He wanted peace. Enough was enough. He wanted calm. He was glad to be home. It had been a long trip, sneaking out of Wellborn Ranch, the long hike through the snow in socks. He almost froze his fucking feet off. Then the drive home. It was stressful.

"Stop. Lulu. He's Masha's family. It's no big deal. He's cool. He is. Masha is cool. Trust me. She is. She's the one who protected me. From the time I was little. Like eighth grade." His eyes were fighting to stay open wide. "They're, like, family now."

"So what?" said Lulu. "Your mother was family."

"We wouldn't be here without Masha."

"Are you sure?"

"Trust me. Put the gun down." Josh turned to Nikolai. "Right? We're friends? Everyone chill?"

The doctor watched this and wanted to cry.

Her son was as high as she'd ever seen him. He slurred his words and nodded off as he tried to find words. She was surprised he was upright, still standing. The therapist had told them over and over that when Josh was this high, he was no longer the son they knew. He was, instead, the manifestation of whatever cocktail of drugs he had taken, possessed by heroin, meth, Oxy, weed, or crack cocaine. Whatever he had sniffed, shot up, or swallowed.

"I don't see how this works with a narc," Lulu said. "We can't have a witness."

"We can't have noise," Josh said. "We'll wake up his mom. Let's just clean up and stick with the plan." Josh turned to Nikolai. "You and your mom and Masha can stay—if you keep this all on the down-low. Stay out back. It's fine with us. We can all live together. Nothing, nothing…has to change. Just my mom. She had to go."

"What if he calls the police?" Lulu said.

"He won't. He's cool. Right?"

Nikolai nodded. "We…we can't call police. We don't have papers. The police will deport us."

"What? You're Mexican? You don't look Mexican," Lulu said.

"Russian," said Nikolai, and suddenly Amory yelled from the stairs.

"Josh! Josh!" She was running down fast. Josh and Lulu turned their heads as Amory ran in, breathless and scared. "She's gone! She's gone!"

"Who?" said Josh.

"Somebody stole your mother from us!"

"What? What?"

"Somebody stole your mother's body!"

CHAPTER 34

SOMEONE STOLE HER dead body?

The doctor almost laughed when she heard this. How stupid could this girl Amory be? Did she really think someone picked up the doctor's body, dragged it off, and carried it out?

Josh went bug-eyed and followed Amory out of the kitchen. They headed upstairs to check out the bathroom, to solve the case of the missing dead mother. The doctor realized that as soon as they flipped on the lights, they'd find her trail of bloody prints.

She turned on her heel and headed for the basement door. She'd go through the bushes, climb the fence into the actors' garden, go to their house, and call 911.

Bandit stopped barking and whimpered as she approached the basement door.

"Shush," she whispered. Bandit fell silent as she wrapped her hand around the knob. Bandit was huge. The dog and the doctor weighed the same. "Quiet," she said softly again, "we're okay," trying to convince him that they were safe. She turned the knob, cracked the door, and Bandit pushed his nose through and pawed.

"No," the doctor whispered. "Stay."

She wedged her bloody hip through the doorframe, and Bandit, like a good dog, backed downstairs, but only a step. He squirmed and jerked his body in protest, ready to run, ready to pounce. The doctor knew this. He knew this. Only the door was in his way. Bandit barked.

"Back," she whispered, pulling the door closed behind her. "Back, back." But he bent his head, trying to nose her aside. "No, no," she whispered, but Bandit writhed and slithered past. "No!" He nudged the door and bolted through, scampering to the left and down the hall, scenting the air, teeth bared and barking.

"Bandit, back!" the doctor yelled. She couldn't help it. She'd lost control, and knew in that moment she'd stupidly revealed she was still alive, and right down the hall from a girl with a gun.

Dumb dog! Dumber doctor!

But she was so dizzy and so unsteady from all the lost blood that she turned and ran after the dog. It was purely instinct. Like a drunken lech, she chased after him, fell toward the walls and caught herself, left then right, and kept lurching forward. She was chasing her dog toward death, and only then did wet, hot tears start to pour down her cheeks. She felt the dried blood lift from her skin in tiny rivers.

This was grief.

Her home, the house, couldn't protect her the way she'd thought. Strangers, robbers, had broken in: first, they took Steven, then Josh, and now they were trying to take her, too, and Bandit. Noble, courageous, loyal Bandit; the real keeper of the house.

But one more thought occurred to her in the seconds as she lumbered toward the brain-dead kids:

Bandit might go for Lulu's head.

If she didn't shoot him first, Bandit would lunge for Lulu's neck, find her head, and lock-on tight. He might tear her pretty little face from her skull.

It was the doctor's only hope.

CHAPTER 35

BEFORE SHE COULD even reach the door, two earsplitting short sonic pops exploded over the kitchen table: *Pop! Pop!*

Bandit cowered and scurried back, only to freeze and stare at the stunned and fish-mouthed girl.

Wide-eyed and frozen, Lulu pointed the gun straight at Nikolai. Straight arm. Straight wrist. Just like she'd learned to do it on YouTube. She looked confused and a smidge regretful there in the dark, with two gaping holes below her neck, to the left, her left, near her heart.

Her eyes seemed to register shock first, then indignation. Then offense.

How dare someone shoot her. And then the light behind her eyes darkened, her face lost expression, her knees buckled. Dark liquid ooze bled through her bra and tank-top. Her long, pretty fingers, witchy and white, nails polished black, released the gun, and it fell to the floor. Then she fell forward, dead, on top of it.

Nikolai looked as surprised as Lulu.

He turned his head and looked past the doorway, at the doctor out in the hall. She lifted her hands and shook her head. She didn't have a gun. It wasn't she who had shot the gun.

He lowered his arms and turned around.

In the mudroom doorway, Sophie stood barefoot in a nightshirt. Her long blond hair fell over her shoulders and to her waist, her legs in a triangle stance. She gripped Masha's gun tight in her hands.

"Oh, my God!" said a voice from across the room. Dr. Parks and Nikolai and Sophie all turned their heads.

No one had noticed Amory standing there, frozen, staring at her best friend on the floor. She hadn't followed Josh upstairs. She'd doubled back down.

"Oh, my God!" she cried out again, in shock, and looked up at Sophie. Sophie was still pointing the gun, so Amory turned and ran out, squaring her back as a perfect target.

No, the doctor thought, don't run! Amory, no!

And *Pop!* again. Another shot rang through the kitchen, straight from the hands of the ghostly Sophie.

Amory seized, arched her back, and belly-flopped straight to the hardwood floor. Her cheekbone landed with a dull flat *thwack*.

"What happened? What happened?" A panicked Josh yelled from the stairs.

Seconds later, he ran in and froze over Amory's body. Then he saw Lulu, dead on the floor. He looked confused and suddenly exhausted, like he might fall asleep. Nikolai shook his head and raised his hands in surrender: It wasn't him. His face swore it. "My mom," he whispered. Josh spotted Sophie and they squared off, holding each other's gazes in fright. Masha's gun rested at her side, out of sight.

Sophie knew the doctor loomed to the left of the boy, at nine o'clock, and she knew in an instant that Josh was her son—the one she had sent away to get clean. Sophie had seen him in photos in frames around the house. How many times had she wiped down the glass protecting his image, dusted his books, and polished his trophies?

She stood and waited.

"Who are you?" Josh cried. He stared again at Amory's body, then Lulu's, covered in blood. "What have you done?" His friends had been alive two minutes ago. He was so confused, he started to cry, and his voice choked. "What did you do? Why did you do that? They were my friends!"

"This is my mom," Nikolai explained again, in a whisper. "I told you. She was out back."

"What are you doing in my house? You have no right! Where's Masha? Where's Masha?"

Sophie's eyes shifted across the kitchen island and landed on the doctor, who was stepping into the doorway. Josh slowly followed her gaze.

His mother, a blood-soaked ghoul, was alive. Like a demon in the doorway, she'd risen, half dead.

Josh mumbled, "No," and turned around, like Amory had, to run off to who-knows-where.

"Josh!" said the doctor, as Sophie raised her gun and aimed.

CHAPTER 36

"NO! PLEASE!" DR. Parks shouted, hoping that Sophie would spare her son.

But Sophie had already made up her mind. She stood her ground and let Josh run. She didn't move an inch, and finally the doctor stepped into the kitchen, revealing herself in her full ghastly state.

"Go," she said to Sophie and Nikolai. "Same as before. But this time for good. Go! Hurry!"

Sophie crossed to Dr. Parks. "No, we'll stay. We have to call 911 for you."

"No. I'll call. I will. Go first. Hurry. Leave. Take all your stuff, all of it, leave nothing behind, and get out of here."

"Your son might kill you."

"Give me the gun. I'll say I did it. I'll say I shot them, like with the coyote."

Sophie shook her head no.

"Please," begged Dr. Parks. "Wait, the bullets. What about the bullets? They'll check the bullets." She couldn't believe she was thinking this straight. "Your fingerprints are on the bullets."

"No," Sophie said. "I wore gloves. We never touch nothing. Masha told me to always wear gloves. She always wears gloves."

"For germs? For the virus? Right? To protect herself?"

"No," said Sophie, shaking her head. She paused. She would tell the doctor the truth. She owed her that. "For fingerprints. We never leave them on nothing."

Fingerprints? The doctor was stunned.

"Where are you bleeding?" Sophie said, approaching her, but the doctor backed away for fear. "Why would your son do this to you? Why would a son murder his mother?"

"Why would a father murder his son?"

Sophie gently held out the gun, and the doctor saw that she indeed wore the silicone gloves that Masha bought and kept under every sink in the house, to protect from germs, she always said, from bringing them in or taking them out of the house; and of course to keep her manicures safe, the gel and glitter, the rhinestones.

She wore them to hide her fingerprints?

Clearly and gravely, the doctor realized, she had completely misjudged her maids.

CHAPTER 37

NIKOLAI AND SOPHIE turned and fled through the mud-room door.

"Sophie!" the doctor called after them. They stopped and turned, and listened.

"Go out over the garden wall, behind the grove at the top of the hill. There's a wood back there and then a ravine. Walk. If you see or hear a car, hide. But keep walking. Head toward the valley."

"Thank you," said Sophie, "I'll pray for you."

The doctor nodded, sure she would never see them again. There were no goodbyes. She watched them through the patio doors as they ran across the backyard and headed down the path to the pool.

Her focus shifted to the kitchen floor, the massacre, the bloody, silent mess of youth, and something else that now caught her eye.

Amory's chest was rising and falling.

She was still alive. She'd survived the bullet. Wherever it had lodged, it may have missed a vital organ or a major vessel. The doctor could save her.

She methodically turned and grabbed a pair of kitchen shears from the utensils pot and fell to the teenage girl on the floor.

"Amory, Amory," she quietly said, feeling lightheaded as she kneeled. "It's Elizabeth. Josh's mom."

Amory groaned.

"You were shot, and I'm going to cut your shirt for a second, to examine your wound." She took hold of Amory's bloodstained blouse, made a quick slice, and ripped through, exposing Amory's back.

Sophie had nailed the teen below her shoulder. The bullet had fully cleared her heart, but might have punctured her left lung. The doctor checked her airway, her breathing. She balled up the blouse and applied pressure to the tiny gunshot wound. Not clean, but all she had, and time, in this case, would mean life or death. The doctor had met Amory's mom once.

"Stay with me, Amory. Stay," she begged, trying to save the skinny redhead. She rose to find a phone but hesitated and looked out back. She wanted to make sure the Poplovs had time to clear out before the entire circus arrived.

It would be madness: police, ambulance, media maybe—especially if Veronica and Drake showed up. And where had Josh run off to?

She had to keep her thoughts from him, otherwise the truth would be too much to bear. Her son had tried to kill her.

Her child.

In her own house. The home that she had made for him.

The doctor's mobile was bedside upstairs, so she rose and then turned for the kitchen landline. Where was it? She couldn't find it. She looked around. The receiver was missing. She pressed the red locator button. The handset sounded an inch from the base. She was confused. It was right there.

Her heart was still beating and pumping blood, but the

beating had quickened to push more oxygen into her brain. She could feel the rush. Sense it. Her bodily systems were working in tandem, trying to cover for one another's loss, trying to save the sum of itself. She picked up, dialed, and waited a moment.

Then another. The line rang. And rang again.

Finally, a man said, "911, what's your emergency?"

And that's when the doctor started to sweat.

Her hands and palms turned from cold to warm, to clammy and moist. Her forehead, her spine, behind her knees, inside her elbows, sweat poured. Suddenly a deep headache set in, and all she wanted was a drink of cold water. A sip. Ice. To clear her head. She couldn't think.

Her head was bleeding profusely again, wrapping her up in a warm liquid blanket and lulling her to sleep. It told her to close her eyes and relax. It said to let go.

"Ma'am? You there?"

"Exsanguination," she said to him, curling her fingers around the handset. This was her lifeline.

"'Scuse me?" he said. "What was that?"

She couldn't find the words to explain. Her brain could no longer connect to her voice.

"Ma'am? You all right?"

She couldn't find sound and dropped to her knees. The handset was still pressed to her ear.

"Can you hear me, ma'am? I need you to talk. What's going on?"

"I'm bleeding out," the doctor mumbled.

"Ma'am? I'm sending the police right now. I've got officers and EMTs on the way. What color's your house?"

"My head got hit with a hammer. Someone—someone . . ."

"Stay with me, ma'am." The doctor had said those same words—*stay with me*—to Amory. "What color's your house? Is there a gate?"

"Yes, a gate," the doctor said. "The code is...I forget."

"Tell me the code," the man said.

"I can, I can." She then had a moment of clarity. "Four seven two..."

"Four seven two."

"Zero, zero, five." She thought that was it. She wasn't sure, wasn't even sure of her own name. Then she said barely, "It's my son's birthday."

"Today?"

"The code. The code's his birthday."

"Ma'am, the police are on the way."

"No," the doctor told him, annoyed. "Forget the police. We need an ambulance. Me and the girl."

"What's your name?"

"Josh."

"Can you give me your name?"

"Josh," said the doctor.

"Your name is Josh?"

"Tell the police to find my son."

And that was the last thing she said on the phone. She dropped the handset, fell to the floor; all went white, and then all went black.

Epilogue

CHAPTER 38

THREE MONTHS LATER

IF A GROUP of men appeared out of nowhere and headed toward her, Sophie Poplov knew to run.

She ran down the sidewalk, past the broad lawns of Hudson Street in Hancock Park. The Hollywood flats.

Back toward the Sumners' house. She was fast. The older suits sent the young one ahead to chase Sophie. The blond one who looked like a boy. Who looked like he was Ivan's age. Why was she running? He was bewildered.

The tallest pressed in on the driver's side of Masha's car, and the thicker one guarded the front bumper, so Masha was stuck. She couldn't drive off.

"Mrs. Poplov!" the boyish man called from down the sidewalk. Transforming into a track star, he gained on her fast.

Sophie ducked behind the Sumners' tall hedge and sprinted up the driveway toward the garage. It was wide open. She knew it would be.

She would outrun him. She would not let this gentleman catch her. No one would harm her, or her son, ever again. If any man stood in her way, or any girl, she'd do what she had to do. Again.

In the garage, she wound her way through the bicycles, boxes, and trash bins. In the back, she ducked behind a trailer that held a sleek wooden boat. She squatted and slipped her hand into her purse. She felt for her gun, gripped the handle, and whispered, "Commend me, commend me to thy gracious protection..."

The young suit followed her into the garage, panting and looking around. How could he have possibly lost this woman? He took off his shades.

"Mrs. Poplov?" he called. "I saw you run in here. Please come out."

From behind the boat, Sophie stood and pointed the gun straight at his face.

"Leave me alone," she said. "Or I'll shoot."

"Whoa," said the frat boy, and lifted his hands. "Please don't. My name is Jeremy. Jeremy Klein. I'm an attorney. Dr. Elizabeth Parks's attorney? I'm not here to hurt you. I'm here to help. With good news. I swear it."

Good news? Sophie stared at the boy, confused. What good news?

"Please put the gun down." He laughed nervously. "My God. Please..."

Sophie studied him. He seemed genuinely frightened.

And unarmed.

"What do you want?"

Klein looked around. "Do you know these people? Are we—could we be trespassing here?"

Suddenly Sophie felt foolish. How would the bikes and the woodwork protect her? Jeremy's English seemed perfect. No trace of a Russian accent.

"Can we speak out here?" he kindly asked. "I work for Tolles and Associates, a law firm? We handle trusts and estates for the Parks family?"

Sophie took a deep breath and nodded. Quietly, calmly, she rounded the boat and wove through the garage toward the bright light of day, holding the handgun at her thigh.

Jeremy stepped back and gave the young mother a little room. He turned and walked toward the sidewalk, pulled a handkerchief out of his pocket, and wiped his brow. Then blew his nose.

Sophie approached and slipped the gun back into her purse.

"Wow," he said. "I've never been held at gunpoint before. Geez. That was intense. Thanks."

"It's not loaded," Sophie said softly.

"That's good for me. Good for you, probably, too. Anyway. Let's walk back to your sister."

"Cousin," said Sophie.

Unless this was a trick, she wasn't in trouble. They headed back down the block in step. Sophie studied Klein's face for a moment. He was so young, around Ivan's age.

"Sorry to scare you, but now we're even," Jeremy said. "I know this is strange, but we've been looking for you for quite some time. You worked for Dr. Parks, correct? In Bel Air?"

Sophie nodded.

"And you know about the break-in? The girls? The robbery?"

"Yes. It was all over the news," Sophie said.

"Then you heard that Dr. Parks shot the two girls, in self-defense? The girls and her son were trying to rob and kill her?"

Sophie nodded. "Yes. It was sad. Her own son. They said he was high on drugs."

Jeremy nodded. "Yeah," he continued. "He was. And he was

in a fatal accident later that morning. Did you know that? He passed away from his injuries, after driving off a cliff on Mulholland Drive."

"No," Sophie admitted. "No. I hadn't heard that. We haven't cleaned for her lately. No."

"Right." Jeremy's face darkened. He sensed that Sophie knew less than they had assumed. He stopped walking.

"And Mrs. Poplov? Are you aware that Dr. Parks is dead, too?"

CHAPTER 39

SOPHIE STOPPED IN her tracks, dismayed, as Jeremy kindly explained what happened:

"Josh Parks hit his mother with a hammer that night. It was the same weapon Amory Banks had used twice before, in two other murders. Dr. Parks went to the ER and survived her injuries. She came to. Gave statements. Spent a week in the hospital, in the good hands of her colleagues at UCLA. She was discharged, but three days later she suffered what they call a 'traumatic' late death."

"Late?" Sophie said.

"A certain percentage of trauma survivors, they die later. From complications. Sometimes long after the event. After discharge from the hospital. Dr. Parks had a heart attack."

"I didn't know," Sophie whispered. "Sorry to hear it."

"I'm sorry to be the one to tell you."

"She was a nice lady. Kind. Giving."

"And she liked you, too. And your son. Did Dr. Parks tell you she'd adjusted her trust a month before the night of the attack?"

"Her trust?" Sophie said. She was confused. What did this have to do with trust?

"A trust is a legal instrument, like a will," Jeremy explained. "Without the courts."

"No," said Sophie. "She never mentioned something like that. Not to me. Why would she ever?"

"Well," he said, matter-of-factly. "She left you her house. The land. The gardens. All of it now belongs to you."

CHAPTER 40

THE SPRING BEFORE, this young paralegal from the downtown law firm had graduated from Stanford Law.

Jeremy Klein was clever.

Jeremy had called Sophie's mobile every day for over a month. When she didn't return and ignored his texts, he asked a female associate to call and pretend she needed a housekeeping service. The associate asked for a reference or two, and Sophie finally texted back.

She gave them Ellen Sumner's number.

Jeremy then called Ellen Sumner.

As Sophie and Masha spoke to the lawyers, Sophie found it hard to focus.

It was hard to remember the details of all they said and explained, before Jeremy and his colleagues gave the cousins their business cards, walked off, and climbed back into the Escalade.

It was all a blur.

The whole discussion of how Dr. Parks had reverted her trust back to a will, how she and Steven had written Josh out of their wills, per his therapist's request. Then there was something called probate, they said, and a three-month deadline to find and tell Sophie; how she could own real estate here, in the US, even as a foreigner, it was legal, and in California she could inherit property, too. Jeremy reassured her that US estate law doesn't discriminate, and that even if Sophie were here illegally and did get deported, the house would remain, as an asset trust, hers.

Sophie had just one question.

"Anything at all," said Jeremy Klein. "That's what we're here for. To get this all done for Dr. Parks. Whatever questions you have, we're here."

"What happened to Bandit?" Sophie asked. "Dr. Parks's dog?"

Jeremy smiled ruefully. "Bandit went to live with Steven Parks. Dr. Parks's ex-husband."

"Oh," said Sophie. "Oh, I see. I never met him."

"I did," said Masha, and nodded knowingly.

After this, the men drove off.

Masha headed out of the neighborhood, too, and Sophie rode along in the Chevy.

They sat in silence for different reasons, lost in thought, numb from the shock, imagining the future, and deeply awed.

Sophie wouldn't live in the Bel Air house. That she knew. She could barely afford the utility bills, much less a yearly property tax.

She stared out the window, and Masha, at the wheel, forgot about Glendale. She forgot about Gor. She forgot about Ellen Sumner's diamond, sitting snug in her apron pocket.

Instead, she drove to Pasadena, so they'd be on time for their afternoon cleaning. They were usually late, but today, Masha thought, they'd even be early. They would be good. Respectful. She'd steal nothing.

Sophie said a silent prayer for Dr. Parks, and for Josh. She thought of Nikolai and what he would say when she told him the news.

They wove through downtown, and Masha merged onto the twisting Arroyo Parkway, heading north.

They'd spend the rest of the afternoon cleaning. They'd dust chandeliers, polish silver, scrub bathtubs, and mop the floors of a hundred-year-old French-style château, built in the 1920s by an infamous American bootlegger, a dear close friend of Joseph Stalin's (which they couldn't know). The central AC in the house was broken. The women would switch rooms around the electricians, and sweat as they scrubbed until nine o'clock.

Off of the Arroyo, Masha pulled onto the ramp of Orange Grove Boulevard. She broke Sophie's reverie and muttered in Russian. At first, she was incomprehensible.

"He must've freaked out," she mumbled in her native tongue.

"Who?" said Sophie, and turned her head and looked at her cousin.

"He must've been frozen."

"Who? The attorney?"

"The boy."

"Josh?"

Masha nodded. Sophie was lost.

"Frozen? No. The lawyer said he lost control," Sophie recalled from the conversation. "He went to the garage and drove away in Dr. Parks's car. He lost control and went over a cliff. You know Mulholland. He was on drugs. I saw him that night."

"But it's not like the movies," Masha said.

"What movie?"

"If you're in your car—"

"I don't own a car."

"Now you will."

This was true. Now Sophie would buy her van and drive away. The rich kind. A Sprinter with a Mercedes chassis.

Masha continued. "If you suddenly see your brakes are cut loose. That someone, you know, cut the lines. As a trick. You find yourself pumping, but they don't work. Rear or front, or maybe both..."

"My brake lines? Why?"

"If your brake lines are cut, pull up the parking brake, on the side. Shift from Drive to Park. It stops the car. I mean, use your head!"

Sophie stared at her cousin. She studied her face. Was Masha crying? Were those tears streaming down her face?

"Did you cut the brakes in Dr. Parks's car?" Sophie asked. Masha had helped her clean the garage the day of the break-in. They'd spent the whole day in there, cleaning around the doctor's Audi.

Masha glanced into the rearview and turned on the blinker. She changed lanes toward the coming exit. Then she mumbled guiltily: "Dr. Parks sent me away. Accused me of crimes I'd never do. I'd never steal drugs. I hate drugs. I'd never kill an old man. In his home, in his bed!"

Sophie stared in disbelief. She was totally bewildered. She shook her head, looked away out the window, and whispered a prayer.

"May God have mercy on our souls."

Masha sighed and rolled her eyes.

"It wasn't my fault. I only meant to give her a scare. And think of that boy."

"What about him?"

"He deserved it. For all he did. It's justice. It is. And it turned out well for you. For us. Because of your prayers. On Sunday I want you to take me to church."

Sophie nodded. That was fine. She had discovered an Orthodox church in the Silver Lake section of East LA, the Church of the Holy Virgin Mary. She took Nikolai and taught him to pray, to feel and stay connected to God, and to Russia.

Rachmaninoff himself, the Russian composer, had worshiped in this parish in the 1940s. And Sophie joined the Sisterhood there. They protected her and it felt like family. For free, she'd go and scrub the tile floors, wipe the pews, and polish the altar. It made her feel pure, as if she could scrub away all of her sins.

Maybe the world's.

At East California Boulevard, Masha turned right and headed east toward the Langham hotel. A few blocks on, a château sat waiting for them, behind a gate on Charlton Road.

ABOUT THE AUTHORS

James Patterson is the world's bestselling author. Among his creations are Alex Cross, the Women's Murder Club, Michael Bennett, and Maximum Ride. His #1 bestselling nonfiction includes *Walk in My Combat Boots, Filthy Rich,* and his autobiography, *James Patterson by James Patterson.* He has collaborated on novels with Bill Clinton and Dolly Parton and has won an Edgar Award, nine Emmy Awards, and the National Humanities Medal.

Duane Swierczynski is the two-time Edgar-nominated author of ten novels, including *Revolver,* and *Canary,* as well as the graphic novel *Breakneck,* many of which are in development for film/TV. Most recently, Duane co-scripted James Patterson's *The Guilty,* an Audible Original starring John Lithgow and Bryce Dallas Howard. He lives in Southern California with his family.

Bill Schweigart is a novelist and a Cybersecurity and Infrastructure Security Agency executive. He lives in Arlington, Virginia, with his wife and daughter.

Julie Margaret Moulin has a master's degree in journalism from Columbia University. A novelist, she spent her twenties writing the Golden Globe and Emmy Award–winning series *Party of Five* and *The West Wing*.

JAMES
PATTERSON
RECOMMENDS

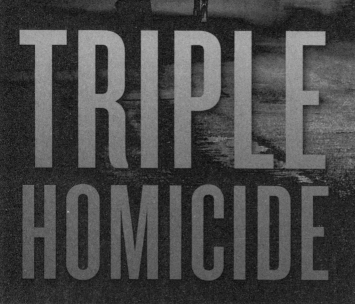

JAMES PATTERSON

TRIPLE HOMICIDE

FROM THE CASE FILES OF **ALEX CROSS, MICHAEL BENNETT,** AND THE **WOMEN'S MURDER CLUB**

TRIPLE HOMICIDE

I couldn't resist the opportunity to bring together my greatest detectives in three shocking thrillers. Alex Cross receives an anonymous call with a threat to set off deadly bombs in Washington, DC, and has to discover whether it's a cruel hoax or the real deal. But will he find the truth too late? And then, in possibly my most twisted Women's Murder Club mystery yet, Detective Lindsey Boxer investigates a dead lover and a wounded millionaire who was left for dead. Finally, I make things personal for Michael Bennett as someone attacks the Thanksgiving Day Parade directly in front of him and his family. Can he solve the mystery of the "holiday terror"?

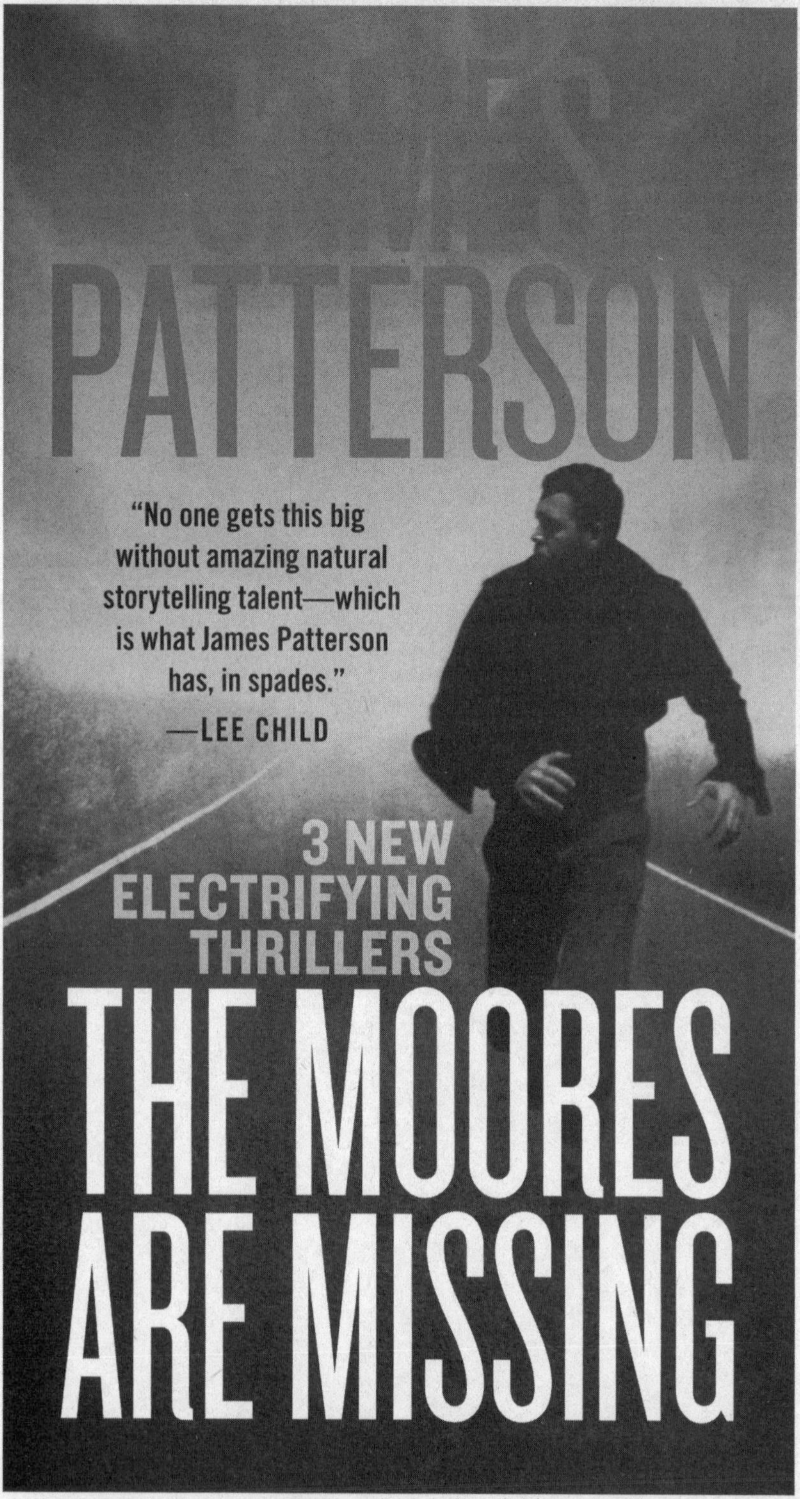
PATTERSON
"No one gets this big without amazing natural storytelling talent—which is what James Patterson has, in spades."
—LEE CHILD
3 NEW ELECTRIFYING THRILLERS
THE MOORES ARE MISSING

THE MOORES ARE MISSING

I've brought you three electrifying thrillers all in one book with this one. First, the Moore family just up and vanishes one day and no one knows why. Where have they gone? And why? Then, in "The Housewife," Maggie Denning jumps to investigate the murder of the woman next door, but she never imagined her own husband would be a suspect. And in "Absolute Zero," Special Forces vet Cody Thurston is framed for the murder of his friends and is on the run, but that won't stop him from completing one last mission: revenge. I'm telling you, you won't want to miss reading these shocking stories.

JAMES
PATTERSON
THE HOUSE
NEXT DOOR
THE
WORLD'S
#1
BEST-
SELLING
WRITER
BRAND
NEW
THRILLS.
SUSPENSE
THAT
KILLS.

THE HOUSE NEXT DOOR

The most terrifying danger is the one that lurks in plain sight; the one that is always there, but you don't notice it until it's too late. Here are three bone-chilling stories about exactly that.

In "The House Next Door," Laura Sherman is thrilled to have a new neighbor take an interest in her, but what happens when things go too far and things aren't really as they seem? In "The Killer's Wife," six girls have gone missing and Detective McGrath will do anything to find them, even if that means getting too close with the suspect's wife. And finally, "We. Are. Not. Alone." proves that we aren't the only life in the universe, but what we didn't know is that they've been watching us . . .

JAMES PATTERSON

THE 13-MINUTE MURDER

The perfect murder takes only a few minutes.

THE 13-MINUTE MURDER

I've really turned up the speed with three time-racing thrillers in one book! In "Dead Man Running," psychiatrist Randall Beck is working against a ticking clock: he has an inoperable brain tumor. So he'll have to use his remaining time to save as many lives as he can. Then in "113 Minutes," Molly Rourke's son has been murdered and she's determined to expose his murderer even as the clock ticks down. Never underestimate a mother's love. And finally, in "The 13-Minute Murder," Michael Ryan is offered a rich payout to assassinate a target, but it ends in a horrifying spectacle. But when his wife goes missing, the world's fastest hit man sets out for one last score: revenge. Every minute counts.

JAMES PATTERSON

THE RIVER MURDERS

& JAMES O. BORN

THE TRUTH LIES PAST THE POINT OF NO RETURN. TO MITCHUM, RETURNING IS *NOT* IMPORTANT.

THE RIVER MURDERS

Mitchum is a relentless man and I've cranked up the tension with three stories just about him. In "Hidden," after being rejected by the Navy SEALs, he becomes his small town's unofficial private eye. But he never could've imagined that investigating a missing teenage cousin would lead to a government conspiracy. And then, in "Malicious," when Mitchum's brother is charged with murder, he'll have to break every rule to expose the truth—even if it destroys the people he loves. And finally, in "Malevolent," Mitchum has never been more desperate after, one by one, his loved ones become victims. Now there's only one way to stop the mastermind: go on the most dangerous hunt of his life.

JAMES PATTERSON
& RICHARD DiLALLO
THE PARIS DETECTIVE
THE WORLD'S #1 BEST-SELLING WRITER
THE BEST DETECTIVE IN NEW YORK CITY IS FRENCH!

THE PARIS DETECTIVE

French detective Luc Moncrief joins the NYPD for three thrilling stories that will put his skills to the test! In "French Kiss," someone wants to make his first big case his last. Welcome to New York. Then, in "The Christmas Mystery," in the heart of the holiday season, priceless paintings have vanished from a Park Avenue murder scene, making Luc Moncrief a quick study in the art of the steal—before a cold-blooded killer paints the town red. Merry Christmas, Detective. And finally, in "French Twist," gorgeous women are dropping dead at upscale department stores in New York City. Detective Luc Moncrief and Detective Katherine Burke are close to solving the mystery, but looks can be deceiving...

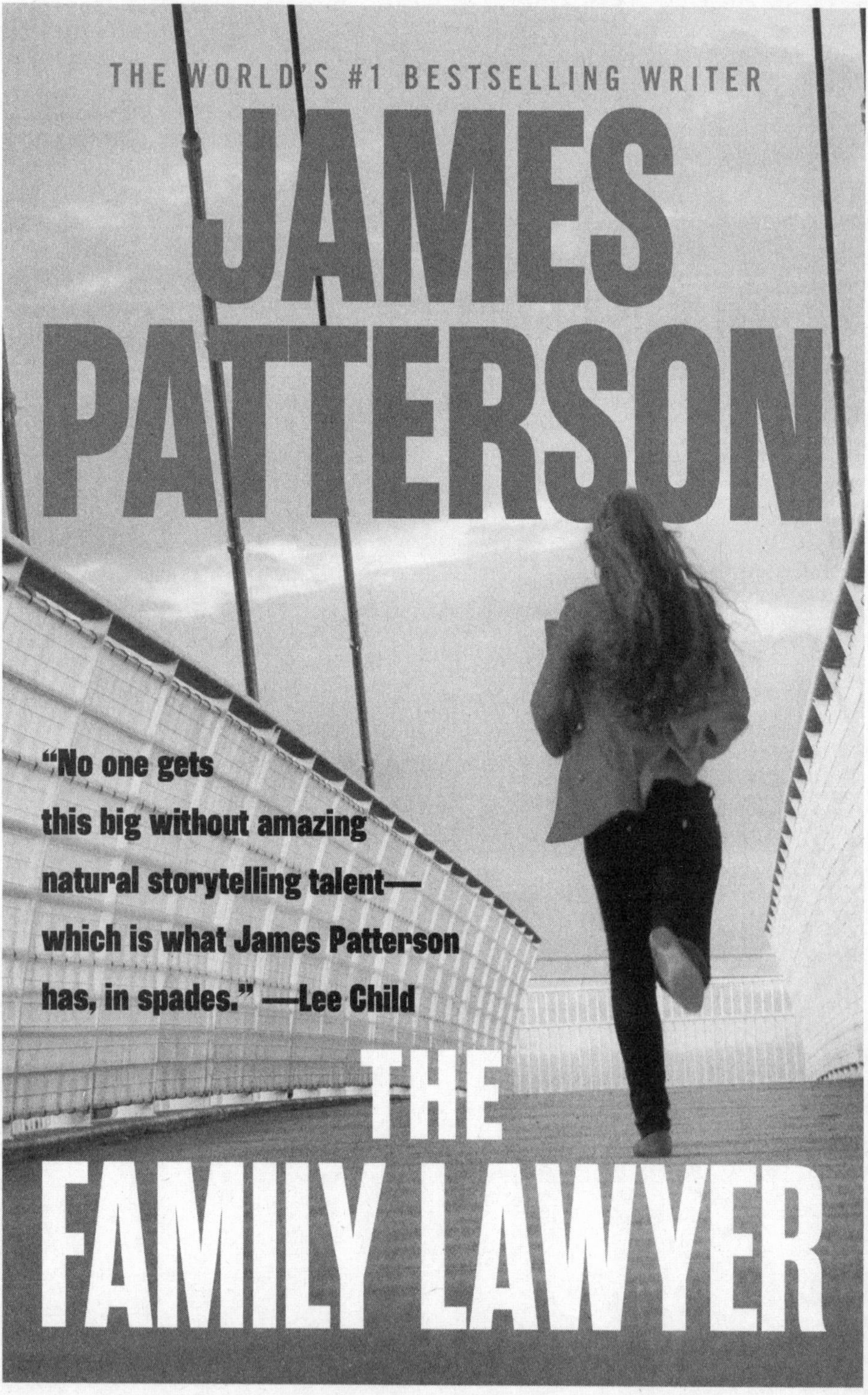
THE WORLD'S #1 BESTSELLING WRITER
JAMES PATTERSON
"No one gets this big without amazing natural storytelling talent—which is what James Patterson has, in spades." —Lee Child
THE FAMILY LAWYER

THE FAMILY LAWYER

The Family Lawyer combines three of my most pulse-pounding novels all in one book. There's Matthew Hovanes, who's living a parent's worst nightmare when his daughter is accused of bullying another girl into suicide. I test all of his attorney experience as he tries to clear his daughter's name and reveal the truth. Then there's Cheryl Mabern, who is one of my most brilliant detectives working for the NYPD. But does that brilliance help her when there's a calculating killer committing random murders? And finally, Dani Lawrence struggles with deciding whether to aid in an investigation that could put away her sister for the murder of her cheating husband. Or she can obstruct it by any means necessary.

For a complete list of books by

JAMES PATTERSON

VISIT
JamesPatterson.com

 Follow James Patterson on Facebook
@JamesPatterson

 Follow James Patterson on Twitter
@JP_Books

 Follow James Patterson on Instagram
@jamespattersonbooks